Sovereign:
A Journey to
Peace

JANICE MARCKMANN

WESTBOW
PRESS®
A DIVISION OF THOMAS NELSON
& ZONDERVAN

Scripture taken from the American Standard Version of the Bible.

This is a work of fiction. All of the characters, names, incidents, organizations, and dialogue in this novel are either the products of the author's imagination or are used fictitiously.

WestBow Press books may be ordered through booksellers or by contacting:

WestBow Press
A Division of Thomas Nelson & Zondervan
1663 Liberty Drive
Bloomington, IN 47403
www.westbowpress.com
1 (866) 928-1240

ISBN: 978-1-9736-2633-6 (sc)
ISBN: 978-1-9736-2632-9 (hc)
ISBN: 978-1-9736-2634-3 (e)

Library of Congress Control Number: 2018904653

Print information available on the last page.

WestBow Press rev. date: 05/08/2018

Acknowledgements

There's never been a story told only in isolation, as far as I know. I have had the privilege of having wonderful friends and family encourage me from the beginning of this story to the end. Some characters have a slight resemblance to some of the people in my circles of work, church, groups and social. I especially want to thank Judy and Marilyn who read my chapters in the beginning and waited anxiously for the next one. Sometimes they made gentle suggestions. My pastor, Robert Solon and my Bible study group have cheered me on each step of the way. Thank you to Pastor Elissa Dodge for the photography. My Red Hat sisters listened to the first chapter and applauded when I finished reading. My brother and cousins supported me all the way to the day it became real. Everyone contributed to my experience. Thank you.

Chapter 1

The hair on the back of Melissa's neck tingled as a brilliant flash of lightning lit up the living room. The thunder that immediately followed reverberated throughout the house as she knelt on the floor in front of the couch to search through the last carton for a flashlight that she was sure she'd packed. *Maybe coming here wasn't such a great idea,* she thought for the hundredth time. *Maybe I should have stayed in Chicago.*

Another flash of lightning foretold a crash of thunder seconds later. The lights flickered and threatened to go out. "If I don't find that flashlight soon," she said aloud, "I'm going to be stuck in the dark."

Just then, lightning was followed by deafening thunder, and the lights did go out. Something banged outside, and the branches of the oak tree scraped the roof. "Where is that flashlight?" she cried as she sat back on her heels.

The front door creaked. She jumped. Her pulse raced, and her chest tightened. *I'm sure I locked that door,* she thought wildly.

Forgetting the flashlight for the moment, she raised herself on her knees and looked toward the entryway. While peering through the dark, she watched in fascinated terror as the door burst inward, and a man silhouetted against the flashing lightning and driving rain stepped into the room. Maintaining her position behind the shelter of the couch, Melissa watched as he raised his flashlight and scanned the room. She held her breath and waited as the light brushed past her, and then she jumped when he demanded, *"Who's there?* I know there's someone in here. Come out where I can see you."

The words of her self-defense instructor came to mind. "Act brave!

1

Talk brave! Stay alive!" Determined not be a victim, she scanned the room in her mind. She remembered the fireplace on the right and scrambled frantically, stumbling toward where she pictured the poker was waiting in its stand. Fanning the air with her hands, she heard the clang of the irons before she could wrestle the first one out of its holder. She held it and turned toward the intruder, only to find he'd crossed the room and now stood towering over her, shining the light in her face.

After taking a deep breath, she challenged in her bravest voice, "Back off! I'm not afraid to do whatever I have to." She stared at the man behind the flashlight, willing herself not to show fear.

Thankfully, she realized it was working.

The man hesitated and then backed away one step, and then another and another, until the distance between them was more comfortable. He shined the light up into his own face and said, "Hold on. I'm not here to hurt you. I just want to know what you're doing in Emma's house."

"Emma?" Melissa said in surprise. "Did you know my grandmother?"

He seemed to take a moment to let the words to sink in. "You're Emma's granddaughter?" His voice reinforced his surprise. "I beg your pardon, miss. I didn't know you were living here." And then as if remembering her question, he said, "Yes, I knew your grandmother. We were good friends. I've always checked on her. Even before ..."

As he talked, Melissa watched his face. She tried to recall her grandmother's remarks about her many friends, but she didn't remember her sharing about any close male friends, especially not one so much younger. But then, Grandmother always said a few secrets made one much more interesting. Could this man be one of those secrets?

The storm continued to boil about the house, and there in Emma Wainsworth's living room, a small tempest was brewing between Melissa and the stranger. She curbed her desire to chide him about barging in on her, still not sure of his identity or intent. She was about to invite him to leave when the storm door suddenly pulled loose of its latch and hammered back and forth between the porch wall and the doorframe. Startled, she cried, "What next?"

Without answering, he crossed the room to the entry and secured the door back in place. "Man!" he said in the darkness, the swing of his flashlight and the flashes from the storm marking his movement back into the room. "That is some storm. Good thing this house is sturdy."

"Humph!" Melissa replied, her mind racing through possible scenarios. *Who is this guy? How am I going to get rid of him?* While she watched him across the room, she moved to keep the overstuffed chair between them.

As if he could read her mind, he offered gently, "I am really sorry that I scared you. I didn't mean to."

She listened to his quiet words and could only think of the patronizing way others had spoken to her before. After a moment, she let go of her control and raged openly at him. "You barge into my home in the dark, in the middle of a storm, and you say you don't intend to hurt me? You have no dishonorable intentions?"

Melissa paused for a reaction, and when one didn't come, she continued. "People don't break into other people's homes if they are honorable. You claim to have known my grandmother, but you don't tell me your name." Melissa felt her anger growing. All the hurts from the past seemed to gather in her heart, and she directed the brunt of it toward this man. "You come in here and scare me out of my mind during this awful storm, and then you have the audacity to say you're sorry and you didn't mean to scare me. I certainly hope this isn't Sovereign's idea of a welcome wagon!"

He stood silently, head tilted down with his face covered in the shadows. Without a word, he listened to her angry tirade until she finally sputtered to a stop. He then held up his right palm forward and simply offered, "Peace."

Melissa stared at this simple gesture, speechless for a moment. Then the absurdity of the entire evening caused her to stare at him wordlessly. Shaking her head, she started to speak but could only let out a snort of laughter followed by giggles. She laughed until her belly ached, and then she laughed some more. Aware of his laughter joining with hers, she felt less afraid for the first time. She felt at ease.

When their laughter stopped, they stood quietly together. "Shh," he cautioned. "Listen."

Melissa listened and then asked, "What? I don't hear anything."

"The storm is passing. It's quieter. The lights will be back on soon. The crews from the electric company are probably already working."

Melissa listened to this information and felt the weight of the awkward moment. *What do I do? What should I say?* She had never felt comfortable around strangers, and standing here in the dark with this man was a bit unnerving. Suddenly, she remembered the candles she'd seen on the ledge over the fireplace. "I think there are candles on the mantle." He shined his flashlight so it swept to the mantle. "Let me light these, if I can find a match."

"Top drawer of the side table there," he said as he shined his light in that direction.

Melissa slid the drawer open and found a box of kitchen matches. She turned, struck the match, and lit the candles. After picking one up, he turned to place it on table where she'd found the matches. She looked in his direction and could see a little more of this man with whom she was sharing a stormy night. "How did you know where Granny kept the matches?"

The flickering lights gave evidence to a pleasant, bearded face much younger than she had originally thought. He smiled and said, "I told you. I spent a lot of time out here with your grandmother."

"I don't recall Granny mentioning having a suitor." She instantly realized her mistake. "I'm sorry. I didn't mean that you ..." She felt embarrassed, and her words got mixed up. "I don't know why I said ..."

She heard subdued laughter in his voice as he spoke. "It's okay. I should have clarified my friendship with your grandmother."

He continued to watch her as she placed candles around the room. The room took on a pleasant golden glow, and it helped to lessen the fear of the unknown a little.

He cleared his throat. "Let me introduce myself," he said in his most soothing voice. "My name is Aaron Chambers. Your grandmother and I became friends through a shepherding group at church. She spent a lot of time helping me through some difficult times." He smiled and extended his hand in a gesture of friendship.

Melissa warily watched him. He seemed calm, and a sense of strength and kindness emanated from him. Remembering her manners, she smiled and reached out to accept his handshake. "Nice to meet you, Mr. Chambers. I'm Melissa Blakesly. Emma was my maternal grandmother."

He nodded and shook her hand gently. "Your grandmother told me about you. She loved you very much, and she was very proud of you."

When she looked into his eyes, she noticed how kind his face seemed in the candlelight. She blushed when she realized she'd stared a bit too long. She ducked her head, withdrew her hand, and backed away. "I miss my grandmother a lot. She was a very important person in my life. She offered me stability when there wasn't much of it."

Upon feeling the tears of grief well up in her eyes, she turned away to wipe her face with her sleeve. She thought she had herself back under control, but the events of the last year, the last month, and even the last hour seemed to weigh heavily upon her. Instead of helping her feel calmer, she felt the confusion and sadness of everything break through the dam of her self-control. Instead of stopping, the tears flowed freely down her face, and she felt her body begin to tremble. Trying to stop the flow of emotion was useless, and even worse, she was embarrassed to realize she was sobbing out loud. The harder she tried to stop the crying, the more pronounced it became.

She felt Aaron move closer to her and heard him say, "It's okay. Just let it go."

She shook her head no, but when he laid his hand gently on her shoulder, she could no longer contain her sorrow. She sobbed, and he guided her down to sit on the sofa and sat next to her, lending her his red bandana handkerchief to mop her tears with. In a moment, she leaned back and said, "I'm sorry. I guess I'm not over losing her yet." She wiped her eyes with his handkerchief. "Thank you for listening." Then she looked at him through teary eyes and said, "I can't remember the last time I have seen a red bandana." She stifled a giggle, sniffed, and then said, "I think I'm okay now." She chanced a look up at him and found him smiling down at her with kindness and concern. She relaxed a little. "Would you like something to drink? I have some tea bags and some instant coffee. I don't think the gas has been affected by the storm."

"Sounds wonderful," he said. Melissa had just entered the kitchen when the lights came back on. She turned to look back at Aaron and finally saw the man in full light. His dark hair and neat beard framed a pleasant and intellectual face. The laugh lines at the corners of his brown eyes made him look as though he was thinking of something amusing. She had to look up at him, and so she imagined he must be well over six feet tall. The way his clothes fit made him look as though he regularly worked out.

"Melissa?"

"Hmm?"

"I said I'll take a look at the door latch to see if it's broken."

"Oh!" Melissa said, startled. She felt as though she'd just been caught daydreaming in school, and she felt her cheeks warm as the potential for embarrassment overwhelmed her. "Sure. I'll start the water boiling."

He nodded, looking pleasantly amused as he turned back toward the door. As she entered the kitchen, she thought she heard him whistling a familiar tune. Was it one that grandmother used to hum?

When the water was simmering, Melissa arranged the coffee mugs, a box of herbal teabags, and a jar of instant coffee on the table. She also opened a container of cookies she had brought with her on a plate and placed that on the table too. The whistle of the teapot must have alerted Aaron, because he crossed from the living room to the kitchen. "The latch on that door is in pretty sorry shape, and the hinges are sprung from being thrown back and forth in the wind." He sat in the chair opposite of Melissa. "The inside door is still in good shape. If you'd like, I can come back out in the morning and make the repairs."

"Thank you. That would be nice. I don't know anyone around here to ask, and I'd appreciate your help." As she talked, she watched him stir the instant coffee crystals into the hot water she had poured for him. She noticed that his hands were smooth and didn't appear to belong to someone who was a carpenter.

Her thoughts were interrupted by his words. "I'm not the handiest guy, but I think I can make the repairs your door needs."

She nodded and said, "I was just thinking that you don't look like you work with your hands."

"No, I don't," he said, "but I've always had a great admiration for those who do." She could hear the smile in his voice and looked up to meet his kind brown eyes. She was startled for a moment to realize how truly pleasant he seemed, and she decided that Iowa might be just the tonic she needed to sooth her stressed-out life.

Chapter 2

"Mmm, I think you inherited your grandmother's knack for making cookies. These must come from the same recipe as hers," Aaron said with a smile as he dunked a third cookie in his coffee.

Melissa chuckled. "Granny used to dunk her cookies too. I loved to follow her example as a child, but my mother told me it was rather uncouth and scolded me when I did it at home. Fortunately, I got to visit Grandmother a lot, and we both promised to never tell my mother." She laughed at the memory.

"It seems we have some similar memories of Emma." He smiled at her, and they sat at the table in the cottage with their own thoughts keeping them company.

"Okay, now that we've both survived our stormy encounter, may I ask you some questions?"

"Fine with me. Just don't move that plate of cookies." He grinned. "Ask whatever you want."

She nodded and then said, "First, why did you break in my door? I was so frightened. If I had had a gun, I could have shot you." Her green eyes widened, and she pressed her fingers to her mouth.

He shifted in his chair and said, "Well, I had a pretty bad day and decided to come out and walk in the woods behind the house. I wasn't paying attention to the weather, so when the sky darkened, the wind picked up, and the lightening was threatening, I came here. Emma always said to consider this my home too."

He watched her face, not sure whether he should go on. After a short moment, he continued, "I didn't know that anyone had moved in here, so when I saw the lights on, I was startled and wanted to see who was here and what was going on. I knocked, but no one answered. Then I thought I saw the shape of a person in the light of my flashlight. I jimmied the knob until it opened." He sat waiting for any response. When she said nothing, he continued. "Then I saw a movement and heard the clanging of andirons, I knew I either had to face the intruder or get out. I decided to find out who was squatting in Emma's house."

He paused, seeming to gauge her reaction. She nodded as if to give him permission to continue. "Anyway, I was really surprised when you were a woman—and one that was so bold in her defense. I had no problem backing away, but I wasn't willing to leave without knowing who you were, what you were doing, and how you got in to the house."

She nodded again and then finally spoke. "I was so involved in settling in, and when that storm came up so suddenly, I knew that I needed a flashlight in case the lights went out. I remember being here in the past when storms knocked the electricity out for a while. It always seemed so magical when Granny was here. But then you pushed in the door! I was scared, but I was not willing to be let someone commandeer my home." Her eyes were wide, and her voice intense. "I guess I was ready to defend what was mine."

He watched her and then bit off a small piece of cookie. He chewed and seemed to be in deep thought when he said, "You remind me so much of Emma. You both have such intensity and passion." He paused to take a sip of coffee, swallowed, and then said, "Have I answered your questions? Do you feel safe now?"

She rolled his question around in her mind. After a minute, she said, "I think I'm okay with it. I'm feeling better now that the storm has passed. But I don't know what to do with the door tonight. I hope I can sleep knowing it's broken."

"I think we can still lock the storm door. Then, if we close the inside door and push the buffet in front of it, you'll be fine for tonight. I'll leave through the back door, and you can fasten the screen door and lock up behind me."

"Yes, I think that will help. Thank you." She waited a minute and then cleared her throat. "Um. It's starting to get dark. Maybe you should think about leaving." She smiled "I don't want you getting lost in the dark."

He chuckled. "You're right. Let me barricade the front door, and I'll get on my way." He stood up, moved to secure the door, and then paused. "You do feel okay staying here alone?"

"Of course. I have a car, if for some reason I don't; I can sleep in it with the doors locked. I don't think anything will bother me. Anyway, I've got my fireplace poker now." She smiled at his concern. "I will be fine."

"Well, if you're sure. There are accommodations in town. I know the guy in charge. If you want, I could check it out for you."

"No, that's not necessary. I'm fine." She waited while he processed her statement. Then using her most confident tone of voice, she added, "Please, I don't want you to be out walking to your car so late."

"Okay, then. Well, I doubt anyone is going to be able to push that buffet out of the way, and you're right: you are safe here." He grabbed his flashlight and turned to go. "Be sure to lock the door behind me."

"Don't worry—I'm not taking any chances." As she followed him to the back door, she said, "I'm glad I've met you, Aaron. I hope to see you again." Surprised at her candor, she blushed and hoped he wouldn't notice.

"I will come out in the morning and take care of the damage. Sleep tight. Sweet dreams." He turned to go. "It was nice to meet you too, Melissa." With that, he was gone, and she watched the swish of the flashlight as he made his way down the drive and toward the road. She closed the door, locked it, and smiled when she saw him flash the light as though to signal his approval.

While walking down the driveway, Aaron couldn't help chuckling to himself as he replayed the events in his mind. The day had been a long one with several counseling sessions with his clients and soothing the hurt feelings of his daughter, Joseline. His concern for her still flared a bit when he thought of her account of her little friends taunting her, saying he would be sent away from her. Then after settling her in and assuring her that Mrs. Mason would stay with her, he escaped to his favorite spot, the woods behind Emma's house.

When he reached his Jeep, parked in the field entry down the road, his shoulders shook as he laughed at the memory of his encounter with Melissa. He really hadn't known that anyone had moved into Emma's house, so the whole incident had been just as he'd told her, a complete surprise. He laughed harder as he remembered the expression on her face when he confronted her in front of the fireplace. Emma had always said her only grandchild was a feisty one. Emma had spoken so proudly of Melissa. Even after meeting her, he felt amazed that she was settling in. Didn't Emma say something about a failing relationship? *That poor guy is probably licking his wounds, full of regret right about now.* He smiled at the thought. Melissa Blakesly didn't seem like someone any man would easily let slip away. It must have been some breakup to have her move all the way out here.

As he drove toward town, the rain started again. *Well, she sure is pretty.* He smiled as he drove into town, thinking all the while of tomorrow's repairs at Melissa's cottage.

Chapter 3

Melissa slept surprisingly well that night and awoke early to the sun in her eyes. Granny's words came to mind: "The sun is the best alarm clock." She could imagine her dimples and impish smile. She lay back against the mounds of feather pillows, relishing the memory of her grandmother. How lucky she felt to have such good memories. After standing and stretching, she moved through the living room and toward the kitchen to make her coffee. She was startled to see the buffet pushed away from its normal place to against the front door, but then the events of the previous evening—the storm, the terror, the rage, and finally the emotional release—played vividly in her mind. *Oh, my! What a weird sequence of events.* Aaron came to mind. She shook her head, put him out of her thoughts, and moved on to make the coffee. Thankful that the electricity was on, she filled the coffee maker with grounds and water and set it to a strong brew.

Over her morning coffee, she made a quick call to her parents to let them know she had survived her first thunderstorm since returning to Iowa. She quickly shared with them the events of the evening, and her dad reacted to the story with a plan to come there to fortify the house so that she didn't have to endure any similar problems. She assured them both that she and the cottage were fine, and that she had a plan to fix the door.

"Well, honey," her mother started, "your grandmother left that property to you to do with whatever you want. Her desire was that you would be safe and have a cushion to be able to live your life as you wanted. You don't have to feel obligated to stay there, or even keep the farm. Your dad and I will help you find an estate dealer to take over ..."

"I know, Mom. And please understand that I appreciate your sentiment. But right now, this is a good place for me." She smiled and then said, "I love you both! I'll keep you involved. Don't worry." After a few more words of endearments and encouragement, they let her go.

Later, as she blew her curly blonde hair dry, she imagined a scrolling list of all the things she wanted to get done today. Unpack the boxes, tidy up the house, find the planter boxes for her front window sills—the list rolled on and on. Once dressed, she pushed the bureau back into place, opened the back door, and breathed in the clean cool air. *Oh, Granny. I hope this is where I need to be right now. It seems so peaceful here.* She sighed, started unpacking the box of food she'd brought, and placed it in the empty pantry cupboard or frig. The coffee smelled wonderful, and so she poured a cup; filled a bowl with cereal, a sliced banana, and milk; and sat down to enjoy her breakfast. The birds chirped and tweeted, seeming to assure her that here was a good place to be.

After swishing her dishes with cool water, she left them to gather the few boxes to take to the car for a trip to the recycling center later. She stepped out the back door and heard a car pull into her driveway and stop. She recognized Aaron getting out of the car, and she stepped off the porch as he approached.

"Good morning."

"Hello, Melissa. Getting an early start?"

Melissa laughed. "Well, the east windows in the bedroom let in a lot of early light. It didn't seem I had any other choice."

Aaron smiled and nodded, his brown eyes glinting in the sun. "I remember Emma saying something about the advantage of rising early. Did you sleep well?"

"Yes, I did. I think I was asleep within minutes of you leaving, and I didn't move until this morning. What a luxury to sleep so comfortably and peacefully."

Aaron nodded again, then said, "I stopped at the hardware store and I think I have everything I need to fix the door. Is it okay if I go on through the house?"

"Sure. Do you need me to do anything?"

"No, I just have to look it over and measure a couple of things. I should be okay."

She watched as he let himself into the back door, and then she put the boxes in the car. The garden shed set just to the back of the garage, and she thought she would find the window boxes there. The door to the garden shed groaned as she pulled it open. The sun shined through the dirty windows, and she cringed as she searched inside the door frame for a light switch. She made a face as she imagined spiders and other creatures watching her from the rafters. Finally, she found the switch and flicked it on. The interior was illuminated with dim, dusty light bulbs centered on the rafters. After letting her eyes adjust, she slowly perused the shapes of tools and equipment hanging on the walls or leaning up against other tools. On the table adjacent to the door, she found a hammer, a handsaw, and lots of containers of screws, nails, and bolts. A can in the corner had a variety of paintbrushes standing upright, all covered with dust and cobwebs. Finally, she saw the window boxes stacked against the wall on a couple of sawhorses.

Thankful that they were there, she lifted one and decided to carry it out to the front of the house. By the time she had brought the second one out and returned to find the braces, the drill, the extension cord, and almost every tool and fastener in the shed, she was ready to get this job done. She tried to attach the braces to the house using the existing holes, but they were all worn too big and wouldn't hold. Sighing, she decided to drill new holes next to the old ones. After studying the placement, she was almost ready to drill a hole when she heard a twig snap behind her. She jumped and turned toward the noise to see Aaron watching her.

"That won't work. You have to drill into the stud," he said.

"Oh, goodness! You startled me. I didn't know you were standing there."

"I'm sorry. I guess you were concentrating and didn't hear me step out. But you have to put the new holes above or below, so they go right into the structure, or they won't hold. I could help you with it."

Melissa watched him as he spoke. "That sounds tempting, but I hate to impose on you. I could pay you. I didn't expect you to ..." Feeling her face grow warm and fearing that she was turning as red as the petunias she wanted to plant in the boxes, she sighed and shook her head.

Aaron watched her struggle and then said, "Melissa, please, I'd like to help. It would really help me work through my feelings of loss to help you."

She sat for a moment, processing his offer and realizing the sincerity of his words. She looked up and smiled. "Okay, I'd appreciate it. Thank you." She stood up and asked, "How about sharing a cup of coffee first? It's fresh, and I still have cookies."

"That sounds like an offer too good to pass up. I'll get these braces attached. Go ahead, and I'll be right there."

Melissa found the mugs in the cupboard, rinsed them, and dried them. She opened the container of cookies and placed them on the tray. While listening to the whir of the drill and the grinding of the screws being tightened through the braces and into the wall of the house, she waited for Aaron to enter before pouring the coffee.

When he tapped on the door frame, she waved him on in and invited him to sit at the table where they had shared a similar fare last evening. "I wish I had something else to offer you. I haven't been to the store yet."

He waved her apology away and said, "This is wonderful." He picked up a cookie and said, "These are great. I think even better today." He bit off a piece and chewed, closing his eyes as though he was relishing the taste and texture. "Mmm. These are so good." He looked across the table at her. "So, Melissa, how long have you been here?" He took another bite of cookie and watched her as he chewed. He seemed to be studying her face, and Melissa wasn't sure whether she could stand the scrutiny much longer when he said, "Forgive my intrusion. Sometimes I'm just too direct."

"It's okay," she said. "I just moved in a couple of days ago. I just brought clothes and a few other things. Everything else is Granny's, and my stuff is stored in Chicago."

"I see," he said, chasing a butterscotch chip along the edge of the plate before popping it in his mouth. "Plan on staying here long?" He looked into her face, his brown eyes shining.

Melissa shrugged. "I honestly don't know right now. I'm kind of starting a healing process. I'm dealing with a few things that I need to work through." She smiled at him and said, "Thank you for everything. Granny always told me that God sent angels unaware when we needed them."

Aaron chuckled and rose as if to go. "I'm not sure about the angel part, but I am sure that God was here." After stretching to his full six-foot height, he continued. "My name's in the book. Don't be afraid to ask for help. Everyone needs someone to talk to."

"I guess you're right. I've been too busy figuring out my next move, and I haven't had much of a chance to meet anyone."

"Then it's time to change that. Tomorrow's Friend Day at Peace Community Church in town. That's my church. Why don't you come to the morning service? Ten thirty. It would be a great way to meet some of the locals. Emma attended there. Everybody would be glad to know you are living in her house. You'd be welcome."

"Well," Melissa hesitated. "I've got lots to do this weekend, and I hadn't planned on church, but yeah, I'll see you there."

"Great! I've got some stuff to take care of, so I'll be going." He smiled and then added, "See you tomorrow." After a wave of his hand, he was in his car and backing out onto the road.

Church, she thought. *Well, guess it would be a way to meet my neighbors.* She watched Aaron's red Jeep disappear around the curve. *If they're all as nice as him, it might be a very good idea. I'll see tomorrow.* She went to gather the bags of soil and red petunias and bright green sweet potato vines she had purchased for her flower boxes.

Melissa spent the rest of the day working in the yard and garden. When she finished, she stood back and took a long look at her accomplishments. It was amazing how much work there was to do here. The window boxes looked nice and would be beautiful once the petunias were in bloom and the vines had a chance to grow and drape over the sides. It was starting to look more like home, more like it used to be when she was younger. *I think I can be happy here,* she thought. She ran her hand through her hair and thought of a nice, warm bubble bath. When she stretched out her fingers, she decided they needed some TLC to clean the grime from her hands, and a manicure would fix the broken nails. *Nothing like the Melissa of a month ago,* she thought. Her life in Chicago had been a whirlwind of activity that included weekly manicures and pedicures and monthly trims, colors, and hairstyles. *Oh, well. Let bygones be bygones.* She sighed. "Maybe it's good riddance," she said out loud. That lifestyle had been a burnout for a couple of years. This was just what she needed right now. And who's to say that the future wouldn't include some of that again?

After pushing those thoughts out of her mind, she finished putting tools away and carrying garden waste to the compost pile. "Boy, I'm tired!" she said to herself. She thought about church the next morning and admitted she was looking forward to seeing Aaron, but it might also be nice to renew that Sunday morning tradition. Church had not been a regular part of her life recently. Sunday had been a "sleep late, catch up" kind of day. She remembered how Granny had always said the best start to the week was a beginning with God and fellowship with his people. Anyway, a shampoo followed by a good soak in the tub was calling to her. A quick supper followed by pajamas and that old-fashioned bed promised a well-earned night of sleep.

That evening, as Aaron went over his notes, his mind kept drifting off to Melissa. It was his nature to feel empathy for others who were hurting. God knew he'd experienced enough of his own in the past years. He hoped Melissa would be at church in the morning. He found himself smiling at the thought of seeing her again. She was nice to look at, but he felt a connection with her because of Emma. What a good friend Emma had been to him through those hard times. She'd been his counselor and shoulder to cry on. She'd been his supporter and encourager. She'd made him laugh when he couldn't cry any longer, and she gave him and Joseline endless hours of her time. *Yes,* he thought, *I certainly hope Melissa Blakesly is at church in the morning.*

Chapter 4

On Sunday morning, Melissa woke up with a feeling of anticipation. Aaron's invitation came to her mind, and she thought, *Will he greet me at the door, introduce me to his friends, and ask me to sit with him?* He hadn't really invited her as his friend, but he had issued the invitation. As she prepared for the day, she thought about how good it felt to not have to put the business face on each day, but a little makeup was kind of fun. Working out in the sun yesterday had given her some color, and the makeup enhanced her face and eyes. People had always told her she had a wholesome, country girl look, and it did seem that the fresh air and sunshine was doing wonders for her appearance and feeling of well-being.

She selected a pretty pink and lavender print dress. It was still early in May, and so she grabbed a blazer. When she glanced at the clock, she was surprised to see it was only 8:05. "Wow! I really moved around," she noted. It was refreshing to look forward to something so simple as church service. It reminded her of her extended childhood visits to Grandmother's house and how they looked forward to going to town or trying something new. It was such a different feeling from the past few years, when the unfamiliar seemed all too normal.

Because she was ready with time on her hands, she decided to drive to town for breakfast. She would have time to buy a paper and catch up on the news outside of Sovereign. She thought, *Funny. I've been here almost a week, and I haven't missed the world at all!*

She drove the mile into town and parked in front of the hotel coffee shop, where she planned to have breakfast. She climbed the steps to the entryway and paused in front of the newspaper vending machine while she searched in her coin purse for the right change.

"Here, why don't you take mine?" a familiar voice said. Startled, she turned toward the voice and met Aaron's smile with one of her own. "I'm done with it. It'll save a tree and some change."

"Oh, thanks, Aaron." She took the paper and tucked under her arm. "It's so nice to see you again."

"I'm glad you're here." He started down the steps, turned, and said, "I hope this means you'll be joining us at church?"

The *us* caught her off guard. She hadn't thought about his family. She mentally scolded herself for not considering the possibility that he had a family. "I-I'm looking forward to it," she stammered. Then, trying to recover her confidence, she turned toward the restaurant door and entered without another word to him.

Inside the restaurant, Melissa took a seat at a table for two next to the window. She watched Aaron taking long strides down the street. After admiring his strength and vitality, she reminded herself of her recent breakup with Sven and the many days that followed of awkward encounters and nights of feeling bereft and betrayed. *I'm not putting myself through that again.*

Her thoughts were distracted by the waitress requesting her beverage order and handing her a menu. The woman followed her line of sight and smiled. "Some pretty nice scenery comes and goes by here."

Melissa felt like she should feel embarrassed. She quickly looked at the menu and gave the woman her order. To cover her feeling of discomfort, she made a big deal of looking at the paper. Everything seemed like a soap opera. Even though she hadn't read a paper or watched the news for several days, nothing had changed. There were still wars being fought, children abused, people hurting one another— all issues she wanted to leave behind her. And to think that she had lived in the middle of that life for too many years. She turned to the business section and felt her stomach cramp when she spotted the picture of Sven Johanssen smiling out at her. The caption read, "Sven

Johanssen, son of Nels Johanssen of NorAM Inc, will be taking over more control of the business. Insiders expect the company to change directions and expand into several new fields." Melissa sat frowning at the picture and remembering the ups and downs of her relationship with Sven. *Thank you, God, for giving me this nice, quiet time away.*

She was sure that she had just thought that to herself, but she was surprised when the waitress remarked, "Makes you want to go away and hide, doesn't it? Boy, am I glad that I live in Small Town, USA. You couldn't give me that city stuff for nothing." After setting the plate down in front of Melissa, she smiled and winked then said, "Here's your breakfast. Hope you like it."

"I'm sure I will. It looks delicious." Melissa smiled and turned her attention to her meal. Before taking up her fork though, she took just a moment to remember Granny's mealtime prayer. *Thank you, God, in every way for all you give to us today. Amen.* She smiled to herself. It seemed a childish thing to do, but it made her feel better about everything.

Halfway through her meal, the waitress came back to refill her coffee cup. "I hope you don't mind my asking, but are you new here? I don't recall seeing you around. Of course, we do have folks stop by on their way through, but not as often since the new highway went through south of here."

"I don't mind at all. I should have introduced myself earlier. I'm Melissa Blakesly. I'm living in my grandmother's house west of town. Her name was ..."

"Emma Wainsworth's grandbaby! Of course, I should have known. Why, you look just like her when she was a young woman. Well, welcome to Sovereign! Wait until I tell folks that Emma's granddaughter is living in her house."

Melissa smiled at the extent of the response this news had brought on. She'd never thought her presence could make much difference. *I guess Aaron's right about everyone knowing and liking Grandmother.* She suddenly felt less lonely. "I'm very pleased to meet you, uh ..."

"Shelia Granger. Why, I knew your grandmother all my life. She used to sew for my children. Oh, my, she and I used to have the best talks. She and my mama were good friends. I remember thinking she had the sweetest face. I was sure she must be what angels looked like. Anyway, after my mama died, I spent lots of time with Emma. Oh, honey, I'm so glad you are here!"

Melissa smiled. "Thank you, Sheila. It means so much to know others who loved Grandmother. Her loss left a big hole in my heart. I appreciate your kind words." She left the last bit of muffin. "I'm on my way to church, so I'd better go. I'll leave my money with the check, if that's okay." Sheila nodded and wished her a good day.

While driving east on Main Street, she soon spotted a white church gleaming in the sunlight. The flower beds carefully prepared for planting around the foundation spoke of someone who cared a great deal about this little church and its people. The signboard in front of the church confirmed that this was Peace Church and proclaimed that all were welcome there in the name of Jesus Christ.

She parked half a block away and watched for signs of others arriving. Suddenly the bell rang, and almost immediately children burst out from the side doors as though they had been let out of school for summer. Parents and other adults moved out of the annex building, greeted them, and gathered them into family groups while waiting to enter the sanctuary. Melissa thought, *I never think of Sunday School being for adults.* She sat for a while longer, watching the groups change and grow and slowly merge into the door leading to the main church area. She looked at her watch and decided at 10:25 that it was time for her to move on toward the building too. She looked around for Aaron but didn't see him. *Well, I'm here, so I guess I can go to church by myself.* After taking a deep breath, she left the car and walked to the church steps. She positioned herself behind the group filing in and mentally tried to convince herself that she wasn't nervous. After all, she only had to do this once.

Her thoughts were interrupted by a voice saying, "Excuse me, but I don't think I know you." Melissa looked up into the smile of a pleasant-looking lady. She smiled, and the woman said, "My name is

Linda Bodine, and this is my husband, Jim; my son, Robert; and my daughter, Julia." Melissa shook hands all around and couldn't help smiling at the children's shy smiles and obvious curious stares.

"You're beautiful!" the little girl said, ducking her head as soon as the words were out.

"And so are you," Melissa returned the compliment. "Where did you get such pretty red curls?"

"From my mom and dad," she replied. "Where else would I get them?" She giggled.

"I guess that's a good question," Melissa returned. "My name is Melissa Blakesly, and I'm living outside of town in my grandmother Emma's cottage."

"Oh, so you're the new tenant. I've noticed signs of life there, but I hadn't heard who was living there. Didn't you used to visit Emma during the summers when you were younger?"

"Yes, I spent many wonderful summer days with Granny as a child. Unfortunately, I didn't spend as much time as I would have liked as I got older. The years sped by, and I couldn't hold on to them tight enough. I wish I'd spent more time with Granny."

"I know what you mean." After placing a comforting hand on Melissa's shoulder, he said, "We all miss Emma too." Melissa nodded and wiped a tear that was threatening to slide down her cheek. Linda continued, "I'd love to visit with you more. We live down the road, not too far from your place. Let's talk after church."

Melissa nodded her agreement and moved on into the sanctuary. A tall, gray-haired gentleman walked toward her. He offered a bulletin, smiled, and said, "Welcome to Peace. May I help you find a seat?"

She nodded and followed him to a seat on the center aisle a few rows from the front. She heard friendly murmurings around her and noticed smiles on faces turned toward her. She smiled in return and then turned her attention to the bulletin. The swell of organ music interrupted, and she heard a male voice welcome all to Peace Church. She looked up and almost lost her breath when she looked into the smiling eyes of Aaron Chambers standing at the front of the church.

His smile widened a little as he noticed her. Melissa wondered what he was doing up there. She tried to listen, but her mind was going in circles. She decided to focus on the bulletin and gasped out loud when she read the heading: "Aaron Chambers, Pastor."

After the initial surprise, Melissa smiled at the memory of her less than charitable thoughts and words to Aaron last evening. She stifled a giggle and joined the congregation in singing some choruses and hymns that were familiar, as well as some that were new to her. After the last song, Aaron encouraged the congregation to greet each other and make guests feel welcome. Melissa sat quietly, uncertain of what to do. Fortunately, Linda Bodine offered her hand and introduced her to her neighbor, Lucy Mason, and the tall man and his wife seated in front of them. The greetings continued for several minutes, and it appeared everyone in the church had made an effort to shake hands, speak, or smile and nod to Melissa. As the organ music swelled, everyone returned to their seats, and Melissa continued to return smiles with a smile of her own. Finally, everyone's attention turned toward the front of the church, and Aaron led the congregation in prayer, followed by a group recitation of the Lord's Prayer. Aaron stood held out his arms and said the altar was open for anyone who wanted individual prayer. Melissa watched as a few people filed up and silently kneeled and bowed their heads. Some were smiling, and some were very solemn. Aaron kneeled and prayed with each one, comforting some and smiling with others. When each had been ministered to, they all returned to their seats.

Aaron took his place behind the podium. The sermon that followed described God's love for his people and his example in a way she had never heard before. He spoke sincerely and from the heart, charging each person to show that same kind of love to others in their community. Melissa couldn't help but sense a feeling of true respect and love being generated between speaker and audience. As she looked around, she often saw people nodding in agreement. But more than that, there was a sense of deep spiritual love in this church.

It provided a feeling of warmth and safety. Surely this was how God wanted his love professed.

After the sermon and a final prayer and song, Aaron moved to the back of the church to give the benediction. He stayed near the foyer to greet each person on the way out.

Melissa waited until others near her stood to file out and found her place in the chattering crowd. She smiled and spoke to those who greeted her on all sides. "Glad you came. Come again," was heard over and over again.

Slowly the procession inched closer to the exit. Occasionally she caught glimpses of Aaron as he said goodbye to each one. Most paused for a moment to compliment him on his sermon or to thank him for a visit or other deed. He gave each person his attention before the next one grabbed his hand, patted him on the back, or hugged him.

When it was her turn, she offered her hand in greeting. He smiled and grasped her hand in both of his. "I'm so glad you decided to come, Melissa. Did you get a chance to meet some of our people?"

"Everyone was very gracious" Melissa returned. "I'm glad I came too. I enjoyed your message, Reverend."

Aaron squeezed her hand and grinned at her formal address. "I'll be in touch. Take care now. Be sure to call if you need any help."

Before she could reply, he was greeting the couple behind her and listening to the woman's suggestions about some activity the church was planning. Melissa squinted in the bright sunlight and moved down the steps that were still crowded with parishioners. She was stopped for a few minutes to visit with Linda and Jim Bodine and their children, and she agreed to drive over to their place later in the week for coffee. After excusing herself to move to her car, she reached into her purse for her keys and stopped when she heard a voice calling her name.

"Miss Blakesly, Miss Blakesly! Wait a minute." She turned toward the voice ad saw a middle-aged woman. "Just wanted to say again that we're glad you came. You'll have to come back tonight. We'll be showing our pictures of our visit to the Holy Land. By the way, my name is Rayleen Ralston. My husband, Donald, and I were sitting a couple of rows behind you."

Melissa replied, "It's very nice to meet you, but please call me Melissa." Rayleen nodded. "And thank you very much for the invitation, but I'm not sure I'll be able to come tonight."

"Oh, that's too bad. Well, what are you doing for lunch? Why don't you come over to our house? We're having some friends over, and we'd love it if you'd join us. Our farm is straight west of your little house. If you follow the road around the section, you can't miss us."

"Well, I really should …"

"Oh, please come. We'd love to have you join us, and this will give you an opportunity to talk to some of the neighbors you met this morning."

After a moment's hesitation, she agreed. "All right. Thank you. That would be very nice. I have a few projects started at home, but I guess they will wait for me."

"That's a true statement if I ever heard one!" Donald Ralston had moved closer to the two women. "I'm glad you're joining us for lunch. It's always nice to have new people in church. Makes us feel we're doing something right." He ended with a chuckle that rumbled up from deep within his sturdy body. Melissa took an immediate liking to this man as he continued. "I hear Aaron gets credit for inviting you." Melissa nodded, but before she could add anything, Don said, "That Aaron Chambers is a good pastor." He gave an impish smile. "And a good man. We'll see you in a little while."

"Bye," called Rayleen as she pulled Don toward the car. "We plan to eat around 12:30, but just come over when you can."

She checked her watch: 11:45. *Well, I guess I could go home for a few minutes,* she thought. *I know! I'll stop at the grocery and pick up a bottle of wine to take along.*

She took her time selecting just the right wine. She considered a nice dry wine or maybe a Chardonnay, but then she decided on a full-bodied, sweet red wine that would go well with whatever they served. Feeling satisfied that she wasn't going empty-handed, she drove quickly past her house and then on to the Ralstons' home.

Chapter 5

Melissa easily recognized the farm from Don's directions. The house was a modern sprawling brick ranch with white farm buildings neatly arranged in a separate yard several yards behind the house. Beautiful landscaping surrounded the house and a white rail fence separated the house from the buildings and farm fields.

Her eye caught a flash of red in her rear-view mirror, and she looked up to see Aaron's Jeep following her into the drive. She stopped behind other cars along the drive and waited for Aaron to pull in behind her. Once out of the car, she stood waiting, purse on one shoulder and the bottle of wine in the other hand. She watched Aaron get out and was surprised when he opened the back door and helped a little girl scramble out. She took his hand and skipped along beside him as they walked toward her.

"Hi." She hoped the surprise she felt wasn't too obvious.

"Hi!" Said the cute little brown-haired girl. "What's your name?"

"Melissa. What's yours?"

"Joseline Sara Chambers." A wide smile pushed he cheeks up into rosy little mounds, and dimples popped out on either side of her mouth. She twirled around and giggled. Then Aaron picked her up and held her against his shoulder.

He nodded at Melissa and said, "Nice day." Melissa nodded in agreement. When he pointed his finger across the fields, she followed his line of direction. "Look over there. You can see the roof of your house just on top of the hill."

"That's where Granny lives!" came Joseline's childish reply.

"Right you are!" he said to the little girl, placing her on the ground.

He bent down to straighten her dress. "Josie, why don't you go in and tell Don we'll be right in."

The little girl responded, "Okay, Daddy," and she skipped up the drive toward the house.

After watching her progress, he turned back to Melissa. "I see you found your way out all right."

"Yes, no problem at all." She scanned the yard and said, "This is a beautiful place." She turned back toward the house and added, "Rayleen said they'd eat at 12:45, so perhaps we should go on in."

"In just a minute," Aaron said as he moved around in front of her. He smiled at her. "I wonder if I could offer you a suggestion?"

"Sure, anything." Melissa looked up at him, wondering what he was about to say.

He took a deep breath and then said, "It's about your gift."

"My gift?" Then she remembered the wine. "Oh, you mean this?"

He was about to say something when Rayleen yelled out the door, "Come on, you two. Dinner's ready!"

Aaron waved at her and said, "We'll be right there, Rayleen." Then he said to Melissa, "It's just that Don and Rayleen are not drinkers, and I'm afraid they might not appreciate your gesture."

"Oh, my goodness!" Melissa quickly tried to conceal the bottle under her arm. She looked up at Aaron and caught him smiling at her, and she started to giggle. "What am I going to do? I don't think I will ever drink it"

He joined in her laughter and said, "Just put it under the front seat of your … No! Here, give it to me. If anyone asks, I'll tell them it's for communion." Melissa handed the bottle over to Aaron as subversively as she could, laughing behind her hand as he stealthily moved it to the back of his own car. She followed him and watched as he opened the rear door, concealed it under a blanket, and then jammed the whole bundle under the seat. He grinned at Melissa and said, "Joseline shouldn't find it there."

Shaking her head at her blunder, Melissa said, "I never stopped to think that they might not care for wine. Thanks. I would have been so embarrassed."

"Don't mention it. Come on. We'd better get in there before Rayleen comes looking for us."

They entered the house through the back door and were greeted by Rayleen. "Well, it's about time. What were you doing out there, anyway?"

"I was just accepting a donation for the church from Melissa."

"Oh." Rayleen smiled at Melissa said. "How nice."

Melissa looked down at her shoes to hide her smile. Then she asked, "Is there anything I can do to help?"

"No, no. You just have Aaron introduce you to everyone. I've got everything under control in here."

Aaron gestured toward the room she had mentioned, and they moved in to a large family room. He stood with her and in turn introduced her to everyone in the room. Even though the couples were not sitting next to each other, he managed to pair them up in his introduction. In the corner opposite the TV, Don sat in a big, soft recliner with Joseline on his lap. Melissa greeted them each in turn and thanked them all for having her join them for lunch. Don gave her a big smile and said, "Well, we're glad to have you, Melissa. How do you like it over there at your granny's place?"

"Fine, thank you. Better when it's not storming out." She smiled and added, "That was really a noisy storm the other night. But I've only been there a few days. I'm just getting settled, but I think it will be very relaxing."

"Daddy says you live in Granny Emma's house," Joseline inserted. "Granny went to heaven to live with Jesus." She looked up at Melissa with wide brown eyes and turned down lips. "I miss her."

Aaron swooped her up in his arms and hugged her close. "We all do, Josie." Joseline suddenly turned shy and buried her face in Aaron's shoulder.

"She's darling," said Melissa. "How old is she?"

"Oh, I can't remember," Aaron teased, bouncing the girl in his arms. "I think she's thr ..."

"Four!" insisted Joseline. "Daddy, you always forget! I'm four years old, and next year I go to kindergarten."

"That's right," Aaron said, smiling at her, "I just can't believe my little girl is growing up so fast." He placed Joseline back on her feet and stroked her hair as she leaned against his leg.

"Okay, folks! It's as ready as it's gonna be," came Rayleen's invitation.

When all the diners were gathered around the table, Don asked everyone to join hands and bless the meal. Melissa listened as Don thanked God for all the guests; for Rayleen, who had prepared the food; and most of all for God's amazing gift of salvation through his son, Jesus. He closed with asking that the food and fellowship be blessed. Everyone murmured, "Amen." The conversation immediately centered around the beauty of the food and presentation. Heavy bowls and platters were passed so that everyone could take what they pleased. As the flurry of words and passing slowed, the conversation lulled into silence with only words of praise for the food. Melissa hadn't eaten that kind of food since she was a child visiting her grandmother at Christmas. Each bite was better than the last.

The talking slowly increased as the eating decreased. So many topics brandished around: economy, politics, farming, community, church, and family issues. Melissa felt like her head was spinning with all the chatter. Then one of the guys at the table said, "Hey, Aaron, how's that speed monitor working?"

The whole table dissolved into a fit of laughter except for Melissa. When the laughter finally subsided, Rayleen said, "We have to remember we have a guest at our table. We must be boring her to death with all our talk."

"That's right. My apologies, Melissa," said Don. "Tell us how you like living over there in Emma's house. Is everything working okay? Any problems? We've got some pretty handy people in this neighborhood, if you need help with anything."

"Don, for heaven's sake, give her a chance to answer."

Melissa smiled. "Well, I haven't been there too long. I just drove here from Chicago the end of last week. Everything is fine. Thank you for asking."

"Any time, Melissa. We are happy to have you in the neighborhood."

"That's right!" Rayleen interjected. "We don't want to be nosy Nellies, but we don't want you to be a stranger either. You come by anytime you need someone to talk to."

"Thank you." Melissa smiled at her hostess. "I will. And please feel free to stop in whenever you want. I would be happy for company so that I get to know everyone."

"Do you have a pet?" Joseline asked. Melissa shook her head no. "I have a cat. Her name is Paisley. She is my best friend, and she is so soft." Joseline continued to bombard Melissa with questions. "Do you like cats better than dogs? I don't, and Paisley doesn't like them at all. She gets really scared when dogs bark at her. Maybe we could find you a cat."

"Josie!" Aaron interrupted. "Give Melissa a break. You're going to wear her out with all your chatter."

"But, Daddy, how am I s'posed to get to be Missa's friend if you won't let me talk to her?"

The group giggled at the girl's pointed question. "She's going to keep you on your toes, Aaron." Don said between chuckles.

Aaron smiled and shook his head. "She's a curious one, and you know what curiosity does to kitties?" He bent to his daughter and lowered his face even with hers. "It tickles them!" With that, he gently tickled her under her chin and laughed as his beautiful daughter dissolved in a fit of giggles."

"Josie, sometime you and I can have a long talk. We could have a tea party, like ladies do," Melissa offered.

Joseline's eyes grew large and round, and she nodded enthusiastically. "I'll come see you at Granny Emma's house. We used to have milk and cookies together."

Melissa smiled her approval and met Aaron's eyes over the little girl's head. She was relieved when he smiled and nodded. "Sounds like a plan to me," he agreed.

Rayleen said, "Okay, everyone. We have red raspberry two crust pie or rhubarb cream pie for dessert. Just let me know what you prefer."

Melissa groaned and rubbed her stomach as she heard others call out which they wanted. When it came to her turn, she shook her head and said, "I can't eat another bite. It was all so good, and I think I overdid."

As she listened to the conversations around the table, she imagined her grandmother as a part of this group of friends. No wonder she'd loved it here so much. When one of the ladies asked what plans she had for the cottage, Melissa shared how she was enjoying the peace and solitude of the house for now, but she did want to sort through and organize Granny's things to figure out what to do with everything. There were no close relatives, and so she was searching for ways to reuse or find new homes for things.

"So are you going to stay, or do you plan to get it ready for a sale?" Rayleen asked.

Don interrupted her. "Now, Rayleen. Give the girl a chance. I'm sure she will tell us what she wants us to know when she ready."

Rayleen made a face at her husband and then said, "I'm sorry, Melissa. Don's right. I get so curious that it just takes over. But you remember that we are here for you. Now that our kids are grown, well, we could use a chance to help someone out. It gets awfully quiet around here."

Melissa promised to call them when she needed anything. Then she smiled at Don. "Maybe I'll even tell you the deep secrets of why I came here and left my exciting life in Chicago."

"Well, just make sure those secrets are worth repeating!" Don teased her. "Otherwise, they'll look pale in comparison to the stories that are probably already going around."

"Don Ralston! You know none of us tell stories; we just share information."

"Honey, I know you just share. It's all those others who gossip. Not you!"

Rayleen smiled sweetly and said, "You just wait until you want to know something, mister, and then we'll see who won't share."

The group laughed good-naturedly at their bantering. By the time desserts were finished, Joseline had crawled up on her daddy's lap and was dozing off. Suddenly, she pried her eyes open and said, "Don, can I ride your pony now?"

Aaron smiled and said, "No, little girl. You are going to take a nap before you do anything."

Joseline immediately screwed up her face and said, "But, Daddy, I wanna ..."

"Hey, Josie," Don said softly. "Rusty always takes a nap on Sunday after lunch. I don't think he would come out of his stall, even for you. We'll see what he's doing another time, okay?"

"Okay," she said as she lay her head against Aaron's chest and closed her eyes.

Aaron smiled his thanks to Don and stood with Joseline in his arms. "I think I'd better take her home. She's had a couple of late nights this week, so she's pretty tired."

Others took their cue to leave too. There were lots of thanks and hugs and handshakes all around. Melissa gathered her bag and made ready to leave with the others.

Rayleen drew her into a hug and thanked her for joining them. "Now, you think about coming tonight, won't you?"

"Well, I'm not sure. I may see you there."

"Don't forget to come back." Don said. "We're always glad to have company."

On the way back to town, Aaron sang little songs of comfort for Joseline, who was fighting sleep in her car seat. Once he was certain she was finally asleep again, he drove on in silence and thought about the day. He'd been so glad Melissa had shown up, and he'd been a little surprised at her reaction to his being a pastor. It had never occurred to him that she didn't know, but thinking back now, he realized that he'd never mentioned it to her. He smiled at her honest error of the wine, and then his smile broke into a grin when he tried to visualize Rayleen's response to her gift. Chuckling to himself, he realized he was very glad Melissa had come today.

His thoughts were interrupted by Joseline's question. "What are you laughing at, Daddy?"

"Oh, not too much. I was just laughing at your funny face!"

"Daddy, you're silly!"

He smiled. "I thought you were sleeping. Did you have fun today?"

"Uh-huh." Then she proceeded to tell him everything that her Sunday school teacher had said this morning, as well as all the children's behaviors in class.

Aaron listened to the sweet sound of his daughter's voice. Suddenly he realized she was talking to him.

"Daddy."

"Yes, honey?."

"Missa's really nice, isn't she?" He nodded. "I think Missa's really pretty." He nodded. "Do you think she's as nice as Granny?"

"Oh, probably. In her own way."

"Do you think she will let me play with Granny's toys?"

"I think so. Why do you ask, Josie?"

"Well, Granny always did, and we visited her a lot. And if Missa's nice like Granny, we'll probably visit her a lot too."

Aaron smiled at his daughter's logic and had to admit that there might be a strong possibility of that very thing.

Chapter 6

Melissa spent some time in the afternoon walking the perimeter of her property. The fences all appeared to be in relatively good shape. There was thick green grass in the meadows, and the woods were clear of dead trees. She made a mental note to read through her grandmother's business diary to see who had been renting the land for grazing, who farmed the tillable land, and who maintained the structures of the little farm. *I'll see Mr. Miller tomorrow. He'll probably have a copy of the rental agreement.*

When she returned to the house, she went to the antique secretary in the corner of the living room and opened her appointment book. She thought about how ironic it was that this little book had been her lifeline a few weeks ago. Now it had been unopened for several days. She flipped through the February and March calendars and noted how the scheduled events she had been responsible for had dwindled. When she came to the big red star on April 30, she smiled at the memory of the tremendous courage it had taken to leave her job.

It had been her dream job for the first few years. When she had applied for a position at Olson Marketing Inc., she was so proud to be hired. She'd never imagined what living in a large city among millions of people would be like. The job and lifestyle took her a long time to get used to. She quickly was promoted into more prestigious projects, but she never made many personal connections. After a few years of lots of hard work but only a few disappointing (and sometimes hurtful) personal relationships, she seized the opportunity her Grandmother offered her, if only for a while. It seemed surprising that so far, May remained empty except for the appointment with Mr.

Miller, Granny's attorney, and Mrs. Gleason, the financial advisor. However, she reminded herself that she had only been in Sovereign a short time, and she had already met several nice people who seemed eager to include her in their routines. She wrote in her promised morning coffee on Thursday with Linda Bodine and wondered whether interesting encounters might be coming her way.

Later that afternoon, Melissa jumped when her cell rang. She smiled at the picture of Brad's smiling face. "Hello, Brad!"

"Melissa, wow, it's nice to hear your voice."

"Oh Brad, I can't tell you how good it is to hear your familiar voice." She felt a lump form in her throat and willed herself not to let her voice waver. "I was just looking back through my calendar, and … Oh, it's so nice to talk to you. How are you? I miss you guys."

"Hey, is everything okay?"

After taking a second to ensure she was composed, she said, "Yes, of course I'm okay. Is that why you called? To make sure I'm doing all right?"

"Well, yeah—and to make you an offer. Are you sitting down? If not, you should be. Wait till you hear the deal I have for you."

Melissa made a face and then said, "Oh, do I have to? Go ahead. I'm sitting and probably won't fall out of my chair, no matter what the deal is."

She waited for a dramatic moment and then listened as Brad said, "Remember the account you were working on when you decided to leave?"

"How could I forget? What a headache. I'd just as soon forget about that one."

Brad hesitated and then continued. "Well, they've made some interesting changes that may help you change your mind."

"I can hardly wait." Biting the sarcasm in her voice back, she said, "I'm sorry, Brad. I don't mean to sound so rude. I just don't want anything to do with business, and especially that account, for a while. I was hoping I'd have a few weeks before I would have to meet my obligations as a consultant."

"I know." Brad paused for a moment, and Melissa smiled at the picture she had of him rubbing the palm of his hand over his red hair. "I know things with Sven were hard for you before you left, but he says he really wants you on the team, and he said to tell you he'll mind his manners this time."

There was a long pause again, and Melissa ran her last few months over in her head. Most of it centered round Sven Johanssen. He'd been the man of her dreams: good looking, wealthy, debonair, and oh so sensitive—until she expressed a need to have friendships other than his. Then she was treated like an errant child whom he had trouble tolerating.

Her thoughts were interrupted by Brad again. "But you haven't heard this deal. Come on. At least listen to me. Please? I promise that if you don't like what you hear, I won't bother you anymore with it. Just listen. Please."

"Oh, all right. I'll listen, but I'll not make any promises."

"Well, hold on to your hat. Old Man Johanssen decided to turn the deal entirely over to Sven. He gave him full reign and told him to make the decisions. Sven has ideas that are much more workable than dear old Dad's. He has plans for expansion that fit right in with the ones you and I had been collaboration on when you decided to hit the road. In fact, when I presented these ideas, he was really impressed." Melissa rolled her eyes toward the ceiling as Brad continued. "I told him you were a major contributor to this plan, and he told the boss he wants you to work on the account as a consultant. What do you think of that?"

Melissa felt icy chills move up her back. After thinking about her friend's proposition carefully, she finally said, "Sounds great for you, but I don't think it's for me at all. I'm just beginning to heal from the last trauma with the Johannsens, and I'm not ready to break open the wounds so soon." She paused and then added, "Besides, Brad, you are perfectly capable of carrying out this work on your own."

"That's where you're wrong. You're the idea person. I'm the one who puts feet to it, but you come up with the creative ideas, and together we make a very good presentation. We were a great team and could be again. Look, I'm not trying to make you move lock, stock, and barrel back to the big, bad city. Just consider the consulting part. Sven says he wants to go with these ideas and is willing to make it worth your while if you can deliver on these plans I showed him."

I bet! Melissa thought. *I doubt if making it worth my while means the same to him as it does to me.* "I don't know, Brad. I really don't feel up to getting back into it."

"Listen, Melissa. I don't know everything that went on between you two, but he seems earnest about wanting you to be a part of this project. Just think about it, okay? We could work it out so that you wouldn't have to spend more than a few days here every month once we get this off the ground. The ideas are ready. They simply need your touch to polish them off."

"I'll give it some thought," Melissa conceded. "But I'm not promising. Give me some time." *Why am I even considering this? I don't need the money. But still, it was an important assignment for me. I put a lot of work and time into that project. If I don't do it, will I be happy knowing I left it half completed? I don't want my professional career to end because I wanted to avoid Sven. I loved working with Brad and that creative team. I guess I need to be able to deal with Sven on a business level. I just need to remember that I can always come back to Sovereign if things get difficult.*

"Great. Only one problem. Sven wants some assurance of how we are going to proceed by the end of the week. I'll fax the specs in the morning tomorrow. You should have it soon enough to review it and think it over. Uh, you do have access to a fax machine, don't you?"

Melissa and said, "Yes, Brad. I'll give you my lawyer's fax number. He offered it to me for any use I needed." She rattled off the number and then listened as he repeated it back again.

"Okay, I'll send it out first thing in the morning."

"All right. But, Brad, please don't put me in a corner. I have to think this through carefully. I promise I will let you know by Tuesday afternoon. Okay?"

"Sure. You know I'm on your side. But this is a great deal, and if

Johanssen really pushes it with Mr. Cohen, you know he'll try to talk you into joining us. Mr. Cohen's a good boss, but he also wants to please the clients."

Melissa groaned and said, "I never thought of that. It would be just like Sven to force the issue too."

"Really, it wouldn't be so bad," Brad consoled. "We could work around your little hiatus out there in Cowtown."

Melissa laughed at that remark. "Not Cowtown, Brad. Sovereign. It's a nice place. You might like it here too. Fresh air, nice people, and a pace of life a human being can endure. You should drive out for a visit, or fly. There's an airport within an hour's driving distance. Not much worse than getting to O'Hare. Think about it, Brad, before that city life eats you whole."

"You make it sound downright pastoral, kind of like one of those commercials for a weekend getaway. But who knows?" Then in his best John Wayne drawl, he said, "I might get a hankering to see ya, Missy."

Melissa laughed at his silliness and responded, "I miss you too, Brad. You made working there bearable. I'll always be thankful to you for your friendship. That's why the invitation to visit is sincere. I'd really like you to come for a weekend. You'd be surprised how nice it is here."

"Well, maybe I will. What do you do out there, anyway?"

"I haven't been here too long, but I've put up some window boxes and planted some flowers and a couple of pots of herbs. This morning, I went to church and met some really nice people."

"Oh, be still, my heart! I don't know if I can stand the excitement."

Melissa could imagine him patting his chest and feigning a fainting spell. "Be quiet." She giggled. Then in a serious tone she said, "Brad, it is so nice to talk to you. Please come to see me."

"Good to talk to you too. I had tried to convince myself that I didn't miss you, but I do. I don't have anyone to squabble with, or anyone to share my great moments with. That's why this deal would be so great for us, Melissa. It would keep us in touch."

"I promise I'll give it serious thought, and I'll have an answer for you by Tuesday afternoon."

"Okay. I'll chat with you then."

As Melissa hung up the phone, she realized that Brad's familiar voice made her feel lonely for familiar faces. But the thought of working with Sven Johanssen again sent chills scurrying up her spine. She absentmindedly twisted her fingers together as she thought about her relationship with Sven. *Relationship,* she scoffed to herself. *All one-sided.* He had liked her ideas and thought she might be a nice diversion on the side in between trips to other companies. But when she didn't meet his personal performance standards, his attention turned from sweet to sour. She shivered at the memory of their last evening together. She grimaced at the memory of his temperamental outbursts and her hurt rebuttals. Then he was done with her, and he cast her aside like something unwanted and unimportant. He had hailed her a cab and almost pushed her into the backseat. She remembered the pain and disbelief as she watched him turn his back as the cab whisked her away. To make things worse, at work he refused to acknowledge her or her ideas in project meetings, causing lots of speculation and gossip among her co-workers. She remembered feeling so embarrassed by his reaction to her. Now to pick up and work for him again …

She jumped when her phone rang, answered it on the first ring, and was surprised to hear Rayleen's voice on the other end.

"Melissa. My, I was about to give up. Have you been on the phone? I kept getting voice mail."

Melissa tried to think of a way to avoid giving Rayleen too much information. After searching her mind, she answered, "An old friend. We were just catching up."

"Oh, that is nice. I just wanted to check to see if you'd changed your mind about coming to church this evening. We could pick you up. It's not out of the way at all."

Rayleen's request caught Melissa off guard and at a time when she really didn't feel like staying home alone. "Well, I guess I could. But there's no need for you to pick me up."

"Oh, we'd be happy to. We'll be over in just a few minutes. I'm so glad you decided to come. I know you'll love this presentation, and of course, Aaron will be pleased to see you too."

Melissa hung up feeling as though she had been maneuvered by a pro.

She was ready when the Ralstons arrived. The ride to church went quickly, and she felt right at home with Don and Rayleen. They both chattered all the way about their wonderful experiences in the Holy Land.

The church was almost as full as it had been that morning. However, the dress and manner of the people was more informal. Melissa was glad she had chosen her cotton sweater and jeans. Several people made a special effort to come over to visit with her. The atmosphere was one of a large family. Several people shared about friends who were in the hospital or other problems. Their genuine concern was evident, and their joy over someone's success or happiness was greeted with sincere smiles and comments. *This is nothing like my world in Chicago,* she thought. There had been plenty of gossiping, and successes were usually met with a gloomy forecast. *That's not all true,* she reminded herself. Brad had been a really positive friend, and Betsy and Sue had always seemed happy for her when she'd impressed a new account or earned an award. The big difference was the size of this whole group. So many people seemed truly interested in each other.

Melissa saw Linda Bodine waving to her from across the room. Linda said, "Come sit with us." Melissa made her way through the groups of people. "Did you have a nice afternoon?"

"Yes, I had a lovely time. The Ralstons invited me to join them and some guests. The food was delicious, and I enjoyed getting to know Don and Rayleen. I also visited with the Mikkers, the Matthews, and the Fellows. Don and Rayleen have a beautiful place."

The last comment brought a big smile to Jim's face. "It's good to know that we have some nice things that rival the ones in the city."

"Believe me, Jim, you have lots of things that are as nice as those in the city. The quality of life here seems to be very good."

"Was, uh, Aaron there?" Linda asked with an unmistakable gleam in her eye.

"Yes, as a matter of fact, he was."

"Isn't he just the nicest guy? I just think he'd make someone a great match …"

"Now, don't be butting into people's business," Jim interrupted.

"Oh, Jim. I'm just interested." Then she said to Melissa, "I apologize if I seemed out of place."

Melissa smile. "That's okay. Don't worry about it. Actually, he does seem like a very nice person, and I do want to make some new friends."

"Well, we're looking forward to getting to know you. Don't forget to come for coffee Thursday morning," Linda reminded.

Melissa nodded and looked toward the front of the room. She saw Aaron leaning over the organ, conferring with the young woman sitting in front of it. Momentarily, he straightened, smiled, and walked to the center podium. The din of conversation started to wane when the organist started playing. "Good evening!"

The group responded, "Good evening."

"It's been a beautiful day. I'm glad you're all here, because we have a special program tonight. Most of you know that Don and Rayleen are going to share their pictures and stories tonight. I've seen this presentation, and I promise you, you will be very pleased. However, before we get started with the show, we have some special music for you. The preschool children have a song for us."

Everyone watched as ten little boys and girls filed up on stage. Each one was a little more reluctant than the first, until they realized that they were the center of attention. Once they saw moms and dads in the audience, they turned from shy little children to pint-sized hams, waving and smiling at their very proud parents. Melissa was pleased to see that Joseline was among the little performers. She appeared to be reenergized and was posing and smiling for her daddy.

Their leader, a young woman, guided them into their proper places and reminded them of their purpose. She spoke quietly to them and, when she had their attention, signaled the organist to start the music. Almost on cue, they all sang "Jesus Loves Me."

When they finished, the audience applauded, and their little faces lit up with the joy of accomplishment. Aaron joined them on stage and said, "We are so blessed. I am thankful for each one of you! Let's give Nancy, our preschool teacher, a hand of applause." The audience responded with clapping and words of encouragement. Nancy dismissed the children, and they rushed to join their parents. Melissa watched Joseline skip happily to join her father. Aaron picked her up and whispered proud words in her ear.

When the noise settled, Aaron led the group in a brief prayer and then turned the evening over to Rayleen and Don. Melissa listened to Don's humorous account of their trip and didn't notice that Aaron and Joseline had slipped into the pew next to her until Joseline whispered, "Hi, Missa."

"Hi yourself," she whispered. "Did you have a good nap?"

Joseline nodded and snuggled up to her dad. Melissa smiled at Aaron, and he said, "I'm glad you came. I think you'll like these pictures and videos that Don and Rayleen have brought in tonight."

She smiled her agreement and turned her attention back to the big screen and the stories her new friends were sharing. She was impressed at how nicely the video was sequenced and staged. Melissa learned things about the Holy Land and surrounding areas that she never knew. She found herself becoming more and more fascinated with the pictures of ancient places where the Old Testament stories took place and where Jesus was known to have walked.

When Don brought the show to a close with one last witticism, the congregations was dismissed, and groups gathered into bunches before saying good night. Aaron turned to Melissa and asked if she had enjoyed her afternoon.

Melissa nodded and told him about her walk and her decision to rent out her pasture for grazing. She said she planned to come to town tomorrow to see Mr. Miller about some legal matters.

"Why don't you meet me for lunch, if you're going to be in town?" She agreed to meet him at the hotel coffee shop at 11:30. When Aaron stood, he smiled and said, "I'll look forward to it."

Melissa went to find Don and Rayleen for the ride home. Before she made her way across the room, Linda stopped her. "Looks like you two are getting along," she said with a big smile.

Melissa laughed and said, "Yeah, we are."

Linda's smile widened, and she gave Melissa a thumbs-up sign and said, "Good for you! Don't forget. My house, Thursday, at 10:00."

On Monday morning, Melissa drove to town to pick up some items from the hardware store and check out a variety store that seemed the same since the last time she had shopped there with her grandmother.

When she arrived at the lawyer's office, Mrs. Branson, his secretary, greeted her with a smile. "Well, Miss Blakesly, right on time, I see. I'll tell Mr. Miller you're here." She called him on the office phone and then said, "He'll see you right away. Oh, by the way, here is the fax that came this morning for you." She handed her a manila folder.

"Thanks, Mrs. Branson. You have been so helpful." She put the envelope in her bag and stood to enter the inner office.

Mr. Miller met her at the door and motioned her to a chair in front of his large oak desk. "Good to see you, Melissa." The older gentleman smiled at her over his half-lensed glasses. His smile, rosy complexion, and graying hair remind Melissa of a mischievous leprechaun.

"Nice to see you too," she replied as she made herself comfortable in the leather winged-back chair.

"Well, what can I do for you today? I've reviewed your grandmother's file, and it seems that things are moving along as expected."

"I'm not here just because of the grandmother's trust. I need your advice on something. Yesterday, I walked around the property and decided that I should check on renting part of it out for grazing. I thought I would talk to you first to make sure I have a legal right to do that."

"I am sure that your grandmother did rent that land, and that those renters are probably wanting to know if you will let the rent it again. You need to know that when your grandmother named you in the trust, you automatically became the sole owner of property. You have the legal right to do whatever you want with the land."

"Oh, I didn't realize that. The cottage, the land, and all the property are mine?"

"Yes. So if you want to rent it, lease it, or sell it, you have the legal right." He watched her as the knowledge of what her grandmother had done for her sunk in. Then he asked, "Do you know to whom she rented it?"

"I have read through her business diary and have found notations about renting the grazing land and the crop land to two different people. The notation also indicated that the agreements were in her lockbox at the Sovereign Security Bank."

"Let me review these pages again. No, I don't see any rental agreements here, so she must have kept them at the bank. Do you have a key to her lockbox?"

"Yes, there is one taped to the inside cover of this diary, so I will go there later today to see what's there." Melissa blinked back a couple of tears and then said, "Granny was pretty organized, so I'm sure I will be able to figure this out."

Mr. Miller listened intently and then said, "Let's see ... Don Ralston's land backs up to yours. Maybe he'd would know who had rented it last. You might ask him."

Melissa nodded. "I just met Don and Rayleen yesterday at church. Thanks, I'll do that. You do feel, then, that it would be legal for me to rent it?"

"Oh, sure. I see no problem. After all, your grandmother left it all to you in her trust." He leaned back in his swivel chair, placed his fingertips together, and appeared to be deep in thought for a moment.

"So, you met Don and Rayleen, huh? Nice people. Let's see … they go to Peace. Is that where you're attending?"

"Yes, or at least I did yesterday."

"Well, there are a lot of nice people who go to that church. They perform many wonderful services for the community. What do you think of the preacher, Chambers?"

"He seemed very nice and gave a wonderful sermon yesterday. The people of the church really seemed happy with him."

"He's certainly well liked in the community. Sad about his wife, though."

Melissa felt her attention focus sharply on Mr. Miller's words. "What do you mean? Is she ill or something?"

"Ill? Oh, no. Well, not unless you call plain poor judgment being ill. She and Aaron came to town about five or six years ago. They seemed happy enough—hard-working, dedicated couple. Then they had that beautiful little baby, and before she was a year old, that woman seemed to lose her mind. I don't know what happened for sure. But the story goes that Aaron came home one afternoon and found the baby screaming her head off with no sign of the mother. He came to find out that Tanja—that was her name—was out looking for something more exciting than staying home with a baby. She started running around with different fellows. Aaron was stressing out between checking on her, phoning her, and running home to check on the baby. He found the baby home alone a couple of times, and sometimes he took her into the office with him. He tried to get Tanja to go to a counselor with him, but she didn't want any of it. Finally, she ran off with some sales rep from Ohio."

"Oh, my goodness! Poor Aaron! Poor Joseline! Whatever happened? Has she kept in touch with them at all?"

"No, I don't think so. Aaron worked extra hard to make a good home for them both. He hired a housekeeper, Mrs. Mason, a widow, to take care of the little girl when he couldn't. It worked out well for both of them. Mrs. Mason lives just across the street, so she's pretty handy. She took those two under her wing. Couldn't find a better woman. I think it's kept her young. Probably couldn't tear her out of there with a team of horses."

"So Aaron never hears from his wife?"

"Oh, well, there's more to the story. About a year ago, her parents called, heartbroken. They had been notified of Tanja's death. Automobile accident, I guess. Terrible news. But I say it's better to have it resolved than never settled. You see, Aaron never filed for divorce. He always prayed that Tanja would come home. He made sure that Joseline knew her grandparents, but some things just work themselves out. It gives Aaron a chance to start his life over again. Strong man, that guy. He never wavered in his faithfulness to her all the time she was gone."

Melissa sat quietly absorbing all this information about her new friend. She'd never imagined that he had endured such agony.

Her thoughts were interrupted by Mr. Miller's words. "Fine man, Aaron Chambers. I imagine there are plenty of women who would like to keep him company." He leaned back in his chair again. "The lady who lands him will be one lucky woman, but she'll have to be willing to share him with the community. Yes, sir, it'll sure take one special gal."

Melissa was processing all this new information about Aaron and didn't notice the gleam in Mr. Miller's eye. She heard the clock chime eleven times and feared she had taken too much of his time. "Oh! Mr. Miller, thank you for your time and advice, and for letting me use your fax machine." Rising and moving toward the door, she said, "I've got to be going. I have another appointment at 11:30."

Mr. Miller followed her through the outer office and held the door for her. "Goodbye, Miss Blakesly. Keep me posted on any legal agreements you make." He turned back toward his secretary, smiling.

"Well, you seem pleased with yourself," Mrs. Branson commented while watching him. "What are you up to now?"

"Oh, nothing much. Just planting a few seeds." He smiled at the serious-faced woman and winked. "Just planting and waiting to see what blossoms." He chuckled to himself as he entered his private office.

Mrs. Branson shook her head and mumbled, "Old man gets sillier every day."

Melissa arrived at the restaurant at 11:10 and told Shelia that she was meeting Pastor Chambers. The waitress grinned and said, "Good going, gal. No point wasting time, I always say." Melissa laughed but asked her to show him to her table when he came in. She had a few extra minutes, and so Melissa decided to scan the fax information that Brad had sent her. The specifications, statistics, and ideas were all familiar to her. She and Brad had worked many hours on this proposal, and they both felt that it was a good one and would promote growth for the Johanssen Company. The last page was a scribbled note from Brad encouraging her to consider working on the project with him. All her thoughts were about the project, Sven, and Brad.

Melissa was just putting the papers back into the folder when Aaron arrived. "Hello. Looks like you're busy here. May I join you?"

"Of course, please do." Melissa smiled back at him.

All the while, Shelia was standing and watching this interaction with interest. When Aaron sat down, Shelia handed them both a menu and said, "Hot beef sandwiches are the special today. I'll be right back with water. You two take your time ordering."

Melissa stared down at the menu for a minute, and when she looked up, she and Aaron spoke at the same time.

"It's good—Oh, excuse me. You go ahead."

"No, you go first."

They both laughed, and the Aaron led off. "It's always nice to see you Melissa. Did you get everything on your list done this morning?"

"Yes, it was quite profitable. I feel like I accomplished a lot." All the time she was talking, she was thinking of the sadness he must have endured over the abandonment of his wife.

"Why the sad look?" Aaron asked with genuine concern.

"Oh, nothing really. Just one of those things. You know, ups and ..."

"Well, here's your water." Shelia stood, pencil poised. "You two have a chance to decide what you want?"

"Yes, I'm ready," Aaron replied. "How about you, Melissa?"

Melissa nodded and said, "I'll have the chicken salad croissant, and hot tea."

Sheila turned to Aaron, and he ordered. "I'll have the special please, and coffee with ..."

"Cream," Shelia finished for him. "Will this be one order or two?"

"Two," Melissa responded.

"No, please. My invitation, my treat." Aaron smiled at Melissa and then said to Shelia, "Please put them both on my bill."

"Okeydoke," she said. "That'll be right up."

"Oh, by the way, Shelia, I'm still waiting for you and that brood of yours to show up at church again."

"We'll be there. It's just hard with so many of us working and having so many different schedules. You know where my heart is, Pastor. My Nancy gets there regular."

"Yes, she does. She does a fine job with the preschoolers. Joseline just loves her. I can't count the times I've heard how Nancy says this or Nancy does that." He finished with a laugh and then added, "I'll be out to see you all this week, same time."

"We'll count on it. I'll go put in these orders." She left in a rush to take orders from the next two tables.

"Shelia's a great gal. She has a big family and a big heart. I try to get out to see them once a month or so. Since her husband, Herb, was hurt and can't work, it's put an extra burden on the whole family."

Melissa nodded in agreement. "She and I had a nice conversation Sunday morning. She knew my grandmother well. I enjoyed talking to her."

"Well, hello there." Melissa looked up to see Mr. Miller. "So, this was your appointment?" Then he turned to Aaron and offered his hand. "Nice to see you, Pastor. Hope you're enjoying your lunch with this young lady."

"Indeed," Aaron said with a smile. "Nice to see you too, Mr. Miller. I hope Mrs. Miller is well."

"Why, yes. In fact, she's waiting right over there, so I'd better get going. Just wanted to say hello." He nodded to Melissa, his eyes twinkling with merriment, and then he moved across the room.

"You seem to be getting acquainted pretty easily," Aaron said.

"Everyone has been very friendly and helpful. I feel as though this is home. It's so different from Chicago. There, I only knew a few people, and some of them weren't friendly. Here, everyone is open. I really like it."

Aaron nodded. "It is a friendly community." After Shelia brought their beverages, they sat sipping their hot drinks silently. Then Aaron broke the silence. "So do you have your week planned?"

"Well, nothing definite. Linda Bodine invited me over for coffee Thursday morning. I'm looking forward to that. She seems very nice, and I could use the company. A good friend of mine from Chicago surprised me with a call yesterday, and since then, I've been feeling kind of alone."

"I'm sure that's part of the process you're going through with mourning your grandmother's death. And besides, you've made a major life change by moving here." He leaned forward and said, "You know, I'm a pretty good listener."

Melissa smiled and nodded. "Yes, I know. But there's something important about having a woman for a friend right now. Linda seems so warm."

Aaron sat watching her for a minute and was about to speak when Shelia brought their lunches. "Well, I see you two haven't had any trouble keeping the conversation going." Then she winked at Melissa and said, "He's a pretty neat guy. If I didn't have that passel of kids and Herbie at home, I'd be setting my hat for this one." She finished by patting Aaron on the shoulder and laughing at his embarrassed reaction.

Aaron shook his head and looked down at his plate. "I declare, Shelia, I never knew you had thoughts of such intentions."

"Pastor, you'd be surprised how many of the ladies in the community have expressed the same idea." She chuckled again and then turned to greet more customers at the door.

Aaron rolled his eyes at Melissa and said, "I hope she didn't embarrass you. She is quite a card."

Laughing, Melissa replied, "I must say, I've never had anyone wait on my table who was quite the caliber of Shelia."

Halfway through lunch, Aaron returned to the subject of her plans for the week. "So, you've made plans with Linda for Thursday. What about the rest of the week? Do you have time for a pretty neat guy?"

The rephrasing of Shelia's remark made Melissa giggle. "Sure," she said. "It sounds like I'd be crazy not to. What do you have in mind?"

"I have to drive into Cedar Rapids tomorrow. Joseline needs some new clothes for the spring and summer." He stirred cream into his coffee and then said, "I could really use a woman's suggestions on picking out clothes for her. She very tolerant, but I think she's getting tired of sweat shirts and pants. The other day, she asked me if she could have some pretty clothes like her friends at preschool."

"Ooh." Melissa laughed out loud at the picture of little Joseline asking her daddy for such a favor.

Aaron smiled sadly and said, "Poor Josie. I'd do anything for her, but I don't do the best job of selecting her wardrobe. We could leave around 10:00, do some shopping, have lunch, and be back by midafternoon."

"Sounds like fun. I'd love to."

"Great, I'll pick you up then." As they finished their meal, Shelia stopped to refill their drinks, but they both refused.

"This has been very nice," Melissa said. "Thanks for lunch. You'll have to let me pay you back sometime."

"Well, you can always bake me some of those butterscotch chip cookies you make so well. I hate to eat and run, but I have several appointments scheduled for this afternoon."

"I have to go too." As they both stood, Melissa said, "Please tell Josie hi for me."

"I will. She'll be thrilled. She's already asked when she can come visit you."

Melissa smiled, "Soon, I hope."

Chapter 7

Melissa spent the afternoon going over the proposal that Brad had faxed her. There were several notations and additions. Some were in Brad's familiar handwriting, and some were in a hand that she recognized as Sven's. All the alterations and additions seemed feasible to her, and she spent the rest of the day adding her own suggestions. She was surprised at how enjoyable this type of work still seemed to her. *Makes sense,* she thought. *After all, I never disliked my work. It was just the overpowering need of the business to want more and more from me.* Then there was the relationship with Sven that made things so awkward.

While thinking about the events that had led up to her decision to leave, she created a list of pros and cons. She loved her work and prided herself on doing a good job. But, the more success she had, the more proficient she became, and that resulted in her receiving more recognition—which made her a magnet for more work. It also garnered attention from Sven Johanssen, the project manager and son of the owner of the prestigious Johanssen Inc account that had been using the Cohen Marketing services. He started spending more time in her department and stopping by her desk frequently. He invited her into the planning sessions and often deferred to her during meetings, noting her accomplishments. His attention was very flattering to Melissa, and she was pleased when Sven invited her to dinner one Friday evening. They spent the evening talking and sharing plans. When he continued to pay attention to her and invite her out with him, she agreed. It seemed that he was moving their friendship quickly into a romance, and Melissa wasn't sure she was ready for that kind of involvement with Sven.

One Friday night, however, she told him she had plans to spend the evening with some girlfriends. Sven accepted her refusal but seemed to be unhappy about not being with her. Just as she walked into the restaurant to meet her friends, Sven called her. She took the call and he asked her if she was having fun without him. She tried to soothe his feelings but told him she'd just met up with her friends and had to go. She didn't think too much about his call until she was interrupted again halfway through her meal. Sven's name flashed on her phone's screen. She considered sending the call to voice mail but decided to excuse herself and tell him she would call him in the morning. He responded with irritation and said, "I don't think I am asking too much to just talk to you."

"Sven, I would really like to catch up with these girls. We haven't seen one another in a long time. Please, just let me have a pleasant evening." She hoped she had consoled him.

She was surprised when he said, "You know, Melissa, I can be very nice to you, or I can make you miserable. You'd better think about what would be better for you at work."

Surprised and hurt by his remark, Melissa said, "If that is how you see our friendship, then you must have the wrong idea about us. We probably shouldn't see each other outside of work for a while."

"I don't think that would be a good idea. You don't want to push me away."

"Maybe you don't understand. Sven, I can't take this tonight. I want to go back to the table, and I don't want to talk to you right now. You need to back off and give me some space. I'm going to turn my phone off now. Maybe we can talk again next week. Good night."

As she placed her thumb on the off button, the last she heard from Sven was, "Don't you dare …" followed by her click. She returned and tried to enjoy the conversation and fun of the evening.

She spent Saturday visiting the farmer's market downtown and treated herself to a chair massage from one of the venders. When she got home, she fixed herself a delicious vegetable stir-fry and some fresh peach tea. The rest of the weekend went by quickly.

On Monday morning, she turned her phone on only to find several missed calls from Sven, a text saying he was sorry, and a voice message from her mom. Melissa found Sven waiting in her office. When he stood, she hesitated before moving behind her desk. "Sven, I hope you are here about the latest project, because I don't want to talk about Friday evening."

He watched her silently and then slowly closed the door. "Melissa, you know I think your work in impeccable, and you know that I'm interested in you as a person."

She nodded but didn't reply.

He waited, and when she didn't say anything, he continued. "You see, I'm not used to ladies turning me down. I've never had to schedule my time with them. You perplexed me when you didn't want to be with me Friday." He stretched out his hands in front of him, watching as the fingers extended and relaxed. "I guess I just didn't know how to respond to your rejection." Then he shrugged his shoulders. "I hope we can move past this."

She took a deep breath and said, "Sven, I didn't reject you Friday evening. I simply wanted to stick with a plan I had made with my friends several weeks ago. I meant no injury to you, but I do have friends whom I will continue to see occasionally."

He sat, nodding his head as though he was expressing understanding. Slowly he stood and leaned forward, placing his hands on the edge of her desk. He looked directly into her face and said, "So you're saying that you think I'm too demanding of your personal time?"

She sighed and then replied, "I'm just saying that as friends, we should be able to understand that there are other people with whom we spend time. That's all. No more, no less."

He looked deep into her eyes. "Well, I guess that is so. I hope we can continue to see each other."

"I would hope so." Melissa returned his gaze and smiled, hoping none of the uncertainty she was feeling was evident in her voice.

When he stood to his full height, he grinned and said, "Good to know that." He turned and opened the door but paused to add, "We will probably need to go through the plans for the project this week. I'll let you know when."

She nodded and proceeded to pull some papers out of her folder. "I'll keep working on it and wait for your direction." He saluted her with two fingers touched to his forehead and was gone.

She leaned back in her chair and thought about the encounter. She was very confused about his behavior and having to work too closely with him. She'd have to call her mom and talk to her. Maybe she could give her some ideas.

Just then, Brad stuck his head in her office and said, "Hi, gorgeous! Got a minute?"

Melissa laughed and suddenly felt the stress release. "Of course. Come in." They talked quickly about their weekends, leaving out her conflict with Sven, and then shared some of the ideas each of them had been working on for the current project.

By midweek, Sven called her to meet with the project team and present what she had been working on. When she got to the conference room, she was happy to see that Brad was already there. She settled in a chair, organized her notes, and waited for the meeting to begin. After some preliminary discussion, Sven asked Brad to present his ideas. Melissa smiled at Brad to encourage him, and she listened as he talked about changes in the plans he had worked up. When he finished, Sven asked Melissa if she had anything to add. She shared the data and designs that she had been working on. When she finished, Brad gave her a thumbs-up, and she nearly laughed, but she sobered when she realized Sven was watching her.

"Is that the end of your presentation, Ms. Blakesly?"

She nodded, and said, "Yes, Mr. Johanssen. Thank you."

Sven pressed his lips together and nodded. After a moment, he said, "Very well, then. That will be all for today." Everyone stood and gathered their work together. Then Sven said, "Ms. Blakesly, may I see you for a moment?"

After stacking her papers together and sliding them into binders, she said, "Of course." As others filed out of the room, she caught Brad making googly eyes at her. She had to repress an urge to giggle and return his look. Instead, she forced herself to ignore him so that she could attend to Sven, who she noticed was staring at her.

"Are you and Brad friends?" he asked, watching her face as he waited for an answer.

"Well, yes. We work together and share lots of ideas. We've become friends over that time."

"Were you with him Friday night?" he nearly whispered.

"No, of course I wasn't. I told you, I was with girlfriends; we get together every few weeks to catch up. Brad is my friend here because we support each other in our creative work. That's all."

"I see." He paused to look out the window at the rows of city buildings. "I wanted to apologize for my words Friday night. I was just feeling frustrated. I know that I must have sounded threatening at one point. I'm sorry." He turned toward her and waited.

"Sven … it's all right. I'm fine, and I appreciate your explanation."

"Thank you. I was wondering if we could have dinner together one night this weekend." He turned his attention back to the city view. "I would really like to show you that I'm not so demanding."

"Well, yes, I'm free Friday night. I would like that too."

"Good. Then I'll be at your apartment by 6:30, if that's okay. We'll eat casual and maybe take a ride down to the lake."

Melissa smiled. "I'll look forward to it." She stood to leave and said, "If there's nothing else, I'll get to work on these plans and ideas."

The next weeks went along smoothly. She and Brad worked together, coming up with new ideas to generate more interest in their project. The planning group praised each of their presentations, and Sven seemed pleased and at ease with the way things were moving along. When they made their final presentation and recommendations, the committee overwhelmingly agreed and voiced praise and approval for their work. Sven said he could not be happier and took the opportunity to invite Brad to join Melissa and him for cocktails in the executive lounge a few floors up. Brad expressed his thanks but asked to be excused because of other plans he had made. Sven agreed and then said to Melissa, "Well, how about a drink in my office?"

She had never been to his private area on the top floor of the building, but she agreed to one drink. He escorted her into the elevator, which whisked them up several floors. When the door opened onto a lavish office complete with a fully stocked bar and beautiful leather couches facing a fireplace, Sven said, "Have a seat in front of the fire. How about a cocktail or a glass of wine?"

She nodded and said, "Thank you, but I would prefer sparkling water."

Sven joined her on the couch with her glass of water and his tumbler of scotch. He leaned back, stretched, and said, "It feels so good to be able to send that project on to production. You did a wonderful job, you know." He smiled at her.

She smiled. "Thanks, but it was a cooperative effort with Brad. He gets at least half the credit."

He studied her for a minute. "Nevertheless, I know you put tremendous work into it, and Father and I appreciate it." He ran a finger down her nose, to her lips, and finally to her chin. He tipped her face up to his and leaned in for a kiss.

Melissa was surprised at his mixing business with such a personal gesture. She let herself enjoy the kiss but then leaned away from him so she could take a sip of her water.

"Hmm. Not interested? No one will bother us here. This is a very private area."

Melissa sat up and moved away from Sven. "It's not that. I just don't feel this is appropriate. I think I should go back to my office." Feeling like she needed to justify her choice, she continued. "There are a few things I'd like to finish up. Some notes and such." She stood.

Sven stood also but said, "Oh, Melissa. When are you going to let down your guard? You know I've been patient, and I've tried to respect the boundaries you've set. I think it's about time you be a little more thoughtful of what I want and how much I can help you in this business. If you would be just a little less inhibited and show me how much you appreciate me ..."

Melissa stared at Sven, her mouth gaping in surprise. "Appreciation? I thought that I was working for Mr. Cohen, and that my hard work was how I showed appreciation. Never did I think that our friendship was a part of how I was to be compensated." She set her glass down on the side table and moved toward the elevator.

Once inside, she quickly discovered that the buttons wouldn't respond to her touch. Sven came to the door and smiled at her frustration. "Calm down, Melissa. It reads my thumbprint. You still have time to reconsider, you know. Come back in so we can order dinner brought in and talk this over."

Melissa crossed her arms over her chest, stared past his shoulder, and said, "Please, I really don't feel comfortable here. Just let me go back to my office."

"Very well, then." The elevator buttons lit up, and the door slid closed.

She leaned back against the wall of the elevator and heaved a sigh of relief when it stopped and opened at her floor. She quickly went to her office, gathered her things, and was gone for the weekend.

By the time Monday morning arrived, Melissa had tried to put the incident into proper perspective. She went to her office and got ready for the day. Brad stopped in to talk about the next big project with her. Melissa stared at his blankly.

"Did you get the specs on this new deal? It's going to be a really big one." Not getting the response he expected, Brad continued. "Mr. Cohen must be pleased that Johanssen Inc is giving us so much work."

"No, I don't see anything on my desk or in my e-mail." She checked her phone and found that it was suspiciously empty. "I guess I'm not included in this project yet."

"What?" He rubbed his chin and then said, "This is one I'd really like to work with you on. I'll check with the head of this committee. I'll be back."

Melissa scrolled through her interoffice e-mail again and found no information about that project. There were a few minor projects available, but nothing very challenging.

She was deep in thought and did not hear Sven step into her office. "Good morning, Melissa."

She looked up at his handsome, smiling face. "Good morning."

"You look a little perplexed. Everything all right?" his blue eyes twinkled.

"I don't know. I was just looking for information about a new project Brad was telling me about. I can't find anything."

"Oh, yes, that one. Yes, a very important account. I suggested to Mr. Cohen that we should let Brad stretch himself on this one. Maybe you can take care of those smaller proposals. I think there are two available. They shouldn't take you long to knock them out."

"But I thought I'd proved myself beyond these small projects. I would really like to work on the more challenging ones."

"Well, I just wasn't sure you fully appreciated my influence in these assignments. Just do your best on those little guys for now."

Melissa stared after him in disbelief. Surely he wasn't going to use her work to try to manipulate her to see things his way. But then, he seemed to be doing exactly that.

During all that turmoil, her mother had called and told her she was planning to spend a week with Granny over the Thanksgiving break might. Melissa jumped at the opportunity to get out of the city. She spent a couple of long days working on the small projects that had been assigned to her. She put all her effort into producing an outstanding product. When she showed her work to the committee, they were very impressed with the quality. The clients were so happy with her ideas and presentation that they requested her work on their proposals in the future. She was pleased to receive such complimentary remarks. That afternoon, she sent human relations her request for vacation time to coincide with her mom's trip to Iowa. Later in the afternoon, she received an interoffice e-mail confirming her time off. She felt very happy with herself.

Sven stopped by after her proposal to congratulate her on her accomplishments. She thanked him and replied that she was simply showing her appreciation to the corporation. Smiling back at her, he said, "Maybe you and I can spend Thanksgiving together. I'd like to restore our good relations."

"That would be nice, Sven, but I'm going to be out of town over the holiday."

His eyes narrowed as he studied her. "Melissa, you seem to be resisting all my invitations lately. Won't you reconsider?"

Melissa sighed and said, "I'm going to spend the time with my grandmother. I haven't seen her in a while, and it is important to me to be there."

Sven nodded, smiled, and said, "Well, then, have a great visit. When will you be back?"

She told him she would be back to work on Monday after the holiday.

He smiled, gave her his two-fingered salute, and was gone.

Melissa flew into the Eastern Iowa Airport on Friday afternoon and joined her mother to drive an hour north and spend the entire week with her grandmother. They talked, laughed, and caught up on the time they had been apart. They visited all the quaint little shops, bakeries, and restaurants in the community, and they ended each evening in front of Grandmother's fireplace cozy and warm. When they left on Sunday, Melissa couldn't help but feel that time with her grandmother was slipping between her fingers.

On Monday, she arrived at work to find her e-mail full of work assignments. Not only did she have more requests from the companies she had done the small jobs for before break, but she also had been assigned to work with Brad on the larger project, and she had a request to work up a prospectus for a new company that appeared to be very extensive. Taken aback by the number of projects she had, she couldn't help but wonder if Sven was using all this to punish her for not spending time with him. Nevertheless, she was determined to do her best work. She called Brad and went over what he and his colleagues were working on. They arranged a 1:00 meeting so she could understand their direction. She reviewed the requests from the smaller projects and quickly drafted some ideas with notations. She looked over the data from the new company request, put everything into folders, and typed up notes in files for each. Feeling as though she had accomplished a good base for each project, she grabbed her lunch bag and bottle of water to go to the atrium in the back of the building's first floor for a quiet lunch in the sunshine.

Just as she was taking a bite of her sandwich, a familiar voice said, "Melissa, may I sit with you?"

She looked up into Sven's brilliant blue eyes and handsome face. She nodded, chewing her sandwich and motioning for him to sit down. She swallowed and took a swig from her water so she could say hello. "Oh, Sven. Well, I guess, if you want to."

He smiled and unwrapped his deli sandwich. "I thought you might be here for lunch. I know you enjoy this garden area, so I took a chance that I would be able to catch you."

She took another bite and chewed slowly, wondering where this conversation was going. Why he would eat a cold sandwich here when he could probably have a sumptuous lunch somewhere else? Her thoughts were interrupted by the sound of his phone and his terse hello. She tried not to listen but could tell by the tone of his voice that he wasn't very happy with the person on the other end of the line.

After ending the call with a click, he sighed and said, "I'm glad you are back, Melissa. Your work on those two small accounts is garnering a lot of attention. You seem to be good for business. I know Mr. Cohen wishes he had more employees who had the work ethic you do."

She smiled, happy for the compliments about her work. Then she listened as he continued. "I'm really happy that you are back, because I missed seeing you last week."

She stared at him, curious where this was going. She studied the apple she'd brought, turning it around in her hand. Finally she said, "I had a really good time with my grandmother. My mom was there too. It really made me realize that time with them is passing way too fast. I'm glad I could spend the weekend with them."

"That's good. But I hope you and I can spend some down time together. Do you think we could get together for dinner, a movie, a walk, or something this week?"

She was surprised at the anxious tone in his voice as he talked. She looked at him and saw that he was almost begging her for a date. "Sven, it seems to me that you and I are not on the same level with our friendship ..."

"Not the same level?" Sven interrupted. "I'm not sure we are in the same area. You just don't seem to understand how I feel about you."

"No, I guess I don't." She hesitated. "Sven, I'm not sure this is appropriate for us to be discussing on our lunch break. I have a meeting at 1:00 to go over the project with Brad and the committee. Why don't we postpone this talk until after work? There's a great pizza place down the block from my apartment. I could meet you there at 6:30 for a light supper. Maybe that would be a better environment to talk things over."

She watched him as she talked and waited for his reply. Finally he responded, "Yes, I would like that. Tell me the name of the place, and I'll be there."

The afternoon presented more challenges. The committee, including Brad, filled her in on the project. They had created an amazing proposal but had gotten stuck in some of the details. Melissa listened to their ideas, read the proposal, scanned the diagrams, and spent a lot of time thinking about the project. "It looks like you all have worked very hard on this. But I think you need more research on the mechanics of the company we are trying to market here. I am a good researcher, and I will do some reading and try to find information online to support this plan. Maybe I can find a little more glue and mortar to pull this all together."

"I told them you were the detail person," Brad said as he beamed at her.

"Well, you guys have put in a lot of time and effort. We simply need some more information to nail down the focus of our project. I am so happy to be able to join in with you all."

After a few words of welcome, everyone moved back to their office areas. Brad lingered a moment. "Good to have you back, and good to have you join the project, Melissa."

She smiled, "I'm happy too, Brad."

"I don't understand why you weren't on it in the first place." He shook his head. "Sven said you had other things to take care of. He sure was a bear to be around last week." Brad made an ogre-like face and then laughed.

Melissa could never resist his comical ways and joined in his laughter. Then she looked around, wondering whether Sven might be watching them or listening to them. She said, "Well, I'd better get back to my cell."

"What? What are you talking about? What cell? Your office is just like all of the offices."

"Oh, nothing. Forget I said anything."

Her evening with Sven did not prove to be the solution to their problems. Sven had arrived before Melissa and was waiting at a table in the far corner of the room. He rose, greeted her with a kiss to her cheek, and held her chair for her. He sat across from her and asked if she was ready to order. She nodded and said, "I really like the goat cheese with spinach, red onions, and tomatoes." He smiled and beckoned the waitress, who took their beverage orders. Sven ordered a German beer, and Melissa ordered a glass of sparkling water with a twist of lime. Sven ordered a sausage, pepperoni, and cheese pizza on thick crust and a goat cheese, tomato, and red onion pizza on flatbread for Melissa. It seemed interesting to her that Sven and her tastes were often on the opposite end of the spectrum.

Sven leaned across the table and held his hands out palm up, inviting Melissa to place her hands in his. When she did, he took a deep breath and said, "I'm so glad to have some time alone with you. I hope we can resolve some of our concerns tonight."

Melissa smiled, wondering whether she could feel for Sven what he seemed to be indicating he felt for her. "Sven, I respect you very much. I'm just not sure I understand your feelings for me."

He lifted one of her hands to his lips and said, "What's to understand? You're beautiful, bright, and fun to be with. You intrigue me. I think about you all the time. I love being around you."

They were interrupted by the waitress bringing their beverages. Melissa took a sip of her water, giving herself time to think about his statement. She tried to evaluate her own feelings about Sven, wondering why she couldn't express similar sentiments about him. "Sven, I am so flattered. No one has ever said anything so nice to me."

He smiled at her over the rim of his glass. "I get the feeling that you are struggling with this. Melissa, I'm not asking for a commitment, but I do want you to know my feelings. I think you should consider what I can do for you both professionally and personally."

Surprised, Melissa felt her face flush and mouth drop open. "What do you mean by that? What you can do for me?" She tried to stop herself from popping off and saying what she felt. "What are you implying?"

Sven looked at her unsmiling for a moment. "I'm just saying that when I'm happy, I like to make other people happy. That's all."

"So are you saying that it was your influence, not my ideas and my work, that impressed the clients?"

"Well, not exactly. They did love your work. Your work is exemplary. But you know I dropped those clients in your lap."

"What?" she blustered. "You mean those 'little jobs' that you left me when you wouldn't give me a part of the larger project?"

Sven's face started to become blotchy. He pressed his lips together as if he was trying to hold something in. Finally he said, "Melissa, I know that's what it looked like, but I was just trying to let Brad and his team show me what they could do. I knew you could handle the other two projects on your own, and I was right. You did a superb job—so good that they both threw more work to Cohen Marketing. I would think that should be a good indicator of the influence I have and how I can help not only you but the corporation as well."

Melissa stared at the few bubbles in her glass, trying to control her feelings of frustration with Sven and his assumptions. "Sven, I want to work on projects, big or small, on which I can do my best work. I don't expect you to do me any favors or prejudge me based on our personal relationship."

Sven stared at her, seeming to weigh his words in his mind. They sat in silence until Sven said, "I'm sorry you feel that I would act that way. I don't want to feel at odds with you." He finished with a sigh and leaned back in his chair. "It doesn't seem that we are making much progress toward resolution."

She was trying to think of how to reply when the waitress brought their pizza. It smelled delicious, and she knew it tasted wonderful, but she had lost her appetite. Sven toyed with his pizza and moved a piece to his plate, but he didn't seem too interested in eating either.

Melissa broke the silence when she said, "Sven I don't think this relationship is working for me right now. I just can't separate it from work. I don't think we should see each other for a while socially, until I can have a clear thought in my head."

"If that's what you want, then I will respect that. It's not what I want. But just so you know, I will not assign or withhold projects from you because of this."

"Thank you." Melissa felt like a huge burden had been lifted from her, but she also felt like crying. She took a deep breath, determined not to make more out of this than it already was. She felt extremely awkward at that moment, and she was uncertain of what to do next.

Fortunately, Sven took care of the situation by calling for the bill. When the waitress asked if they wanted to take their pizza with them, he said, "No, I think we've both lost our appetite." He then said, "Melissa, let's not leave this on such an uncertain note. I think we both need to take a break from this. I'll give you as much room as you need. I'll say good night, and when we see each other at work, we will continue with the best interest of the company. Does that work for you?"

She nodded and smiled the best she could. When they stood and walked out to the street, she turned to say good night. He leaned down and kissed her on the cheek. "Good night, sweet Melissa. I don't think you should walk home alone, so I hailed a cab."

"No, Sven, I'll be fine. I'll see you at the office."

He opened the cab door and nearly pushed her into the back seat. After leaning forward, he handed the driver a fifty-dollar bill and told him the address. "Keep the change." He turned and walked away.

Chapter 8

Sven was good to his word, and Melissa's work environment was happy and productive. She and Brad worked together with other team members, and Sven seemed pleased to listen to and add ideas to theirs during planning meetings. As Christmas approached, Melissa received a call from her mother that Grandmother Emma was not feeling well. She was failing, and her mother was dealing with the heartbreaking fear of losing her. Melissa shared the pain of those feelings and talked to the team and to Sven about needing to take a break to be with her mom and grandmother. Mr. Cohen was gracious about encouraging her to take time for her family. She spent several days in the hospital, and as she watched the wonderful woman fail, she regretted the fact that she had been so engrossed in the demanding lifestyle she had been captive to for the past few years.

Emma Wainsworth passed from this life on December 15. Melissa was inconsolable. All too late, she realized that she was not able to hold back time. Granny was gone, and Melissa felt bereft. She had little memory of the visitation or the funeral. She and her parents tried hard to support one another, but the loss was so great. She remembered people coming to share their grief with them. She remembered a service in a small white church in town, but the words said about her grandmother were lost in her grief.

After the funeral, they cleaned and straightened the cottage, contacted the lawyer, and left instructions for a caretaker they had appointed. It was hard to leave, but it would have been impossible to stay. Melissa followed her parents to their home in Cedar Rapids to spend Christmas. They made a tentative plan to return in the spring to sort through the contents of the house. Her mother told her then that her grandmother had left the cottage, the land surrounding it, and a trust fund to her. Melissa was stunned and protested, thinking that her mother should have been the beneficiary.

"Oh, darling," her mother said in a soothing voice, "this was your grandmother's wish. We had talked about it, and she knew that your dad and I are very blessed financially. She wanted you to have a cushion and an opportunity to live whatever life you choose. She chose to give this to you, with her wish that you use it however you want." Melissa knew that she could not handle these decisions now. Her parents promised to help her with anything she needed. After the holiday, she went back to her life with a broken heart, so many memories, and now the responsibility of owning property.

Melissa was sure that work was the only way to cope with her sadness. She went in early and stayed late. She took every account she was offered and made her skills available to Brad and the team. Sven stopped by her office daily for the first week, but she seemed to be so secluded in her cocoon of work that his sympathies were brushed away as she excused herself to return to her current project. Brad also tried breaking through the wall that she had built around herself, but she was only interested in focusing on her current work. Sven, Brad, and team members shared concerns for her well-being, but all decided to allow her time to heal; they would be available when she felt like talking.

Melissa's coping took its toll on her emotionally. When she wasn't at work pushing herself to research and create, she was at home wrapped up in a blanket and only answering her parents' calls. Her friends tried to cheer her up, but she remained in her isolation. While thinking about her grandmother, she remembered the woman encouraging her to pray to Jesus Christ when she had problems. Although she knew a lot about God and Jesus and Christmas, she had never put much thought into praying for anything. Oh, she remembered when she was a little girl, praying that she would find her dog, and she did. But that was a coincidence, wasn't it? Granny put a lot of stock into prayer, so maybe she should try it, just to honor the memory of her.

She bowed her head, closed her eyes, and started talking to God. Even though she was alone, she felt foolish talking out loud to someone she couldn't see. But knowing Granny believed so strongly in it, she continued. "Dear God, I know you know me. I'm sure you heard a lot about me from my grandmother. I'm sorry that I haven't come to you before, but I've been so busy, and now I'm so sad, so lost. Would you please help me move out of this dark and depressing place in which I've found myself? I know that I don't deserve anything, but please, God, help me. I am so sad. I need your help. Amen." She sat for a moment, wrapped up in a blanket with her head bowed, and tears streamed down her face. Somehow, she felt she had been released from some of the grief she'd been carrying around. She sat that way for some time, thinking about God, her requests, her parents, her grandmother, and her life. She was so deep into her meditation that her phone's ringtone startled her. Without looking at the caller ID, she answered it on the fourth ring. "Hello, hello?"

"Melissa? You answered. I'm so glad. This is Brad." Melissa smiled at her friend's excitement—the first time in a month that she had found anything to smile about. It felt good. *Wow, God!*

"Hi, Brad, how are you?"

"I'm fine. I'm just calling to see how you are doing."

"Well, maybe better." She felt her throat constrict and tears well up in her eyes. She sniffed and then said, "I am better. Thanks for asking."

"I've been so concerned for you." There was a long pause, and then Brad said, "Hey, have you had supper?"

Melissa tried to remember if she had eaten anything. She knew she'd lost weight because her clothes were loose. "I don't think ... no, I haven't eaten. I should probably see what I have ..."

"Wait, wait! I made an amazingly delicious pot of Chicago chili, and I would love to bring some over, okay? How about it?"

She could imagine Brad scooping chili into a container as he talked. "That sounds like a lot of trouble."

"No, it's not any trouble. I'll be right there. Can we eat together? Is that okay with you?"

"Of course it is."

"Okay, I'm on my way. I'll buzz you in ten minutes."

Melissa couldn't help but laugh at the picture of Brad. He did live close, and so he could probably walk easily. She caught her reflection in the mirror and noticed that she had a smile on her face. *Wow, God!* she thought for the second time. *Is this real?*

She cleared her table off in the kitchen and put random cups and spoons into the dishwasher. She had just finished wiping down the counter and the table when she heard the buzz. She went to the security screen, saw Brad's smiling face, and typed in the code to allow him inside. She waited by the door until she heard the elevator open, and then she unlocked and opened the door for her friend.

Brad whizzed by her, smiling and asking about the microwave. He put his pack of goodies down on the counter and then turned to her and held out his arms to her. She walked into them and let him hug her tightly. Then with her at arm's length, he said, "Oh, Melissa. You look so much better."

"Thanks." She sniffed and wiped a tear away. "What is Chicago chili, anyway?"

He shrugged and made a silly face that made her laugh. "It's chili that I make in Chicago," he said as he unpacked a huge container of chili, saltine crackers, and a pint of butter pecan ice cream. "I hope you have room in your freezer, or we could eat dessert first and warm up with chili."

Melissa shook her head, smiled at her friend's logic, and took the ice cream from him to put in the freezer. Brad had already put the open container in the microwave and was opening the saltines. "I didn't bring anything to drink."

"Hmm. I can give you water or ice water," she said.

He stared at her dumbfounded. "Melissa, you said something

funny! You *are* getting better." He looked out the window and said, "Thank you, God!"

The microwave dinged, and he made quite a fanfare of pulling out her chair for her. Then he ladled chili into two bowls and brought the opened package of saltines to the table. After filling two glasses with water, he placed one at each place and then sat across from her. "No guarantees. The chili is my favorite, but it's not gourmet. Hope you like it."

She dipped the spoon in the chili and brought it to her lips. "Yum, very good." She followed Brad's example and crushed crackers into her bowl. Then she took another bite and said, "Oh, Brad, this is good. Thank you!"

He smiled, and they ate together, two friends sharing a special moment.

When Melissa finished her bowl, Brad swooped it up and opened the freezer door. "It's a rule that you have to eat ice cream after chili. Otherwise your metabolism will overheat, and you won't be able to sleep tonight."

Melissa stared at him. "What? I've never heard of that." Then upon realizing he was teasing her, she laughed. "You got me, Brad!"

He smiled and said, "Where's your silverware?" She told him, and he brought the pint of ice cream and two spoons to the table. After opening the container, he handed her a spoon and said, "Dig in." They sat eating butter pecan out of a container, and finally Brad said, "Is there anything I can do for you, Melissa?"

She focused on the ice cream and said, "I don't think so. This was so nice of you. Thanks. I think I'm turning a corner." She sat quietly for a moment and then said, "Brad, can I ask you a personal question?"

"Of course, anything you want to ask."

"Well ... do you ever pray?"

She chanced a look up at him and found him smiling at her. "Of course I do. It's a good thing. God's a captive audience. He's always available and is always willing to listen. Best of all, he always has the perfect answer."

Melissa felt tears crowding into her eyes and looked down quickly. She sighed and then said, "That's good to hear." She fished out another bite. "I prayed tonight that God would help me get out of my doldrums. It made me feel better, and then you called."

"I've called lots of times. I was so happy to hear your voice that I nearly dropped the phone."

They talked for a while—some about Melissa, some about her grandmother, some about work, and on and on. When Brad looked at his watch, he said, "Wow, it's 10:30. I'd better get home. See you tomorrow?"

She nodded and then said, "Thanks, Brad. This was good for me."

He smiled and said, "Good for me too. Everyone at work will be happy to see you feeling better."

"Good night." She closed the door and again thought, *Wow, God!*

The next morning, she arrived at work at her regularly scheduled time instead of the early hours she had been keeping. She looked at people as she met them and smiled at their greetings, aware that their smiles seemed to brighten when she made eye contact and said, "Good morning."

Two of her team members, Kristen and Jessica, followed her to her office. She smiled at them and asked if she could help them. Kristen said, "We're just so happy to see you smile. It's been a long time since you have said good morning or taken time to smile at us. Welcome back!" Jessica nodded and smiled and held out her arms for a hug. Kristen joined the two, and the three stood laughing and talking at the same time.

Brad stuck his head in and said, "What's all the commotion about? A man can't hear himself think in this place!"

The three girls stared at him for a moment and then erupted in laughter again. "Oh, Brad! Let's all have lunch together today," Jessica suggested. "How about 11:55 at the coffee shop downstairs?" They agreed.

Brad lingered a minute to say, "Team meeting at 9:45 in the conference room. It will be great to see your smiling face there."

The next day progressed nicely, and Melissa realized that everything seemed so much easier. She thought about her grandmother, but she remembered some happy times with her instead of only grief. She felt productive, and it seemed people went out of their way to say hello.

She felt happier for the first time in weeks. She was working through her grief, she was enjoying her work, and she had renewed her friendships. Early in the afternoon on the following Tuesday, she received a call on her cell. She didn't recognize the number but noticed the area code matched her grandmother's. "Hello, this is Melissa Blakesly."

"Ms. Blakesly, this is Mrs. Branson from Miller, Miller, and Allen Law Office, in Sovereign. Mr. Miller handled your grandmother's legal affairs. He would like to speak with you."

"Of course, thank you."

There was only a momentary pause, and then Mr. Miller was speaking to her. "Ms. Blakesly, how are you doing?"

"Fine. Better than I was, thank you."

"I'm sorry to interrupt your day, but I wanted to talk to you about some legal affairs concerning your trust."

"Okay, I have a few minutes. Go ahead."

"Well, Mrs. Gleason over at Sovereign Savings and Loan called me, and she is wondering if you want to do something with the money your grandmother left you in the trust." He paused. "You know, she is just wondering if you want to keep it at SSL. She's getting a little concerned because some of the investments have dividends that may need to be reinvested."

"Oh, yes, the trust. I didn't think it was a large amount. Did you say investments? Are you sure it's mine?"

"Yes, very sure. Your grandmother was quite adamant about you having this. Didn't your mother mention this to you?"

"Yes, she did. I've just been so overwhelmed with my grief. I knew she left me the cottage in trust. How much money are we talking about?"

"Well, you'd be better off talking to Mrs. Gleason. She's the trust manager at the bank. But I'm pretty sure it's several hundred thousand dollars. It's enough to deserve your attention. And we also need to talk about your land. The renters have been asking if it is available to them again this year."

Melissa felt waves of shock roll over her. She noticed the phone start to slip from her fingers and grabbed it before it fell. She could hear Mr. Miller calling her name. Finally, she gathered her wits and said, "This is such a surprise to me. I will call Mrs. Gleason. Can you give me her number?"

As Mr. Miller supplied the number, she scribbled it down on a pad of paper. She promised Mr. Miller that she would call the bank to discuss matters, and she would keep in touch with him and make decisions about the property rental.

She leaned back in her chair and said aloud, "Oh, Lord. What am I going to do?" A thought came to her. *Maybe I should take a leave of absence and go to Iowa to check out the property and financial trust that Grandmother left me. I'll talk to Mom and Dad and get their thoughts on what I should do.* She quickly wrote out a list of things that would need her attention so that she could leave her job for a few weeks to make decisions about Grandmother's gift to her. It seemed quite a huge responsibility, and she felt she needed to deal with it in person and directly. She called Mr. Cohen's administrative assistant to discuss how to handle personal leave like this.

Of course, Melissa did not want to leave the team without a completed project. She talked to them about her plan to be on extended leave while she figured out what to do with her newfound responsibilities. They were very helpful in working with her to expedite the process, and Mr. Cohen agreed that he would not assign other projects to her. He assured her that included Sven and Johanssen Inc. He did call her into the office when she was clearing her work area, and he asked her to consider staying on with the firm as a consultant. "Since you are asking for a substantial leave away from work, we would like to know you would work with us on specific projects." She agreed that she would consider any project, but she shared that she was feeling overwhelmed with all that faced her. He wished her well but said he would be in touch.

Chapter 9

Tuesday morning, Melissa woke up in her grandmother's home in the country for the sixth time. She realized that she was beginning to feel that it was normal to be there. Even though Grandmother had given this property to her, she had difficulty comprehending that this truly belonged to her. She loved everything about it. The more she worked to clean and organize the house, the more it seemed possible that it could be hers. Yet she still expected to walk into the kitchen and see Granny sitting at the table with her coffee cup and newspaper. She reminded herself to give it time. She and her mother talked frequently, and between calls and visits, Melissa felt more and more comfortable with this life.

She made her coffee and then took a cupful and her muffin out onto the porch, where the sound of the birds greeted her with beautiful songs and trills. She closed her eyes and tried to remember the sound of street traffic and the commotion of people rushing past her on their way to work or school. It all dissolved into a vague memory, and she let herself enjoy the surroundings of nature. It was such a luxury to relax and enjoy the sounds and smells and the feeling of sun on her face.

A feeling of satisfaction wafted over her as she thought about her trip to the bank; meeting with Mrs. Gleason, Granny's financial advisor; and sorting through the safety deposit box. She found the rental agreements Granny had made. Fortunately, the names corresponded with the notations in the diary. A call to Mr. Miller assured her that he would draw up paperwork. All she needed to do was contact each person and have them stop in and sign the agreement. Mrs. Gleason helped her find phone numbers, and they both seemed happy to be offered the same agreement for this year. What a relief to have that completed.

Her phone pinged a reminder that Aaron would be there in an hour. She didn't want to make him wait. At 10:00, his red Jeep pulled into her driveway just as she was finishing straightening her house and checking that windows were closed and doors were locked. Without waiting for him to come to the door, she went to meet him.

"Hi! Isn't this a beautiful day?" She twirled around, holding her arms outstretched. "I wish I could capture this and keep it forever."

Aaron leaned against the front fender of the Jeep and listened to her with an amused look on his face. "Good morning to you too. I agree, a beautiful day—and a beautiful lady."

Melissa stopped and smiled at him. "Thank you. I feel beautiful today. I'm so glad you suggested this trip. I've been looking forward to it since you asked me."

They rode along, chatting about ideas for Joseline. Aaron pulled out a list of measurements and suggestions that his housekeeper, Mrs. Mason, had given him. Melissa looked it over and then said, "You know, this is kind of like the blind leading the blind. I've never shopped for a little girl either."

Aaron turned to look at her, and they both burst out laughing. "Well, at least two heads are better than one, and at least you have the advantage of knowing what you liked as a little girl."

"I loved blue jeans and sweat clothes when I was little. But I also remember a couple of outfits I had that I enjoyed wearing, mostly because my daddy made such a fuss over me when I wore them." She smiled at Aaron and continued. "Daddies have a lot of influence on little girls. So don't worry about it. Trust your judgment. If you like it, chances are that Josie will like it too."

When they arrived at the mall, they took time to stroll through several stores. In each children's clothing department, they checked sizes and prices. The salespeople were very helpful. By 1:00, they had packages containing everything from underwear and pajamas to swimwear, play clothes, sneakers, pretty dresses, and fancy shoes for church. Satisfied with his purchases, Aaron asked Melissa if she had anything she wanted to look for.

"No, I don't need too much. I think I'm fine."

"All right, then. How about lunch? There's a nice place on the edge of town called the Orchard."

"Sounds good to me. I am getting hungry."

Once in the car, Aaron said, "I think you'll really like this place. I used to take my wife here." He watched her reaction to this information.

Melissa smiled and said, "I've never heard of the Orchard before." She turned to meet his gaze. "Aaron, I haven't wanted to pry, but I must tell you that I had been curious about your marital status."

"Had been?"

"Well ..." She swallowed and continued. "Mr. Miller told me about your situation yesterday. I am so sorry that you've had such sadness in your life."

Aaron pressed his lips together as he guided the car into a parking place near the entrance to the restaurant. "Hmm. I should have known someone would tell you. News circulates rapidly in a small town." He sat quietly for a moment, watching people come and go. Then he said, "It was pretty rough. Sometimes I still can't believe it happened." He shook his head sadly. "I always thought Tanja and I were invulnerable. Then when Josie came along, I was sure we had a perfect family life. Did Mr. Miller tell you that she died?"

Melissa wanted to comfort Aaron but didn't know what exactly to do. "Yes, he told me. I'm so sorry."

Aaron smiled at her again—a sad smile of a man who had experienced a lot of pain. "Thank you." He sighed. "I'm glad you know. I don't want to forget Tanja, but I don't want to dwell on the pain either. The Lord is leading me through it, and I'm having more peace about it now." He sat for a moment. "Let's not let this dim the beauty of the day. We both need to eat and enjoy our time together."

At lunch, they recaptured the mood of the morning. They sat at an umbrella-covered table overlooking the orchard covered hills, and they talked of things that people who were becoming good friends found fascinating. When Aaron looked at his watch, he said, "Oh, it's later than I thought. I need to get back for an appointment."

"That's fine. I should probably work on organizing more of Granny's stuff and make decisions about what to keep and what I can throw away, what to shred, and what to recycle. It gets complicated, and sometimes overwhelming." She sat thinking about the task she had facing her. It seemed to be a slow process. She realized it was a task she needed to complete, but she wasn't about to let it dim the wonderful memories of her grandmother.

"I know it's not easy for you. Even though you parents come up and make suggestions, it all seems to fall to you. But prayer does help. It gives God that niche to come into your life and work things out."

She smiled. "I'm ready to let him do that for me, but I know I still interfere because I just don't know how to let him."

"Melissa, I will pray that you find peace in all of this."

She turned to smile her thanks at Aaron and said, "That helps so much. I am just beginning to include God in my daily activities. He has helped me a lot, but I don't always remember to invite him into my life." She felt tears piling up behind her eyelids and willed them away. She knew that Granny prayed for her, and her mom and dad too. Brad had said he prayed. How nice to know Aaron was joining these wonderful people in praying for her.

When he dropped her off, Aaron walked with her to the porch. Melissa unlocked the door and thanked him again for the nice day. "My pleasure," he said. "Well, I'd better go. I have promises to keep. One of my parishioners has been having some problems, and I told him I'd be out this afternoon."

She nodded. "I guess you have one of those jobs that doesn't allow many blocks of free time."

"Yeah, that's true. But the benefits outweigh the concerns. I can't say I mind helping people and telling them about the Lord." He hesitated for a moment and then said, "I meant what I said about praying for you, and about being a good listener. You can call me if you need someone to talk to."

"Thank you, I will. Let me know how Joseline likes her new clothes."

He laughed and headed to his Jeep. "I'm sure you'll hear her all over the county when she sees her haul. Thanks for coming along."

Chapter 10

Melissa worked on her project the rest of Tuesday and all day Wednesday. By Thursday, she was sitting on the kitchen floor and contemplating the piles of cookbooks, journals, and scrapbooks that Granny had stored in the bookcase between the kitchen and dining room. She wasn't sure whether there was anything there she wanted to keep. *I guess I can just box it all up and take it to recycling,* she thought. It was such a beautiful day that she was considering going out to dig weeds out of the flower beds, but she wasn't sure what was a weed and what was a flower. When she heard a car drive up, she walked to the front door and was surprised to see Joseline looking in the screen door.

"Josie!"

She opened the door, and the little girl threw her arms around her legs and said, "Missa, I just rode on Rusty. It was so much fun."

"I'm not sure he will ever be the same," came the teasing voice of Aaron from the porch.

"Hello," Melissa greeted. "Come in, won't you?" Aaron opened the door and entered the living room, where Joseline was still telling Melissa the wonders of Rusty the pony.

"And Don said I could come out every day if I wanted to!"

Melissa covered her lips to stifle a giggle at Aaron's forlorn look, and she watched as he kneeled to talk to Joseline on her level. "I don't think Rusty is up to that much excitement, Josie. Besides, you have all your friends and Mrs. Mason and me to play with. What would we do if you rode Rusty every day?"

Without missing a beat, Josie said, "Oh, Daddy! I'd still play with you." She put her arms around him to reassure him.

"Well, that's good to know," he said with a grin. "Now, let's tell Melissa why we're here."

"We want to play with your toys!" Josie announced.

"You want to what?"

Aaron laughed quietly as he shook his head. "Emma always kept a box of toys that she let Joseline play with when we visited her. We thought maybe you still had them."

"Oh! I did see a box in the pantry. I'm glad I didn't throw them out."

"Me too!" Joseline agreed as she followed Melissa to the pantry. Together they dragged out the box and looked through the collection. "See, here's my granny doll. She didn't go away, and here's my cars, and this is my puzzle."

Melissa kneeled next to Josie as she completed her inventory. "I'm happy that you came to visit Granny's toys. She would be so pleased that you want to play with them."

Aaron smiled down at the two and said, "Whoa, remember, those aren't yours. Only yours to play with when you visit."

"I know," came Joseline's reply as she became lost in her world of imagination.

"This is a nice surprise," Melissa said. "I was just trying to make some decisions about all these cookbooks, and Grandmother's journals and scrapbooks. I guess I'll keep a few and take the rest to recycling."

"Do you mind a suggestion?" When she smiled and shook her head, he offered, "The historical society might be interested in anything about the history of the area. Those journals and scrapbooks may have interest to them. The cookbooks could be sold on the church garage sale. We have some storage space, if you want a place to put them."

"Okay, let me sort through them again, and then I'll let you know. Do you think cookbooks would sell?"

Aaron laughed. "Yes, I've seen ladies grab those up quickly. The proceeds of the garage sale go to missions support."

"That's a very good idea. Say, do you have time for some cookies and a glass of milk? Or I could make coffee. We could take them out on the porch."

"Sounds like a winning idea to me. Let me help." He turned to Joseline and said, "Josie, Melissa and I will be on the porch. Do you want to come?"

"No, Granny wants to go to town, so I gotta take her. She's been very lonely without me."

Aaron stood for a moment to watch his daughter discuss the trip with her doll and then drive the car around the braids of the rug. "Okay, but you come out when you want to." He held the door for Melissa with her tray of cookies and glasses of milk. They settled in the wicker chairs on the opposite end of the porch swing, setting the refreshments on the coffee table between them. The weather seemed perfect: a slight breeze, sunshine, and the promise of a beautiful spring ahead of them.

"When will the farmers start tilling the fields?" Melissa asked.

"I have seen a lot of ground worked up. I imagine they will be planting soon. This is perfect weather for it, and I'm sure they are anxious to get going."

Melissa offered Aaron another cookie and then said, "How did Josie like her clothes?"

Aaron chuckled. "She loved them all, especially the dresses and the cute shorts outfits. She modeled them all for me and Mrs. Mason before supper. She even wanted to wear the swimsuit to bed!"

Melissa joined in his laughter. "I'm so glad she is happy with them."

"Oh, she was. She wanted to wear some of them today, but it's still too cool for shorts, so I promised her she could wear them as soon as we saw tulips bloom. Thanks again for helping me out."

"I was happy to. It was nice to have a diversion. It helps to define the days of the week."

"I remember Emma saying something like that." He stroked his chin and then continued. "If I remember right, she talked about how the days of her life were like an endless circle until she marked them with a special event. I remember several times we would sit here or in the kitchen and talk about the most important events in her life." He paused and seemed to be thinking about a very serious subject. When he continued, he looked directly at Melissa. "One of the events she talked about was the day that she accepted Jesus Christ as her savior."

Melissa thought about her grandmother and some discussions they had had about church and faith. Aaron broke into her thoughts and said, "What about you, Melissa? Do you have a day like that?"

"I … I don't know." She looked at him and then down at her hands. "I'm not sure what you're talking about."

"Let me ask you another question before I answer, if you don't mind."

Melissa shifted in the rocking chair, feeling unsure of what was to come next. Then she looked directly at Aaron and said, "Sure, go ahead."

Aaron smiled the smile that made the whole world a little brighter. "Melissa, if you were to die tonight, would you go to heaven?"

Melissa wasn't sure she was hearing correctly, and she leaned toward him. "Excuse me?"

"I said …"

"I know what you said. But why did you say it? How could I know?" She leaned her head back against the high back of the chair and thought for a moment. "I guess I don't know what you are asking me. I … I think I would. I try to do what is right." She sat up straight and returned his direct look.

Aaron nodded and started again. "What I'm asking is not what kind of a person you are, or what kind of a life you live. I think you've demonstrated that you're a very nice and honorable person. What I want to know is, do you have the assurance of going to heaven when you die?"

Despite not knowing what to say, Melissa sensed that Aaron was completely genuine in his question. After some thought, she said, "Well, I went to Sunday school and church when I was growing up, and I learned some Bible verses; I still remember some of them. I usually say a prayer before I eat, and sometimes before I go to sleep." She looked at him, wondering whether she was telling him what he wanted to know. "Does that answer your question?"

Aaron leaned closer and said, "Let me ask you this: Do you know that Jesus Christ is your personal savior? Is he a part of your daily life?"

Melissa thought about her response. "I don't know. I remember learning that Jesus is the son of God, and that he died on the cross to save me from my sins. But I'm not totally sure that I know him the way you're talking about. I don't know …"

Aaron smiled. "Let me give you an illustration of what I'm talking about." He picked up a cookie and said, "If this cookie represents salvation, and this plate represents God …" He laid the cookie back on the plate and then offered it to her. "If you don't accept that cookie and taste it, you'll never truly know it is a cookie. So, when God offers you salvation through His Son, Jesus Christ, first you have to recognize and accept that Jesus is the son of God." Melissa smiled and nodded. "Okay. So, in your mind, you have admitted that Jesus is the son of God and the way to salvation. But to experience the joy of your salvation, you have to receive Jesus Christ as your personal savior."

"Okay, so knowing about Jesus isn't the same as having him as my personal savior?"

"Exactly!"

"Oh, all right. I understand. Thank you, Aaron."

He smiled. "Well, there are a couple of more steps that you need to know about."

Melissa leaned forward in her rocker, elbows on her knees and head propped on her hands. "What are they?"

"You have to confess it to others." He smiled at her questioning look and continued. "Think about it this way. You made these delicious cookies and offered them to me. I took them home, but I never told you whether I enjoyed them. You'd never know whether I ate them or threw them out the car window."

"So I'm supposed to tell people that I like Jesus?

"Well, yeah, but more than that. You know Jesus is the son of God." Melissa nodded. "You need to pray to receive him into your heart and confess your belief in him as your savior with your words."

Melissa leaned back and continued to rock in her chair, watching Aaron's earnest countenance. After a while, she said, "Okay, I can do all those things. I want to do those things."

"Good! Now, you need to admit that you are a sinner and ask forgiveness for them. After all, we wouldn't have a need for a savior if we didn't know we sinned."

Melissa sighed. "I know that I sin. Not great big ones, but sometimes I have angry thoughts, or I react to people or situations in a mean way. Sometimes I say or do things I know I shouldn't. I do want to change those things. Is that what you mean?"

"Exactly. That's all there is to it." He pushed the chair back and then let it rock forward. "So, Melissa. Is this your special day in your circle of days?"

She smiled at him and said, "It could be. It doesn't seem hard. I don't feel any different."

He reached over and took her hand in his. "Let me share a prayer with you. Lord, I praise you for your works, and thank you for Melissa's life and for her acceptance of you. I pray that you work in her life and give her assurance of your presence and your love for her. I ask that you be with her and assure her of her eternal salvation. Amen."

He gave her hand a slight squeeze, and when she opened her eyes, she was looking directly into his warm smile. "Now, be sure to ask questions as they come up." He pulled a folder from his shirt pocket and said, "This explains what we talked about this afternoon. Do you have a Bible?"

"Actually, I have one, and I have the one Granny kept at her desk."

Aaron smiled. "You might want to look up some of the verses mentioned in the pamphlet and read them in context." He took another cookie and said, "These sure are good. Maybe even better than Emma's."

Melissa smiled and said, "Thank you."

As they sat and enjoyed the sunshine, their conversation turned to other subjects, and their relationship gradually changed again from pastor and parishioner to friends.

Aaron asked Melissa if she missed her friends in Chicago. She replied, "Some I don't miss at all, but others, like Brad, I really miss." She enthusiastically shared Brad's phone call. She didn't notice the serous way Aaron was watching her as she talked. "Actually, we worked together on many projects and produced some great results. Now the company is offering me a job as a part-time consultant. I can work from home. Brad's going to fly out, so we can spend some time together and go over the account sometime in the next couple of weeks. I would really like you to meet ..." She stopped midway in her sentence when she noticed the expression on his face. "Is there something wrong?"

"No, not a thing." He rubbed the back of his neck with the palm of his hand, seeming to study the floor of the porch. "I just didn't know you were involved with someone."

Oh, it's nothing like that. Brad and I have been friends and co-workers for several years. We're collaborating on this project for work that we will present next month in Chicago. We've used Facetime and text, but we want to sit down in the same room and do the fine-tuning. The boss is okay with him coming here."

"Will he need a place to stay?"

"I just thought he would stay here. We'll get a lot done, and besides, we have a lot to catch up on ..." She stopped again because of the thoughtful look on his face. "Don't you think it would be okay for him to stay here? I have plenty of room."

He smiled and said, "Melissa, it's not what I think. But this is a small community, and people see who comes and goes. You've caught the interest of a lot of your neighbors and others in the area. I just don't want you to set yourself up for a lot of questions or conversations." He ended with a smile and then added, "Just so you know, the church maintains a cottage behind my house for visitors to the church—you know, other pastors, missionaries, and extra guests. It's available if your friend wants to use it."

She stared at him, processing his statement. "Thank you, Aaron. I'll think about it and share it with Brad. I'll let you know."

He nodded. "That sounds like a good idea. Consider it prayerfully ..."

He was interrupted by Joseline's perfect timing. Like a small tornado, she burst through the door, letting it slam loudly behind her. "May I have a cookie?"

Melissa looked at Aaron. When he nodded, she said, "Sure," holding the plate to her eye level. "Pick out the one you want."

Joseline picked out the perfect cookie and then joined her dad on the rocker. She cuddled up to him and munched away on the treat. He smiled and wrapped his arm around her. He asked, "Did you put away the toys?"

Josie nodded and after a few more bites said, "I put all the toys in the box and gave the Granny doll a big kiss, so she won't be so lonely." She ended her sentence with turned-down lips that seemed to tremble a bit. "I know she is very sad without Granny Emma." She buried her face in her dad's shirt, and Aaron held her close.

Melissa smiled and said, "I'll be sure to talk to her every day. I get lonely sometimes too." She watched as Josie turned her face toward her. "I know! Maybe you could come out to visit us more often."

At that, Joseline smiled and nodded enthusiastically. "I would like to come out every day, but I have to go to preschool and take care of Daddy and Mrs. Mason." She heaved an enormous sigh. "So I can't come over here all the time."

Melissa grinned and said, "Anytime you want to come, you are welcome."

Joseline finished half of her cookie and then wiggled off the chair, heading out to the yard intent on trying to entice the noisy squirrel to come close. Aaron and Melissa watched her, concerned that the squirrel might try to take a bite. They were amused as it scampered away with Joseline running after, holding cookie out at arm's length. They sat in comfortably together, enjoying the warmth of the breeze.

Aaron broke the silence and said, "There's a new exhibit at the art museum in Cedar Rapids through June. Would you be interested in seeing it with me tomorrow evening?"

Melissa turned to face him and considered this kind man who had challenged both her spiritual and social being this afternoon. Without a second thought, she said, "Yes, I would like that."

Aaron beamed. "Great, I'll pick you up at 7:00. That should give us plenty of time to drive there, enjoy the exhibit, and return without rushing. I guess I should get Josie back to town. Mrs. Mason has left supper for us in the slow cooker, and Josie is going to need a bath after riding Rusty." He wrinkled his nose and laughed. "He's pretty old and stinky, but she thinks he's the wonder horse." He called Joseline to his side and whispered something in her ear.

"Thank you, Missa, for letting me play with Granny's toys, and for the cookie." Aaron waved as they climbed into the Jeep and took off down the road.

Melissa stood to watch them leave and found herself thinking, *Am I being overly concerned about Aaron's reaction to Brad staying here? Am I going to have to be careful about everything I say and do?* She shook her head, walked back into the house, and smiled at the granny doll sitting on top of the other toys. She picked her up and hugged it. "Either I'm too cold or too bold."

Chapter 11

Melissa spent a restless night tossing and turning. Every time she closed her eyes, she could see Aaron's face. Was it her imagination, or had there been disapproval when she'd told him about Brad coming and staying with her? Finally, she gave up the hope of sleep and got up at 5:30. *I don't know why I let things bother me so much*, she thought. *I'm not doing anything wrong.*

She moved into the bathroom to brush her teeth. She stared into the mirror and said, "If I wanted to carry on with Brad, I certainly wouldn't tell Aaron Chambers about it!"

She picked up her hair brush and started brushing her hair vigorously. "Who cares what he thinks?" She slammed the brush down on the counter and shouted into the mirror, "Why does his opinion matter so much?" She shook her head in disbelief. "I must be going crazy! Here I am, talking to myself about a man I've known for such a short time. Maybe I should go back to Chicago and try to save what's left of my sanity."

She thought about the truth of that idea. For the first time since moving here, she had to deal with the reality of living alone in a cottage in the country with very few connections. Although the people she had met were friendly, there was no one around when she opened her door. She wasn't used to not seeing people coming and going once she left her home. She didn't have her friends to chat with, and she missed the camaraderie of Brad and her other work associates. "I don't know. Maybe moving here was a mistake." She held her face in her hands and groaned. "But I don't want to live in that rat race anymore." She thought about the people she rode up and down the elevators with each day: everyone stared straight ahead as though the other didn't exist. After thinking about the adjustment she had made in her lifestyle, she said to no one, "I just don't know."

Forlornly, she wandered into the living room and collapsed into the overstuffed chair. After curling up sideways, she laid her head on the broad upholstered arm. She let her mind go blank as she stared at nothing. Her grandmother's words quietly came to mind. *"Melissa, no matter what happens, and no matter where you are, you always have a friend in Jesus. He will always listen to you, even when others don't have the time or inclination. You take your cares to him and ask him what to do. He'll always listen, he'll never hurt you, and he'll always have the right answer."*

Melissa sat remembering her grandmother's bright blue eyes shining as she told her only granddaughter about the importance of prayer in daily life. *Maybe she's right,* Melissa thought. *Maybe Jesus does care about me.* She quietly started her prayer. "Jesus, please hear me. I'm feeling confused and misunderstood. I don't know whether I'm right or wrong, but I hope you will help me know what to do." She continued to sit quietly and eventually drifted off to a peaceful sleep.

Melissa awoke with a start to the sound of quacking. She realized her phone was ringing Brad's personal ringtone. She grabbed it and answered, "Brad! What's up? Why are you calling so early?"

"Well, it's nice to hear your voice too, Melissa." She could imagine Brad's put-out expression to her greeting. "Some of us have to get up in the morning to go to work. Not that you're currently in that group." He tried to sound grumpy, but she knew her friend too well and was sure there would be a chuckle coming forth. There was. "How are you doing out there? Not up with the roosters, I see." He chuckled again at his own humor.

"Well, I had kind of a sleepless night and, so I guess that I was catching up."

"Hmm, what's keeping you from sleeping? Not worrying about me or Sven or our project, I hope."

"No, not really. Just one of those things." She paused. "So why are you calling?"

"I just wanted you to know that I just faxed the contract for our project to your lawyer's office. I hope that's okay. Anyway, if you can sign it and fax it back to the grumpy guy at the office ..."

Melissa smiled at his sarcastic reference to Sven. "I'll take care of it this morning. So, things haven't changed in the office?"

"Well, not for the better. Sven is always barking orders and pushing everyone to the limit. I'm hoping he'll be happy with this project and give us all a break."

Melissa felt her heart rate increase at Brad's description of Sven's insensitive demands. She closed her eyes and thanked God for this quick answer to her request. "Oh, Brad, I'm sorry you are having to endure Sven's ill temper. I pray that he will lighten up on all of you. I know that I don't want to walk back into that either."

"Well, hopefully once we get this project into the works, he'll calm down. He did almost smile when Cohen told him you had agreed to come back as a consultant."

"I don't know whether or not that is a good sign."

"Who knows? I sure don't. Well, changing the subject, I am calling to check out your accommodations out there in the Wild West. Do you folks have a motel?"

"Actually, we do. But we also have a couple of other options too."

Brad immediately returned with, "You mean a bunkhouse or a teepee?"

"No, don't be silly. I've been attending church, and they have a cottage they offer to guests. I was thinking maybe that would be nice for you. It looks cozy and would be quiet. Or you could stay here with me, but the spare bedrooms are filled with Granny's stuff, and there is only one bathroom here."

"Well, I don't think I should stay with you because Sven has been asking about you and where I would stay. I don't want to antagonize him. The guest cottage sounds nice. We could work together and then have our privacy. Anyway, I can be antisocial before I've had my quart of coffee and a hot shower. I wouldn't want to do anything to offend you."

Melissa felt like a huge weight had been lifted off her shoulders, and she let out a sigh followed by, "Okay, I'll set it up for you. Bye for now. Looking forward to seeing you."

"Me too!"

Melissa quickly made a call to Mr. Miller's office to check whether the fax had arrived. It had, and she told Mrs. Branson that she would be right in.

By 9:00 she entered the law office. Mrs. Branson handed her the contract, and Melissa quickly read it and signed it. She waited to make sure the fax was received, and then she took her original copy. "Thank you so much! This is so nice of you."

"Not at all, we are glad to do it for you. Have a nice day, Melissa."

On the way to Linda Bodine's house, Melissa was engrossed in her thoughts when something the announcer said caught her attention. "And in John 16:24, we receive the assurance, 'Until now you have not asked anything in my name. Ask and you will receive, and your joy will be complete.'"

Melissa stopped and contemplated the passage. *They make it sound so simple,* she thought. Out loud she said, "Just ask, and I will receive. Well, I'm asking again, Jesus. I need some assurance and guidance that I'll make the right choice, and that these doubts I'm having will be eased. Amen!"   Melissa followed the road south two miles. "Third driveway on the right," Melissa mumbled as she remembered the directions.

When she drove into the drive, a huge tan and white collie came running up to escort her car to stop at the side of the house. She sat for a minute, sizing up the behavior of the dog. Then she heard, "Don't be scared—she's friendly."

Melissa opened the door to meet Jim's friendly face. "I'm so glad. I wasn't sure."

Jim waited, holding the dog's collar. "She loves company but gets a little excited when someone new visits. Her name is Poppy. Julie named her after her favorite flower of the day. I think it's a dumb name for a dog, but you know little girls get just about anything if they smile pretty enough." Jim smiled, and Melissa reached out to pet the dog. She was thanked by the appreciative look of soft brown eyes and a lolling tongue.

"It sure is a beautiful day. Nice day for a little drive," Jim said. "Linda's in the house. She's looking forward to your visit. Go right in. She's in the kitchen just inside the back door."   "Thanks."

Jim waved, and he and Poppy headed toward the pickup truck parked in front of the garage. Melissa followed the path around to the back of the house and rang the doorbell.   "Come on in, Melissa. I see you've already been greeted by two of the Bodines."

Yes, and a very gracious greeting," Melissa replied with a smile.

"Would you like coffee or tea, water? Just name it, and I'll try to come up with it."

"Thanks. I just finished breakfast, but maybe a glass of water would be nice." Melissa noticed the farm-style kitchen and the gleaming hardwood floors. But the bay window with a window seat caught her eye. There on the window seat was a group of cushions and pillows, and a Bible open as if someone had just been reading it. Linda joined her at the table with the glass of ice water and her own cup of coffee.

"You have a beautiful place here. It looks like it should be in a magazine."

Linda chuckled. "Well we try to keep it picked up and clean, but it takes all of us to make it work." She paused to sip her coffee. "I'm so happy you came, Melissa. I've been looking forward to getting to know you a little better."

"Thanks. Me too. I hope I'm not keeping you from doing anything."

"Not at all. I need a break about this time of day, so I welcome your visit. We've been up since 4:00 doing chores and looking over the cattle. About a third of the herd are calving, and we need to keep a close eye on them."

"I had no idea your day started so early!"

Linda laughed. "Not many people do. If you're not involved in farming, you have no way of knowing how much work it takes." She sipped her coffee. "Enough about me. How about you? How are you doing over there in the Emma's cottage?"

Melissa stifled a yawn. "Excuse me. I didn't sleep very well last night."

Linda nodded and said, "I understand that. I hope you're not coming down with something."

"No, I'm fine. I just was letting my thoughts take over last night and didn't fall asleep. Very early in the morning, I got up and sat in Granny's overstuffed chair. I remembered that she always told me to pray about things and let Jesus take over. I did, and I felt so at peace. I fell asleep in that chair and felt pretty good this morning."

"You know, Jim and I try to start each day with scripture and a prayer for the day. It seems like things go a lot better when we take that bit of time and include God in our day."

Melissa absorbed her friend's testimony. "So, you think daily prayer helps?"

Linda smiled and nodded. "Believe me, sometimes it's minute-by-minute prayer. If you're interested, a group of ladies meet here on Tuesday afternoon and do a Bible study about prayer, sharing what our concerns are. You are certainly welcome if you want to come. Just drop by, and bring your Bible and a notebook and pen. It's a great time. We keep it to an hour from start to finish, so that we can keep a schedule." Then she chuckled and added, "Well, we pray for an hour, but then we stay for a snack and some socialization. It might be a good way for you to meet more of the ladies in the community." She smiled, patted Melissa's hand, and winked. "Pray about it."

Melissa nodded and smiled. She made a mental note to add to her list of things to consider.

Linda said, "So what do you have planned for the day?"

Melissa grimaced and then said, "There seems to be no end of things to do around the house and the yard. Leaves need to be raked, and I'd like to plant a few flowers and maybe a little garden for fresh salad, and ... Oh, I don't know what all. I'm just trying to decide how much I want to do while I'm here. I'm kind of in a quandary about what I want to do here and keeping some connections with my job in Chicago. Grandmother was very generous to me, so I have choices to make that are different than I've had before."

Linda listened as she added some ice to Melissa's drink and then filled her own coffee cup. She offered her a slice of yummy-looking coffee cake. "Well, have you talked to a financial planner? That could help lift some of the burden of handling assets."

Melissa stirred sipped her ice water and broke off a corner of her coffee cake. "Grandmother had her investments with Mrs. Gleason at Security Bank. I like her and will probably stay with her."

Linda nodded. They chatted on about the neighborhood and how much Emma Blakesly added to the community. "She was well liked and respected. We all loved her and were sad to lose her," Linda said, and then she smiled when she caught Melissa wiping a tear away.

Melissa said, "I still miss her so much. I wish I'd spent more time with her."

Linda grabbed a tissue and handed it to Melissa. "But you did come out as often as you could. And your cards and letters and phone calls were the best part of her week. Don't regret anything. You have a whole life ahead of you, and that's what you need to focus on while you honor your grandmother. She wouldn't have wanted it any other way."

Melissa smiled and nodded. "I know. I just have to keep myself busy."

"Have you thought about a job. I thought I noticed a few things in the paper last night."

"Well, actually, I have a part-time job. My firm in Chicago has hired me as a consultant a few days a month. I'll be doing a lot of work out of my house and an occasional trip into Chicago. I've just been feeling restless—you know, missing familiar faces and all that. Anyway, I got up early, and Grandmother's words came to mind about how important it was to pray. Then when I was driving here, the radio announcer gave a scripture from John about asking for anything and receiving it. I guess I'm searching for answers. And then our conversation about prayer too. It seems obvious that I'm supposed to pay attention to all these cues."

Linda laughed and said, "Well, he isn't being too subtle with you. You just don't know. None of us know how absolutely Jesus loves each of us and wants the best for us."

Melissa sat thinking about the immensity of that statement. She shook her head and said, "Oh, my. It's overwhelming when you put it that way."

"Think about that Bible study. We would love to have you join us."

"I will. Well, I'd better get on with my day." She stood up and picked up her phone and keys.

That evening after raking and digging up the garden spot, Melissa spent a long time in the shower letting the hot water soothe her aching muscles. She towel-dried her hair, finger-combed it into waves and curls, and put on her favorite jams. Before she allowed herself to get too comfortable, she pulled out the scripture verses Aaron had given her and searched them out in the Bible. She read through each one carefully and noted that they all had to do with works God would do in her life if she allowed him to do so. The one that she decided to focus on was Proverbs 3:5–6. "Trust in the Lord with all your heart and lean not on your own understanding; in all your ways acknowledge

Him, and he will make your paths straight." She sat and thought about that passage. *It all seems so simple. This morning it was "ask, and I will receive," and now it is "trust, and he will guide me."* Out loud she said, "Okay, God. I'll give it my best try. I've told you my concerns, and I will wait on guidance. Thank you for being so patient with me." Before she could say amen, she had fallen asleep.

Chapter 12

The sun shone in on Melissa before 6:00 the next morning. Melissa squinted at the light and smile. "Good morning to you too, God." She reread the verses she had marked in her Bible and prayed about her day and the decisions and plans she had. Before she had finished breakfast, the delivery truck drove into the driveway and dropped off a package for her. She was excited to see whether the curtains she had ordered were what she'd wanted, and she tore into the package and held up a panel. They were perfect, a beautiful, subtle fabric that would look pretty but would also block out the sunlight.

Excited to put up the new curtains, she carried them into the bedroom and held them up to the window. They seemed to be the right length and width. Now to hang them. The rods were a little too high for her to reach and take down. She considered a chair but wasn't sure that was a good idea. Maybe there was a ladder out in the shed. Practically skipping, she made her way out of the house and to the rear, where the shed stood. She opened the creaky doors and stared into darkness. After letting her eyes adjust to the lesser light, she moved to where she remembered she had found the light switch earlier. She patted the walls, found it, and then could see a little better. After looking at all the stuff in the shed, she searched for a ladder or step stool of some kind. She had to be careful where she stepped because there were boxes and buckets all over the floor. While scanning the perimeter, she saw a ten-foot extension ladder and a two-step ladder. *That's it! That's exactly what I need.* She worked her way through the maze of boxes and trunks and all kinds of things Melissa wasn't sure what they could be used for. She reached the wall where the step ladder was resting. After grabbing it and lifting it high so that she could move it back to the front of the shed, Melissa made her way back to the daylight. "Phew! This has been a job in itself." She set down the ladder, opened the legs, and tested the sturdiness. She put one foot on the first step and was dismayed to feel it sway violently. *Oh, no! This is no good to me.* She sighed, put the step ladder out of the way, turned out the light, and closed the door.

Dejected, she made herself to the front porch and settled on the swing. She pushed back and let the chair swing gently. "Okay, God. What do I do now? I want to hang my curtains, but I'm not sure I can reach high enough, and I'm afraid of falling. I am sharing my need with you and trusting you to help me find a solution." She paused and then added, "And thank you for your love and blessings." She sat there for a while, wondering if the God who ruled the universe possibly had time for her request.

"You just tell us if you need anything. Just call us we want to help you out." Melissa sat up straight and braced her legs as she mulled over the words of Don and Rayleen.

"Hmm, is that the answer? I guess I could call. They might not answer, or they could always say no." She scrolled through the numbers on her phone and pressed dial.

"Hello?" came the strong, friendly voice of Rayleen.

"Hi, Rayleen. This is Melissa Blakesly."

"Yes, hello. Good to hear your voice. Don and I were just visiting about you, wondering how you were getting along."

"I'm fine, thank you. And how are you two doing?"

"Oh, right as rain. We are happy and healthy and so thankful to God for our blessings. So how are you doing over there? I've been thinking I should call or drop over."

Melissa assured her she was fine. "I was wondering, though, if I could borrow a ladder to hang some curtains? The only one I can find is so rickety that I'm afraid of it."

"Of course we do. Goodness, that's a two-person job, anyway.

We'll just throw the ladder in the truck and be right over. Now, don't you try to do it until we get there. Okay?"

Melissa chuckled and said, "Okay, I won't. Thanks so much."

"Don't mention it. Don was needing something to do anyway, and I'll come along to give orders."

Melissa smiled when she heard Don say in the background, "That's what she does best!"

As she clicked the off button and sat for a moment, amazed at the answer God provided. *Coincidence?* She thought for a moment. *No, I don't think so. Amazing? Yes indeed. Beyond amazing.*

Her thoughts were soon interrupted by the sounds of a truck on the gravel. She could see Don driving and Rayleen chattering next to him. Melissa smiled as she watched Don nod and smile and then open the door.

"Well, hello, Melissa. Beautiful day again." He moved around to the back of the truck as he talked and lifted a sturdy five-step ladder out of the back. He carried it to the porch steps and waited while Rayleen greeted Melissa and chattered on about her latest interest.

"So where are we going with this project?" Don hoisted the ladder on to his shoulder and started up to the deck of the porch.

"The big bedroom, first door to the left. It was Granny's bedroom, and it makes me feel close to her to be in here." She ushered them into the room. Rayleen commented on how nice the house looked and how much Emma had loved her cottage.

Melissa explained that she wanted to take the sheer curtains and the roller shades down. "The new curtains will slide easily back and forth, and they will black out the sun and give me privacy if I want it." She held up the new curtains up for them to see.

"Oh, those are nice. This won't take any time at all," Rayleen said. Then she said to Don, "Now, be careful. You can just hand me the curtains. And the shades. Melissa, where do you want these?"

Melissa said, "I'll just put them in this corner for now. I'm not sure whether I want to keep them."

In short time, the curtains and blinds were taken down, and the new drapes were up. The rods were back in place.

Rayleen pulled the curtains together and said, "My, this will make a huge difference. The sun won't be bothering you with these."

"Very nice, Melissa," Don said as he nodded in agreement. He moved the ladder through the door and back out to the porch then to the truck.

Melissa walked with Rayleen out to the porch and said, "Please stay and visit for a while. Would you care for some lemonade?"

"That sounds good to me." Don's smile stretched from ear to ear.

Rayleen helped Melissa carry out the pitcher and tray of glasses. Melissa also offered a plate of her cookies. Don took one bite and exclaimed, "These are as good as Emma's! She was the best cookie maker around. Did you make these, Melissa?"

Melissa laughed at his enthusiasm and told him she had used her grandmother's recipe.

The shade of the porch was so pleasant that the three enjoyed the early spring weather.

Rayleen sampled "just one more cookie" and said, "Have you talked to Pastor Aaron lately?" She glanced at Don.

Melissa smiled and said, "Yes. He and Josie were here on Wednesday afternoon. Josie wanted to visit Grandmother's toys. They seemed to have quite a strong bond, and I guess Granny's death hurt her deeply. Visiting here and playing with those toys must be comforting to her."

Don nodded. "Emma's passing was hard for a lot of us, but Aaron took it really hard. He and Emma used to visit quite a bit. You know, a young pastor in his position needs someone whom he can visit with and know it won't go any further. They were good for each other. I know Emma loved Josie and helped them both through some difficult times. And Emma knew everyone in the county. She was a wonderful resource for Aaron."

Melissa listened, thinking about how much she was learning about her grandmother. She knew she was loving and caring, but she hadn't realized the influence Grandmother had had with so many people. "Thank you for that. I was so busy with my own life that I didn't spend as much time with Granny as I would have liked. Aaron told me he visited here with her a lot. I didn't know why."

"That Aaron is a wonderful guy," Rayleen gushed. "Why, if I had a daughter the right age, I sure wouldn't hesitate if he showed some interest in her."

"He must have come over here after being at our house Wednesday. Little Josie sure loves that old pony of ours. I don't know when I've heard such pure joy as when she's riding him."

Melissa chuckled and said, "Yes, they stopped by. Aaron and I had a nice visit, and he shared some Bible verses with me and explained the plan of salvation like I've never heard it before. He made it so simple and so clear. He encouraged me to think about the verses he gave me. They were both about prayer and God's willingness to help me out. And you know what? I prayed about what to do about a ladder and those curtains, and your offer came to mind. More than that, you answered the phone, and you were available and willing to help me. I don't think I'd have ever gotten that job done alone. I was afraid of standing on those old chairs of Grandmother's." She paused and looked down at the floor of the porch. "Thank you so much! I love being here, and I'm enjoying the home and everything Grandmother has provided for me, but it's not what I need when I'm not tall enough or strong enough or smart enough to finish a task."

She hadn't noticed that Rayleen had reached over to hold Don's hand. She squeezed it and then said, "Well, we are here when you need us. Don't forget!" She smiled at Don and then at Melissa. "We loved Emma, and we love you too. Just like Jesus does."

Don cleared his throat, and his voice came out a little more hoarse than usual. "Ray's right. We are glad to help." Then he gave a mischievous smile. "I bet Aaron would be glad to help you too." His declaration was followed by a grunt when Rayleen elbowed him in the ribs.

"For heaven's sake, Don," Rayleen fussed.

Melissa smiled and then thought about her plans with Aaron that evening. "Would you mind walking around the yard and helping me know the difference between weeds and flowers? I honestly don't know the difference right now."

"Of course, we'd love to. Emma had beautiful flowers, but she couldn't do a lot with them this past year. I'm sure we can salvage a lot by pulling weeds and putting down some mulch. It will take some time and effort. Let's see what you've got here."

The three of them walked around the house and pointed out to Melissa some of the flowers that would be worth keeping. "Just work at it a little each day, and you'll be surprised how fast you know what you're doing. I bet Emma has some books on perennials in the house that would help you know what to look for."

Melissa stood, not feeling at all sure she would ever know the difference. Don smiled at her and said, "We'll be over to help you. Don't worry; you can't make too many mistakes. I'll bring my mulcher mower over so we can clean up these leaves and overgrowth a little better."

"Well, I really appreciate all you've done. I hope I can pay it back sometime."

"Don't worry about that. Think about paying it forward. Someone else will need a hand sometime, and you can pitch in. It's what we do around here." Rayleen opened her arms for a hug, and Melissa felt the amazing peace of being cared for unconditionally. She knew tears were close and tried to blink them away.

"I will," Melissa promised. "I will." Impulsively she reached over and gave Don a hug too. "Thank you."

Don scuffed his feet and looked at the ground. "We're just happy you called on us. Don't forget to do it again. I have a tiller that would just love to tear through your vegetable garden over there. Looks like you've already worked it up a little. I can turn that into fine potting soil for you. Would you like that?"

"I would love it. Thanks so much. I want a little garden for tomatoes, peppers, and onions, and maybe lettuce and herbs. I would really like that."

She walked them back to their truck and watched as they drove away. When she saw them turn onto the road, she looked up at the sunlight streaming through the trees and said, "Thank you, Lord."

When Aaron arrived for their date, Melissa was sitting in the porch swing and let her legs lazily scrape the floor, absorbed in a picture essay, "One Hundred and One Desirable Hostas."

He quickly got out of the car and took the steps in one long stride. "Hi," he greeted. He smiled. "I'm a little early, I guess."

"That's fine. I'm ready." She found herself smiling up at him, pleased to see him, and looking forward to spending time with him on the ride to Cedar Rapids.

Once settled in the car, Melissa said, "I didn't take the time to check the museum website. What is this exhibit we're seeing?"

"It's a showing of a local guy who has been all over the world with his camera. He does both landscape and human study photography. I've followed his career for a while and wanted to see what he's done in this latest grouping. I think you will enjoy it. I hope you do."

Melissa smiled and assured him she would. "We're going to take some back roads to town tonight. This route goes through several small towns and villages. It's very pretty."

Funny, Melissa thought. *I grew up in Cedar Rapids, and I've been to Sovereign several times, but there's a lot I don't know about the area. Things have changed since I've been away.*

"Penny for your thoughts." She turned to see Aaron smiling at her inquisitively. "You were in another world."

Melissa smiled and felt a blush creep up her cheeks at being caught in her memories. "Oh, I was just thinking how my life has changed in the last few months. It seems like I left here to seek excitement and fulfillment, and now I'm back wondering why I didn't look for it closer to home. Does that seem silly?"

"Not at all. I don't think people know which road to take until they've gone down a few. God assured us in Jeremiah that he knows the plans he has for us—plans for good and not for evil." He glanced at her to gauge her reaction.

She thought about his comment for a moment. "Hmm, that's reassuring, I guess. I wish he'd share more of his plans for me with me."

Aaron chuckled. "I think you are searching just like the rest of us. He may not tell you, but he does make his plans clear to you by his grace. It just takes us a while to understand his plan."

Melissa nodded. "It's so pretty here—prettier than I remembered. Of course, after spending my last several springs in the middle of a concrete oasis, anything this naturally beautiful is a treat."

"You sound glad to be out of the city."

"I am. It was getting to be too hectic. I think when Mother called and said Granny was so ill, I came to my senses about what was and wasn't important in my life." Melissa smiled at Aaron's serious expression. "Anyway, I'm happy here right now, and I don't have to worry about where I'm going to live or how I'm going to pay the bills. I intend to enjoy it as long as I feel comfortable here."

Aaron nodded as though he understood.

The ride was peaceful, and Melissa found herself reviewing the events of the time she'd been in Iowa. The surprise of finding out Aaron was a pastor, meeting so many nice and helpful people, the wonderful feeling of acceptance she had experienced, and all the conversations she had been part of. Suddenly she focused on the one at Don and Rayleen's dinner table about Aaron's speed monitor, and she blurted out, "Aaron, why do you need a speed monitor?"

Aaron put his head back and laughed. "I wondered how long it would take." He glanced at her with an amused look. "I've been a little careless in my driving habits, and they finally came to fruition."

"Really? What happened?"

"About a month ago, I was driving down this very highway,

minding my own business. Actually, I was rehearsing a sermon. A highway patrol car came roaring up behind me with lights and siren blasting. I immediately slowed down and pulled over to the side to let him pass. To my surprise, he pulled off behind me. Well, of course I thought there must be some emergency that he had been called to summon me to for one of my parishioners. But to my amazement, his only intent was to issue me a speeding ticket."

"You're kidding! Why, I would never have guessed. Even a pastor can make an error in judgment."

"Yep. I had gotten lost in my thoughts and wasn't paying attention. Anyway, the officer informed me that I was driving twenty-six miles over the speed limit."

"Uh-oh. That must have cost you!"

"You're not kidding." He shook his head. "I was more than embarrassed when I noticed Don and Rayleen driving by as the good officer was issuing the ticket."

Melissa gasped and then stifled a giggle behind her fingers.

Aaron continued. "Well, anyway, as you can imagine, by the time of the next service, all my loyal sheep were baaing their heads off. I've had to suffer the indignities of their teasing ever since."

Melissa sat thinking about the situation, and then she asked, "Why does it always happen that way? I mean, when you're at a vulnerable point in life, why do the people you want to see least show up?"

"I don't know. Perhaps the Lord's way of keeping us humble. Anyway, I'm sure he has our best interests at heart, if not our pride." He shrugged. "What I don't understand are the hurts that children impose on others." He smiled at her questioning look and then explained. "Joseline's preschool friends told her that I would have to go to jail if I didn't quit speeding." It took some very persuasive talking to calm her down and to make her realize that I'd never do anything to separate her from me, but it made quite an impression on her, and she doesn't forget easily."

They rode on in silence, but Melissa felt pleased that Aaron had been willing to share such an embarrassing incident with her.

When they reached the edge of Cedar Rapids, they drove right to the museum. They had to cross a street, and Aaron put his hand on her elbow as they ran to the building and then up the stairs to the entrance. The exhibit was even better than Aaron had described. The photographs were all well done and covered a wide range of subjects, but they shared a central theme: the struggles of building and maintaining friendships. They laughed at pictures of children's antics with each other and their pets. They came close to tears at the ones of parents grieving over a sick child.

When the announcement came that the museum would be closing in fifteen minutes, they were surprised. "Whew! That went fast," Aaron noted.

"This was wonderful, Aaron." Melissa smiled. "Thank you for inviting me."

"I'm glad you came. I've enjoyed the evening too. But it is after 9:00, and I should get home to relieve Mrs. Mason."

The ride home didn't seem to take long at all. Melissa and Aaron traded stories about their childhood and memories from the past. Soon they were pulling into her driveway. She said, "Well, thank you again. It was a great exhibit, and I enjoyed our visit."

"Me too. I hope we can go out again soon," Aaron said.

Melissa smiled. "I'd like that too." She stifled a yawn. "Oh, excuse me. I've had a long day, and I'm more tired than I realized. I'd better go in."

"I'll walk you to the door." Aaron was out of the car and around to her side. After walking to the porch, Melissa caught her toe on rock, and Aaron caught her hand to steady her.

"Thanks. Clumsy, I guess." She didn't pull her hand out of his until they reached the porch. Melissa found her key and unlocked the door.

When she turned back, Aaron was standing on the edge of the porch, looking up at the moon. "Come look at this. It's so beautiful."

She looked up and gasped. Away from street lights, the full beauty of the moon and the stars was so brilliant and so clear. "Oh, it is amazing! Look at all those stars!"

"Uh-huh!" He moved behind her and placed one hand on her shoulder. Then he pointed to the right of the moon. "Do you see the Big Dipper?"

Melissa nodded, and he pointed out Orion and several other constellations. Melissa realized how safe and at ease she felt. She sighed. "Yes. God's beauty. Such a gift." She felt Aaron's chest lightly pressed against her back as they gazed at the sky. It was a very comfortable feeling.

Finally, Aaron said, "Well, I have to go. Mrs. Mason is so good to me, and I don't want to impose on her benevolent nature too much." Melissa turned toward him, and his hand dropped to her waist. After a moment, he said, "Have a good night, Melissa. It was a lovely evening. I'll see you soon." She waited while he started down the steps, and then he added, "I'll wait until I hear your lock click and your lights go on. Sleep well."

She stood facing him and realized he was waiting for her to say something. Finally she said, "I will. You too. Good night." As she let herself into the house and flipped on the lights, she sighed and thought, *He is nice.*

Aaron put the Jeep into neutral and let it roll down the slant of her driveway. He glanced toward the porch and could see her silhouette. *Is she watching me? Did she enjoy tonight as much as I did?* He moved the gear shift into drive. The memory of the softness of her skin and the clean scent of her perfume stayed with him as he rounded the curve into town. Melissa Blakesly had been taking up a substantial amount of his thoughts lately, and tonight didn't discourage any of them. He silently prayed for guidance and good judgment in this relationship. Faith and an ability to rely on the Lord had grown to become more and more important in his life. Of course, he been raised to believe in God's will in his life, but it hadn't been until his adult life that his faith had been tested so sorely. His marriage in which he'd put so much stock had crumbled just when he was sure it was at its strongest point. The grief he'd felt over the loss of his wife's loyalty, and then eventually her death, had been nearly overwhelming. Amid almost insurmountable bitterness, at one point he'd thought of leaving the ministry, but instead he had turned all his energy toward the Lord. He'd submerged himself completely in the business of doing the Lord's work and in providing the best for his daughter. And God had put Emma Wainsworth in his path too. She had recognized that he needed a prayer partner and a friend. At her invitation for tea and cookies, she asked if he could help her with a Bible study she was starting in her home. She asked if he would bring Joseline along to brighten her day. Under the guise of needing guidance, she shepherded them through the dark days when he could barely see his way. She had provided the touch and love to his little girl. She was his angel. But then she had passed to her reward after a short illness.

He'd kept himself so busy that he'd left little time for personal relationships. Melissa seemed to be a breath of fresh air during his recovery. She was fighting her own ghosts but seemed to be gaining strength every day. Perhaps she was an answer to Mrs. Mason's prayers. He smiled as he thought of the selfless woman who'd spent so much time with Joseline, making sure she felt loved and cared for when he couldn't be with her. She'd been another Godsend to them and made no secret of her intention of seeing him and Joseline part of a family again. To her, Melissa had simply been dropped right out of the heavens for the purpose to be his life mate. He grinned at the memory of Mrs. Mason standing in his kitchen one hand on her hip, waving an index finger in his face, and making the point about God's plans in their lives. Aaron wasn't so sure God had transported Melissa directly into his life, but he did know he didn't mind doing some personal research to see just what part she might play.

Chapter 13

Saturday was beautiful day to clear out the flower beds. By the time she had pulled the weeds, she could see her grandmother's design. Hostas, lilies, poppies, iris, and peonies were pushing out of the soil. *Maybe I can talk to Don and Rayleen about where to get mulch to add to the beds.* The garden spot that Don said he would till for her was cleared of old plants and weeds. She felt pleased with herself for accomplishing quite a lot of work in a short amount of time.

Linda dropped by at midafternoon, and Melissa showed her all she had accomplished the last few days. The two women ended up at the kitchen table and chatted over glasses of tea. Melissa shared with Linda her project she had committed to with Johanssen and Associates. Linda listened attentively and said, "Wow! That sounds like a huge job. I couldn't begin to understand what you are going to have to do."

Melissa laughed. "Oh, Linda, you and Jim run a huge farm with so much capital investment in livestock and land and machinery. What I do is no bigger than that."

"If you say so. It sure sounds overwhelming to me." Linda shook her head. They chatted on about the spring weather, gardening, crops, and the community. Eventually, Linda asked if she was enjoying getting to know people. When Melissa smiled and chatted about people she was recognizing and how friendly many were, the topic turned to Aaron.

Melissa shared with Linda her evening with Aaron and laughed when Linda enthusiastically encouraged her to keep seeing him. "He's a really great guy. I think it would be wonderful if you two kept seeing one another."

She smiled to herself, nodded, and tried to think of how she could broach a concern of hers. "He is really nice, and we've had nice times together. But ..."

"But what?" Linda urged. "Is there something else?"

Melissa swirled the ice cubes around in her glass. "Well, I guess I just don't know what to expect of him. He is a pastor. I mean, do I act the same way with him that I would with any other man?"

Linda stared at her for a few seconds. "Of course. How else would you treat him?"

"It's just that I don't want to do something to make him think I'm not a ... oh, I don't know ... a nice girl."

Linda laughed out loud. "Melissa! What in the world are you thinking? Why shouldn't he think you were a nice girl?"

Melissa raised her eyes toward the ceiling and said, "Oh, let's just forget it. I'm sorry I brought it up."

Linda smiled and leaned closer to her. "I'm sorry I laughed. Come on. Why don't you tell me what's bothering you? I promise I won't laugh, and I won't share this with anyone."

Melissa let out a huge sigh. "It's just that I didn't know Aaron was a pastor when I met him. When I found out, it surprised me. I'd never had any dealings with a clergy other than listening to a sermon and shaking hands at the door. So when he asked me to out with him, I wasn't sure how I was supposed to act."

Linda nodded. "And so you feel uncomfortable with him now that you know he is a preacher?"

"No, I can't say that. Last night, we had a great time talking on the way to Cedar Rapids, and we both enjoyed the exhibit at the museum. On the way home, we talked about growing up and memories. The time flew by, and we were home before we knew it. He walked me to the door and waited while I unlocked the door. When I turned back, he was standing on the edge of the porch and looking up into the sky. He called me over, and we stood there together, talking about the splendor of God's stars and moon. He was standing behind me with one hand on my shoulder and his other arm pointing out different stars. We stood close together staring at the sky, and it all seemed so ... comfortable. Then he said he had to go, and he'd wait until he heard my door lock. Then he was gone. Poof, like vapor."

When she looked back at Linda for her reaction, Linda was staring dreamily off into the distance. Melissa cleared her throat. Linda blushed and laughed. "Oh, you caught me. Last night, after chores and homework, Jim and I went outside and looked up into the same sky. It was amazing. We stood there, caught up in the beauty of it all, and ... well, it was a very romantic moment for us." She smiled at her new friend. "I think Aaron is probably having feelings for you that he hasn't experienced in a while. Give him time. He is probably not sure of what to do. Did he ask you out again?"

"Well, he said he hoped we could go out again, but we didn't make a date."

Linda stood up and patted Melissa on the shoulder. "Don't try to analyze this too much. You are both new acquaintances, and you just need to give it some time. Hey, I've got to be going. I told Jim I'd be home to help with the calf vaccinations, and I haven't even been to the grocery store." After moving toward the door, Linda paused a moment and added, "Your place looks real nice. I'm glad you're here. Just relax and enjoy the peace and quiet while you can. See you in church in the morning?"

"Yes, I'll be there."

They walked out to the front porch. "Oh, has anyone mentioned next Wednesday night's church social?" Linda asked.

"No, I don't think so."

"Oh Melissa, you've got to come. It's the best time. People come from other churches and all around. We all look forward to it every spring."

"What do you do there?"

"Lots of things. But the really fun part is the pie bake-off. Every lady bakes a pie and donates it to the church for an auction, with all proceeds going to our mission fund. Last year, we raised almost two thousand dollars."

"Okay. So, do I bake a pie?"

"Yes! It's a lot of fun if you have one in the bidding. Be sure to bring a salad or casserole to share, for the potluck. The men always make homemade ice cream, and the kids have a ball playing all evening. We all eat supper together at 5:30 and then go from there. I hope you will come."

"Sounds too good to miss."

"Good! Well, thanks for the conversation and tea." She reached over and gave Melissa a warm, friendly hug. "It's so good to have a friend in the neighborhood."

On Sunday morning, Melissa slept later due to the drapes that held back the sunshine. When she looked at the clock, she was surprised to see that it was already 9:00. She thought about staying in bed a little longer but reminded herself of her plan to put some discipline into her life. By the time she'd had breakfast, bathed, and dressed, it was time to drive to church.

Many of the same people whom she'd seen the previous Sunday greeted her, but there were others whom she didn't remember. As she found her way to a pew, she overheard several whispered comments. "That's Aaron's new friend ..." "They've been seeing a lot of each other ..." "Good for him to be going out again ..."

Melissa smiled to herself and thought about the consequences of living in a small community. *Well, at least they all sound positive,* she thought. She looked at the bulletin for a few minutes and noticed the church social was announced. Everyone was encouraged to come and join in the festivities to raise money for the mission projects. When she looked up again, she surveyed the congregation for familiar faces. Linda, Jim, and their children were sitting ahead and to the right. Rayleen and Don sat near the front on the left-hand side. She smiled when Joseline's little face peering over the back of the front pew caught her eye. She could barely see the top of the girl's head and eyes, but Joseline was waving at her quite enthusiastically. Several titters were heard throughout the congregation when she whispered in a loud voice, "Missa, can I sit with you?"

Melissa looked around for some adult who might be in charge of her. An older lady sitting next to the girl turned to look Melissa's way. She smiled at Melissa and then nodded to Joseline, who came skipping back to join Melissa. When she stopped in the aisle next to Melissa, Joseline looked up with those big brown eyes and said, "Mrs. Mason said I could."

Melissa looked toward the older lady and returned her smile with a nod. Then she said to Joseline, "It's nice to see you again. What all do you have here?" She looked at the denim satchel that Joseline had lugged along with her.

Joseline wriggled her way up onto the pew next to her and then methodically began taking out each item and describing it to Melissa. "This is my Sunday school paper, and this is my coloring book, and these are my new crayons, and this is my puppet, and ..." She continued the identification of each item in the satchel then carefully put all back in, except for her coloring book and crayons. "Daddy says it's okay to color in church as long as I stay quiet."

As people noticed the two sitting together, they smiled, commented, and turned to watch their interactions again. Melissa felt a little like a fish in a bowl but reminded herself that she was new and still an oddity—let alone receiving the full attention of the pastor's daughter.

The preservice followed the same pattern as before, and when the organ swelled, everyone quieted down. Melissa turned her attention toward the front, where Aaron was greeting the congregation. He smiled as he scanned the group, and he seemed to hesitate a second longer when his eyes met Melissa's. She followed his lead in songs, listened to the announcements for the week, and bowed her head to listen to his prayer. All the while, Joseline sat coloring, in seeming contented unawareness of anyone around her. The sermon that followed was again about God's love for mankind and his desire for everyone to come close to Him. Melissa listened intently and noticed that Aaron used some of the same phrases and examples he had shared with her earlier in the week. She reviewed in her mind the scripture she had been reading and rereading during the past week, and she found that the ideas were becoming clearer to her.

When Aaron announced that the altar was open for anyone who wanted to come and make a deeper commitment to the Lord, something stirred deep within her. *Should I go up there? I don't know what to do. It seems like the right thing to do, but I don't want to do something foolish. It seems like the right thing to do ...* After taking a deep breath, she thought, *Trust in the Lord ...* She thought again about the past week and her visit with Linda, the radio message, and Don and Rayleen's answer to her prayer of hanging curtains. She decided to follow this silent urging. She was halfway down the aisle when she realized Joseline had left her crayons and coloring book on the pew and had tumbled out behind her. When she reached the prayer rail, she silently kneeled, bowed her head, and prayed that the Lord would continue to work in her life. She thanked Him again for the answers he'd laid before her this past week. She was barely conscious of Joseline standing beside her until she felt her little hand patting her softly on her back.

She continued to pray the words and thoughts that formed in her mind. *Thank you for having me move here. Thank you, God, for bringing Aaron and Joseline, and Linda and Jim, and Rayleen and Don into my life. Thank you for Grandmother and her generous gift of love and prayer and inheritance to me. Thank you for all the answers to prayer this week. I love you, and I am so sorry for not always including you in the minutes of my life. I am so grateful for your love and care. Thank you for your son, Jesus, and his sacrifice for me. Help me to be the person you want me to be. Help me to know how to deal with Sven, to know whether I should stay or move back. Help me to know how I should act and talk. I praise you, Father, for your loving guidance. Amen.*

Before she could rise and return to her seat, Aaron was announcing the benediction. When she heard the noise of people rising, she felt relieved that she wouldn't have to face so many people. The whole experience had been so touching that she found herself sniffing back tears of unexplainable joy. She stood up to return to collect her purse and bulletin, but she was stopped by Linda and Jim. Linda gave her a big hug and looked at her with teary eyes. "Oh, Melissa!"

Melissa smiled and wiped a tear from her eye before saying, "Don't! You'll make me cry."

Linda hugged her again and then said, "I always get so choked up when I see people come to the altar." She stepped back, linked arms with Jim, and then said, "You know you can come to us for anything you need?"

Melissa nodded and stood there sharing with the couple. "I didn't plan on coming up here, but it seemed like the right thing to do. I know the Lord has been working in my life, and I just need to thank Him."

They nodded in unison, and Jim said, "I think that's often the best way to come to God. Just as he moves us to." He offered his hand to her, and Melissa grasped it in both of hers.

"Thank you two. You have been a great encouragement to me. More than either of you know."

None of the three had noticed that Joseline was still waiting close by until she tugged at Melissa's skirt and said, "Come on, Missa. Let's go!"

Melissa smiled and then said, "Looks like I need to go. I'll see you both later."

"Don't forget the social Wednesday evening."

Melissa nodded and assured her she was planning on coming. She followed Joseline down the aisle. Melissa grabbed her purse and bulletin and hurried toward the door and Aaron. "Hi, Daddy!"

"Hi, sweetie," he said as he picked her up in his arms. "You were a very good girl in church today."

Joseline nodded her head, curls bouncing, and said, "I colored you a picture." She whispered something in his ear and giggled.

Aaron laughed and set her down on the floor. "Stay nearby, Josie. I don't want to come hunting for you."

Joseline assured him that she would, and she went down the steps to the sidewalk in front of the church. Aaron turned his attention to Melissa, who was by now the last person in line. He smiled broadly at her and took both of her hands in his. "Melissa, it was good to see you come to the altar today. I would like to talk to you about your experience some time."

"Of course. Any time would be ..." She was interrupted by the laughter of several of the people still visiting on the sidewalk in front of the church. She and Aaron turned at the same time to see Joseline hopping around on the sidewalk, flapping her arms.

"Joseline! What are you doing?" Aaron asked, unable to mask his amusement.

"I'm an angel, Daddy."

Aaron laughed and glanced back at Melissa. He motioned for her to follow him, and they walked down the steps. "I didn't know angels acted like that."

Joseline stopped and turned toward her father, her hands on her hips. "Daddy!" she said in a very exasperated voice. "Miss Nancy said that the angels dance when someone comes to Jesus. I'm just dancing for Missa."

Melissa felt her throat tighten and the tears accumulate against the back of her eyelids. Aaron knelt and extended his arms for Joseline. She moved into his embrace, and he said, "I forgot, Josie. That was a nice thing for you to do." He stood with Josie in his arms and then turned toward Melissa, who by now was losing the battle of fighting back tears.

She smiled at them both and said, "Thank you, Josie!"

Joseline stared at Melissa and said in a concerned voice, "It's all right, Missa. Don't cry."

Aaron explained that sometime people cry happy tears, and that was what Melissa was doing right now. Melissa nodded, unable to say anything else for a moment. Aaron hugged Joseline close, assuring her that everything was fine and giving Melissa time to compose herself. When he felt the time was right, he said to Melissa, "I asked Mrs. Mason to pack a picnic basket for three people. We were hoping we could convince you to join us."

She looked at the sincere face of her friend and the sweet smile of Joseline.

"Of course, if you have other plans, we will understand …" Aaron said.

Melissa hesitated, but then she decided to grasp this opportunity to join this adventure. "No. I mean, I don't … I'd love to."

"Great!" Aaron said. Joseline giggled in delight. "Come on, Josie. Let's go change our clothes. Melissa, we'll be out to pick you up in a few minutes."

Chapter 14

When she heard the crunch of tires on the gravel, she smiled at the memory of expression of joy on Josie's face when she said she wanted to come along. What a wonderful feeling to share in her joy. She opened the passenger door to see Aaron's smiling face and Joseline safely situated in her car seat. "Hi again. What fun this is. Thank you for inviting me."

"We are happy you came along," Aaron said. "Right, Josie?"

"Yes! You make us happy, Missa." She smacked the palm of her hand with her lips and threw a kiss at Melissa.

Melissa reached out to grab the kiss and held her hand to her heart. "And I always feel happy with you two." Josie giggled. "So where are we headed?"

"We're going to Josie's favorite spot at the state park,"

"And I get to wade in the creek!" Joseline interjected.

Aaron smiled and shook his head. "I said *maybe*, little girl. We have to see how deep it is and how cold it is first."

"Well, probably it isn't cold 'cause it was really hot outside yesterday," Joseline hedged.

"We'll see. Now, why don't you watch for black and white cows today? I think we might see some on the way."

They backed out of the driveway and headed out of town on a black-topped road, heading east. They didn't have to travel too far before Aaron turned the Jeep off the highway and headed for the park. It was beautiful place where the glaciers of years ago had left deep crevices formed by creeks in the valley. They found a picnic table under an oak tree near the stream and got ready for lunch. Mrs.

Mason had packed a plaid table cloth with weights to keep it safe from a breeze. The food was packed in plastic containers, and there were colorful plastic plates and spoons, a jug of apple juice, and a jug of water. Melissa helped open and arrange the containers of sandwiches, celery, carrots, crunchy raw cauliflower, a bag of potato chips, and chocolate chip cookies for a sweet treat. The picnic was delicious. They sat together and talked about the birds and stream.

"I hope I see some fishies today," Joseline said. "I hope I don't step on any when I'm wading in the water." She watched her dad with an expression of hope.

"Let's just take time to finish lunch before we check the water. It might be too cold for the fish to come out of their nice, warm homes." He watched his daughter weighing his words and winked at Melissa.

"Well, maybe some of them have coats to wear, and they will come to see me."

"Could be. Did you finish your sandwich?" Josie nodded. "Did you have some vegetables?" Josie nodded vigorously as she stuffed a carrot in her mouth. "Well, I see you've tried some of everything. That's very good, Josie." Then he turned to Melissa. "What do you think? Should we go check out the water in the stream and see if it's warm enough to wade in?"

Melissa smiled and said, "Yes, I think we should."

She laughed when Josie let out a loud, "Oh, yes, yes! Thank you, Missa. Come on, Daddy. Let's go!"

Shoes off and hand in hand, the three carefully dipped their toes into the water and then joyfully splashed along the shallow edges of the stream. "Now, try not to keep any of your clothes dry," Aaron teased Joseline, and they laughed as she splashed water, soaking her to her waist. In a few minutes, despite the warmth of the water, Josie was ready to get out and play on the equipment near their picnic table. She tentatively joined other children her age while Aaron and Melissa settled down on a bench to watch her. Soon, Josie was so involved in the adventures with her new friends that she was oblivious to the adults watching her.

"She's so outgoing," Melissa said.

"Too much so, sometimes," Aaron agreed. "Sometimes I'm afraid she's going to make friends with the wrong person."

Melissa turned to look at Aaron and was surprised at the intensity of the frown on his face. She reached out to grasp his hand and said, "I know it must be scary for you. But you must let her try new things and meet new people. It's only natural."

Aaron smiled and said, "I know you're right. But I'm scared to death for her sometimes. I don't know what I'd do if something ever happened to her."

Knowing there was no appropriate response to his remark, Melissa sat next to him and hoped he knew she understood his concern. She decided to introduce the subject of the Wednesday social. Aaron seemed to appreciate the change in topic and encouraged her to join in with the festivities. "And don't forget to bring a pie for the auction."

"Oh, I won't. I know just what I'm going to bake."

Aaron grinned. "How about telling me which one, so I can be sure to offer the high bid on it?"

Melissa laughed and was about to tell him she would just be pleased if her pie helped to contribute to the mission fund when a chilly breeze wafted across the park. Aaron called Joseline to get a jacket. He rose to meet her and then stopped and asked Melissa, "Do you need a jacket too?"

"Yes, thanks. Mine is lying on the front seat." When they returned, Joseline had on a pink sweatshirt and blue jeans instead of damp shorts, and Aaron had on a navy windbreaker. Joseline ran back to the playground equipment, and Aaron joined Melissa on the bench. He slipped the jacket he had brought around her shoulders and then leaned back and put his arm around her. Melissa smiled and said, "Thank you. This is much better."

Aaron turned to respond to her, and she found herself staring directly at his lips. Any words he might have said remained unspoken as Melissa felt rather than saw him move closer. She closed her eyes just as the soft touch of his lips met hers. For what seemed like minutes, the rest of the world disappeared except for the softness of his lips. When they parted, she gazed at him and returned his sweet smile with her own. She sighed, remembered they weren't alone, and turned to see Joseline still happily playing on the castle with her friends.

Aaron squeezed her shoulder and pulled her a little closer. "She's okay." She snuggled her head into his shoulder. Sitting there with him felt so nice. He gently stroked her hair and commented, "Just like silk. Your hair feels so soft."

She felt his body tense. He moved his arm from around her and she sat up straight. "Sorry. I thought Josie bumped her head." He relaxed and laced his fingers through hers. Melissa looked toward the playground and saw that Joseline was following some of the other children up to the top of the castle. The children were all giggling and daring one another to move farther up the ladder. As she climbed higher, Aaron stood up to move closer. Suddenly the boy in front of her slipped, and his foot came down on Josie's hand. She cried out, pulled her hand away from the ladder, and lost her balance. She fell into the sand. Immediately Aaron was across the lot and bending over her. Melissa followed and moved in beside him to see if there had been any damage.

"Josie, are you hurt?" Aaron asked as he pulled her into his arms. The little girl was crying and frightened, but there didn't seem to be any injury. He took his handkerchief out of his pocket to wipe the tears from her face. Aaron picked her up and carried her over to the bench and held her, consoling her. Melissa sat next to them. Aaron soothed, "It's all right. I don't think you're hurt. It must have been very scary for you, though." The little girl nodded and buried her face in his chest. When the tears subsided, Aaron said, "Melissa and I were having such fun watching you play. You're getting to be such a good climber. Isn't she, Melissa?

Melissa took her cue and responded, "Yes, you are! I was very surprised at how high you climbed."

Joseline sat with her head on her dad's chest and watched Melissa.

She said with a quivering voice, "Someday I will climb up to the top and touch the moon."

"Yes, I'm sure you will," Melissa agreed. "But I don't know whether your daddy will want to watch you."

"That's for sure!" Aaron agreed. "I'd be scared for you, but so proud that you are so brave." The three of them sat there for a few minutes before deciding to start home. By that time, Joseline was over her scare and was back to her chattering self. Once in the car though, the fresh air and exercise took its toll, and she soon drifted off to sleep.

When they reached Melissa's house, Aaron put his finger to his lips as he opened his door and eased out of the car. They quietly walked to the front porch. Aaron took her face in both hands and lowered his face close to hers. "Thank you for coming along." Then he dropped a quick kiss on her lips and said, "Will you see me again soon?"

Melissa nodded and said, "Yes! Please call me when you know your schedule." She raised up on her tiptoes and returned his kiss. "You'd better go before Josie wakes up."

Aaron laughed at her impulsive action. "Yeah, you're right." He hesitated a moment. "I'll call you early in the week."

She nodded, smiled, and waved as he backed up to turn around. Then he was gone.

Chapter 15

Melissa changed into favorite sweats and settled on the couch to watch some TV. She found a movie to watch when the phone rang. After grabbing it from the table next to her, she saw Brad's ID and said, "Hello, Brad. It's good to hear from you. What's up?"

"Well, I thought I'd let you know a tentative date to come out to the land of milk and honey," he teased.

Melissa could almost see the grin on his face and the freckles on his nose that lined up when he did so. "Great. When can you come?"

"How about Tuesday afternoon?"

"That should work for me. How long can you stay?"

"I'll probably catch the plane back Thursday, if we get everything done."

Melissa tried to hide the disappointment in her voice. "I was hoping you could stay through the weekend. I wanted to show you some of the sights around here. Any reason for going back so soon? Hot date? New girl?"

"Well, you know, I have to work for a living." He paused and then decided to tell her about his new significant friend. "I guess I can tell you. There is a special girl."

"Brad, tell me! Who is it?"

"Remember Bonnie Stone, the product rep from the computer services we use?"

"Yes."

"Right before you left, we were starting to go out and it really seems to be working. Anyway, she's having some friends over for a dinner party on Saturday night and I want to be there."

"Brad, that's wonderful. I can't wait to hear all about her."

"She's making some major changes in my life. I'll tell you all about it when I get there."

Melissa could imagine the smile on his face as he talked about Bonnie. They talked about their project and what they needed to accomplish in those days. "Okay. I'll plan on seeing you Tuesday at 12:30 at the airport."

"I'm looking forward to it."

"Me too."

Melissa clicked off the phone and sat thinking about her friend. I should have talked to him about staying at the cottage. He'll probably think I'm nuts. Then she remembered her promise to God to trust in him. She said out loud, "Okay, God. I know I'll just make a mess out of it, so I'll try to let you handle it. No! I *will* let you handle it." She smiled to herself and lay back on the couch to nap in front of the TV.

Aaron called on Monday, and she told him about Brad arriving on Tuesday. Melissa wasn't sure whether there was an extra pause in his response, or whether it was just her imagination. "I'm looking forward to meeting him. He must be pretty special if he's so important to you."

"I want you to meet him too. I thought we could come by and get him settled in the guest house first, and then we'll have to get to work on our project. Does that house have a place where we can work, like a desk or a table big enough for us to spread out?"

"There's a table in the kitchen, or you can always come over to the church and use the tables in the fellowship hall. I'll unlock the door to the cottage after lunch. So just help Brad get settled and feel free to work on your project."

"Well, we really need a place where we won't be interrupted. I think the table would work. Anyway, we will try to get some work done Tuesday afternoon and evening, so that we can finish up on Wednesday. I really want to bring him to the social that evening. I hope you will drop by and meet Brad whenever you have time."

"That would be fine. We need all the help we can get to crank those ice cream freezers."

Melissa laughed and then said, "Aaron, I really enjoyed yesterday with you and Josie."

"I did too. We had fun." He paused and then added, "Well, I will see you on Wednesday. Bye till then."

"Okay, good bye for now." She couldn't help but look up and say a thank-you. *You are so good to me. Thank you, God. Please keep your hand on me, Brad, and Aaron.*

Just as Melissa pulled into the airport, her phone rang. Brad said he could meet her right outside the baggage claim. She pulled up close to the door and watched for him, waiting anxiously to see her friend after several weeks. When he appeared in the doorway, she beeped her horn, and he jogged over, smiling from ear to ear. After opening the back door, he swung his backpack and computer bag on to the seat and then slid in next to her.

"Oh, Melissa! Are you a sight for sore eyes!" His eyes were glistening, and he had the biggest smile. "It is so good to see you." He gave her a hug and then fastened his seatbelt.

Melissa laughed. "I have missed you, Brad. Good to see you too." They chatted on their way towards Cedar Rapids, taking in the different buildings and neighborhoods, the river and bridges,

Brad remarked. "This is a big little city. I didn't realize this area was so developed."

Melissa laughed. "It's not Chicago, but it has lots of interesting history and customs. We're going to grab lunch at a diner up here. It has a lot of variety on the menu. I think you'll enjoy it."

"Sounds good. Lead on." Once settled in the booth, they looked over the items on the menu. There were American, Greek, Czech, and Italian. After discussion and questions of the waiter, they chose sandwiches with small salads and water.

"So, do you think we will be able to finish this proposal by tomorrow afternoon?" Melissa asked.

"I think so. I hope so," Brad said between bites. "We have talked it through and we've covered most of it on our collaborations online. We shouldn't have any trouble finishing up tomorrow." Then he grinned at her. "Why? Do you have a hot date?"

Melissa covered her laughter with her hand. "No, but we are going to a church ice cream social and pie auction. I expect you to bid on my pie so that I don't feel like a failure."

Brad threw his head back and laughed. "You are making a pie? What? Mud pie?"

Melissa laughed. "No, apple walnut raisin pie. You'll like it, I promise."

"I'm sure I will." Brad rose and grabbed the check before she could. "My treat."

Melissa sputtered about him being her guest, but she gave in to his generous gesture.

"So how far to Cowtown?" Brad asked as he waited for her to unlock the car door.

"Sovereign," she corrected. "Not far, about thirty-five miles. We should be there in about that many minutes, unless there is a traffic hold up or something."

"Like cows loose on the highway?" Brad smirked.

"No! Well, I guess there could be. Usually a deer or an accident."

As they travelled, Brad commented on the countryside. "Man, it's beautiful here. Look at all the colors. I thought you saw the most color in the fall, but this is beautiful! Different colored greens, flowering trees, and wild flowers. This place is amazing!"

"I told you so!" Melissa replied. "Evidently, I have to hit you over the head to make you believe me."

Brad smiled. "Ah, Melissa, I promise I'll never doubt you again." He laughed when she rolled her eyes at him. "So, how's life treating you? You look good. A little tired, maybe."

"Oh, I'm doing well. Sometimes I don't sleep too well, but other than that …"

"Something wrong?"

"No, just doing some thinking about the direction I want my life to go. I guess I'm at a point where I need to make some adjustments again. You know the feeling. I'm just not sure that I'm doing the best for me."

Brad turned back to look out the window and said, "I sure know that feeling, but I'm starting to get things sorted out. Bonnie has a lot to do with that."

"Yeah, I want to hear more about this. Are you two getting serious?"

"I don't think there's much getting to it. We're pretty much there." He turned to look at Melissa and continued. "I've never felt so alive and so happy in my life."

"My goodness! What has she done to you?"

Brad laughed. "It's not just Bonnie. It's, well, a lot of things."

Melissa slowed down to enter the city limits of Sovereign. "I can hardly wait to hear more. We'll get you settled and then get to work. I think if we really push, we can still get a lot accomplished and then take a break, and you can tell me all about everything."

Once Brad was situated, they drove out to the cottage that she was starting to consider hers and not just her grandmother's. It would always have Grandmother's essence, but Melissa was feeling more and more at home here. When she stopped the car next to the house, she said, "Here we are. Home, sweet home."

Brad climbed out of the car and straightened his long frame. He paused, one hand resting on the top of the car as he looked around. "This is gorgeous! No wonder you like it here so much. Is all of this yours?"

"As far as that fence to the east, and down the hill to the road on the other side of the stream, and back south to the line fence in midsection. This is three hundred acres, mostly cropland, but some pasture and some timber. Come on in, and I'll fix us some tea and share some of my cookies with you."

Brad whistled softly. "Quite a spread. I've never known anyone who owned such a big place."

She walked with him through the house, pointing out memories and things she was thinking of changing. When she came to the guest room, she paused and said, "And this is where you could have stayed if your conscience hadn't gotten the better of you."

"Not my conscience, Melissa. I know neither of us have anything to be concerned about. You are my friend, and I respect you completely. It's just that Bonnie means a lot to me, and I want her to know that things are on the up and up with you and me, especially because we are going to be working together a lot again. She knows how strong our friendship is, but I just don't want to give her any reason to worry."

"I understand, Brad. Don't worry about it. Actually, this really works out best for me too."

"How so?"

"Well, it's a long story, but it's what made me laugh so hard." As she talked, she poured the tea and put the cookie jar in the middle of the table. She told him about her first encounter with Aaron. "It scared the wits out of me. I was sure I was going to be attacked by some wild man, but by the time he left, I had changed my mind. On Sunday, I decided to go to church, and there he was—the pastor!"

"Pastor? You've got to be kidding!"

"No, I'm not. I about fainted, but then he and his daughter ..."

"Daughter?"

Melissa shared her feelings and experiences she'd had with Aaron. Brad sat back and listened intently, smiling when he could see her emotions surface. She shared how he related the salvation message with a plate of cookies. They laughed together when she told him how upset she was with Aaron when she thought he was trying to tell her she couldn't have Brad stay in her home.

"Did he get mad and order down the fury of the heavens?" Brad joked.

"No. He quietly apologized for prying into my business and told me that he would never try to tell me what to do. So here I am, all irritable, and he really hasn't done anything to cause it. He was just here, not making judgments or trying to make me feel guilty, or any manipulative stuff at all. It was like I had stepped over some invisible barrier or something."

Brad smiled and nodded as though he understood.

"Anyway, that night I didn't sleep because I kept thinking about Aaron's reaction, and then one thing led to another. When I finally got up the next morning, I was thinking I shouldn't be here at all. I started the day in a real funk and fussed around for a bit when I remembered Granny telling me to pray about things that I couldn't handle. So I did. I prayed that God would end my confusion and help me have a clear answer to what I was to do with you. After all, I didn't want you to think that I didn't want you to stay here."

Brad sat watching her and listening to her, and a little smile crept across his face.

"What are you looking so smug about?"

Brad's smile grew wider, his eyes glistening with humor. "Oh, not much. I just wonder if the love bug isn't nibbling at your toes."

"What? What are you talking about?"

"Well, he's taken a whole chunk out of me, and I can really relate to everything you're telling me. I've gone through some of the changes you're telling me about."

"Well, tell me! Don't keep it all to yourself."

"Hmm, where do I start?" He thought for a moment. "Did you ever talk to Bonnie much?"

"No, just business stuff. You know, the in-service programs she offered."

"Well, I hadn't either until we started going out. Actually, she asked me out first. She needed a tennis partner, and so she asked me to join her. Anyway, I think Bonnie's a really good-looking girl, and I was all primed for an afternoon of fun and an evening of romance."

Melissa nodded her head as she took a sip of tea.

"We go to play tennis, but it was a couple's game these people from her church. I thought, *You know, this is okay. I can handle this for a couple of hours.* Well, after the sets, they invite us to their house, and we talked and talked all night. Do you know what we talked about?" He stared at her and then blurted out, "Christianity!"

Melissa clapped her hands together and leaned her head back and hooted. "You're kidding!"

"No! Well, at first, I thought that I couldn't wait to get out of there, but those people were so nice. What they said made sense because it related directly to me and questions I had been asking myself. To make a long story short, I started to go to church with them, and within a month, Bonnie had led me through the steps of salvation."

Melissa sat staring at her friend, feeling that his story was a little too incredulous for words. "That's what Aaron has been talking to me about."

Brad smiled and shook his head as though to clear his mind. "The way Bonnie explained it to me, it's not enough to just say you believe in God, or live a good life, or go to church occasionally. She says you must accept Jesus as the son of God and be willing to receive him as your savior. Then you have to confess him as the Lord of your life, and you must be willing to repent of your sins. That's the only way to heaven and eternal salvation."

"Wow, this is incredible!" she said as she put her glass back on the table.

"I agree. But more than that, I mean it when I tell you that I feel more alive now than ever before."

Melissa watched him for a moment, silently evaluating his statements. "That's just because you're in love. What would happen if suddenly Bonnie wasn't in the picture? Do you think you'd be so enthusiastic then?"

Brad raised both hands high above his head and stretched back in his chair, arching his back. When he returned to his seated position, he looked at her and said, "There's no way I can answer that. The fact is that Bonnie is in the picture, I have accepted Jesus Christ as my Lord and savior, and I feel great. I don't know how one affects the other. All I know is I would love for everyone I know to feel the same way I do."

They sat at the table a few more minutes when Melissa said, "Come on. Let's get you settled in the guest house."

"Good idea! We've got work to do." As they walked down the steps, Melissa touched Brad's arm and pointed toward the side yard to a stand of trees. There stood a doe and two fawns. She put her finger to her lips to warn him not to talk. Brad's eyes widened as he stared. They enjoyed the beauty of the deer for only a minute before the doe moved her babies back into the protection of the timber.

"I can't believe my eyes! This place is wonderful. Melissa, could I bring Bonnie here sometime?"

"I'd love that. Call me when you have a date, and we will plan it." On the way to town, Brad continued to talk about the beauty of the scenery, Bonnie, and finally their project. "I think we can put it together easily. I know you have some ideas, and I've been working on it."

Melissa nodded as she guided the car down the road towards town. She pulled up to the cottage next to church and said, "Well, here we are. Your home for a couple of days." She smiled, slid out from the driver's seat, and met Brad at the side of the car to help him carry in his computer bag. She let him lug in the heavier backpack.

She tried the front door to the cottage and found it unlocked. "Hello, anybody here?" When no answer came, she moved into the foyer of the little house.

"Don't you Iowans lock your doors?" Brad asked.

"Most of the time, but I told Aaron we would be here about this time, and so he probably left it open for us."

The cottage was clean and bright, furnished in a cozy manner that would welcome the guests who needed to use it. Melissa placed Brad's computer bag on the kitchen table and let him go ahead of her to find the bedroom. "Hey, look at this. A king-sized bed and a very nice bathroom." They looked around and found the living room with a TV, and a second bedroom with a smaller bathroom in the hallway. "Hmm, very nice."

Back in the kitchen, Brad arranged his laptop and some written notes on the table. Melissa had brought her tablet too, and the two sat down to review their ideas. Brad shared with her the project plans presented by the development team, and she showed him her ideas of how to change and modify the website to reflect the new ideas they wanted to incorporate into the project.

"Okay, because they aren't changing the product a great deal, they want us to focus on a new slant so that clients and consumers will be more attracted to what they are already producing. You know, make the old new again."

"Sure." Melissa leaned back in her chair and tapped her index finger against top lip. "It seems to me that the way it was presented last season was targeted at people who had the money to buy this product outright. But too many of today's consumers may hesitate to invest in a product that is such a large cost. I think we need to emphasize that the cost is worth it to them, because it will be adaptable over a length of time."

Brad listened and watched her. "That's exactly what Sven said in the development meeting on Monday. Did you talk to him?

"No, of course not!" Melissa stood up and felt a sudden rush of panic rush through her. "I haven't even thought of him since I left." She turned to look out the window and saw Aaron striding across the lawn with Josie close behind.

Brad said, "Melissa, I'm sorry. I didn't mean to upset you."

Melissa turned back toward him, fanning her face with her hand. "You didn't. I just get the strangest feeling when I think of Sven. Never mind. I think we are about to have visitors."

A knock came at the kitchen door, and before Melissa could open the door, Josie rushed in and hugged her around her legs. "Oh, Missa, I've missed you!"

Melissa leaned down to hug her and said, "I've missed you too. I want you to meet my friend Brad."

Josie looked up at Brad and gave her best curtsy. "Hello, Mr. Brad."

Brad couldn't help but chuckle at her sweet reply, and he bent down to offer his hand. Josie shook it solemnly and then charmed him with her best smile.

"And Brad, I want you to meet Aaron Chambers." The two men shook hands, and Melissa continued telling Aaron that she and Brad had worked on the same marketing and development team for several years.

The two exchanged friendly greetings. "You have a little charmer on your hands here," Brad said, tipping his head toward Josie.

"What does that mean, a little charmer?" Josie asked.

"It means that you make people like you because you are polite," Aaron returned.

"Thank you, Mr. Brad," Josie said, and she smiled and curtsied again.

"Why are you doing this curtsy all of a sudden?" Aaron grinned at her.

"Miss Nancy taught us in music today, because we sang a song about bow to your partner and curtsy to your partner. She said it was a very nice way to tell people you like them."

Aaron scooped her up and planted a big kiss on her cheek.

Josie giggled, and Brad said, "Well, it worked for me."

Aaron laughed. "We won't keep you from your work. Melissa has told me you have an important project to finish up. But we did want to welcome you and let you know we are next door in the two-story house, if you need anything."

Brad was about to reply but stopped when he noticed Aaron's gaze at Melissa. She smiled and then ducked her head to look at some notes she had scribbled. Brad cleared his throat and then said, "Thanks a lot. Hey, I was wondering, would anyone mind if I took a run in the morning around town? I mean, being a stranger and all, I don't want to startle anyone."

"No, that would be fine," Aaron said. "What time do you usually get out?"

"Well, probably 6:30 or so."

Aaron nodded. "Why don't I check with you at 7:45, and if you're ready, we could go to breakfast together."

"That would be great. Melissa, you're not coming in that early … or do you want to join us?"

"No, I'm sleeping in tomorrow, and then I have to bake my pie. I'll be in around 10:00."

Brad turned back to Aaron and thought he caught a slight look of disappointment in his face. "Well, okay then, it's a plan. I'll see you at 7:45."

"I'll pick you up right about then. Come on, Josie. These people need to get back to their work, and we have to eat supper."

"Okay." She hugged Melissa again and smiled at Brad. "Good night, Mr. Brad." Then she impulsively hugged him around his legs before joining her dad.

"Bye. We'll see you tomorrow." Melissa watched them leave and then turned back to her computer. She noticed Brad smiling at her. "What are you thinking about?"

Brad shrugged. "It seems to me that Pastor Aaron is very interested in you."

"Oh, he's just being polite."

"Right, and I'm a pepperoni pizza."

Melissa laughed. "Hmm, that makes me hungry, but we have work to do. Maybe we can call for a delivery after we get more done on this presentation."

"Good change of focus. Yeah, that sounds good."

They ordered their pizza at 8:30, and by the time it arrived, they were both hungry and ready for a break from the demands of work. Sharing pizza seemed like such a comforting thing to do. They talked about their hopes for the future, and finally Brad brought up a subject he had hesitated to discuss.

"Melissa, can I ask you about Sven?"

She felt the mood of the evening change, and she sighed. "What do you want to know?"

"Well, you seem to bristle every time his name comes up. I know you two went out." He opened his mouth to start again but hesitated. "I don't mean to stick my nose into your life, but, well, he seems to be around a lot. He brings the company a lot of business ..." He seemed to sense her tension and reluctance to discuss Sven's effect on her.

Silence filled the space between them. "It's hard to describe my reaction to Sven. When he first asked me out, he was rich, handsome, sensitive, and kind. We had a lot of fun together. As we continued to spend more time together and became more romantically involved, I was swept off my feet. I thought we could keep our personal lives and our business lives separate, but Sven didn't seem to be able to separate them. If I didn't make myself available to him when he wanted, then he would punish me at work." She caught a questioning look from Brad. "Remember when I wasn't included in some of the important accounts?"

Brad nodded, and then realization spread across his face. "That was his way of controlling you?"

She nodded.

"He was willing to jeopardize an account by keeping one of the best managers off the project, because he didn't like something you said or did away from work?"

Melissa pressed her lips together and nodded. Her eyes were full of hurt.

"That's crazy. Did that happen often?"

"That was just one of the ways." She told him about her dinner out with her girlfriends, and how he didn't want her to spend time with her parents or grandmother.

"I had no idea. Melissa, I am sorry. You should have told me. Maybe I could have done something."

"There was nothing you could have done. Don't feel like you should have tried. There were so many weird behaviors. I know he had women friends in other cities, maybe in Chicago. I heard him talking to them. Sometimes when he had been away, I found phone numbers or names. So many things he would leave around for me to see or hear, just so he knew I would be aware of his other women."

"Melissa, I am sorry. I will understand if you don't want to work on any of his accounts again. I'm also sorry that you may have to see him when you come in for the presentation."

"I knew it would be a possibility when I agreed to work on this project again."

"Does Mr. Cohen know?"

"I'm not sure. He may know. He has offered me projects with other accounts. But Sven tries to influence him too. It's a difficult situation. I simply have to be assertive and stay firm. It is so wearing, though. Sven always has a way of manipulating things to include me. I pray that he will find some other target for his harassment—or better yet, not bother me or anyone."

Brad moved over to sit next to her. "I'm sorry I asked, but I am glad I know. I will try to run interference for you." He stood up. "Lord, help us. Help Melissa. Protect her."

Melissa smiled and said, "Thank you, Brad.

Despite her plan to sleep in, Melissa was taking her pie out of the oven by 8:30. She grabbed a cup of coffee and a couple to muffins and then headed over to the breakfast table by the window. She was surprised to see how foggy it was. *I'm glad I don't have to be to town before ten. I wonder if Aaron and Brad are having breakfast together?* She smiled at the thought of the two of them chatting over eggs and pancakes. If they went to the coffee shop, Sheila was probably engaging Brad in a question-and-answer session. She giggled at the thought of Brad matching Sheila's witty conversation.

Melissa had securely placed the pie carrier on the floor of the passenger seat when her phone rang. "Hello?"

"Melissa, Aaron here. Have you left your house yet?"

"I was just about to. What's up?"

"It's really foggy, hard to see. Be careful coming into town. We've had some heavy rains, and the roads may be slick. Just be careful."

Melissa smiled at the sincere sound of concern in his voice. "I will, Aaron. Thanks. I will take it slowly. I'll see you in a few minutes."

"Good. Oh, I wanted to tell you that Brad and I will be in the church library. I have some books that he thought he might be interested in. I just wanted you to know where we would be."

"Okay. Where is the library?"

"Go in the side door and take the steps down. We will be in the first room to your left. You can't miss it."

"Okay, see you in a bit."

"Drive slowly. Watch out for deer and slick spots. Everything is different in the rain and fog."

"I will, Aaron. I'll be along." She clicked off the phone, walked around to the driver's seat, and slid in. She couldn't help but smile again at Aaron's concern. *When was the last time anyone, other than my parents, seemed worried about me?* She snapped her fingers. *Oh, the night Brad brought his Chicago chili and ice cream over to my apartment.* She adjusted her seat belt and started the car. She had to admit it felt very nice to have people express care and concern for her. She was quite amazed at the density of the fog. Her bright lights reflected into her face, and the dims did shine down onto the road to give her a short look into the distance. Thankfully, she did not see deer or turkey in the road, and she heaved a sigh of relief when she came to the corner where she turned onto the highway. However, that wasn't much better, and now she had to meet cars and trucks and make sure she was between the white line on the right side of the road and the dotted line in the center. A truck came up behind her quickly, and she prayed that he would stop before he hit her. He whizzed by and disappeared off into the curtains of fog. The streetlights were a welcome sight, but even then, they did little to give much visibility. She was thankful when she spotted the church and pulled in next to Aaron's Jeep.

She hurried to the side door and down the steps. As she proceeded toward the first room on the right, she heard Aaron call out, "Melissa, we're in here." She followed the voice to find Aaron and Brad sitting at a long, walnut library table with several volumes arranged between them.

Brad said, "Hi! I'm glad to see you made it in one piece. It's pretty eerie out there."

Aaron stood and pulled out a chair for her. "Thank you. It is like driving in pea soup. I've never seen fog like that."

She glanced at Brad and sensed that something was awry. *What is he up to?* "This is really nice," she said while looking around the room decorated in warm, comfortable furniture and beautiful wood surfaces. She noticed a large TV and several computers and shelving units filled with books and memorabilia. The walls and ceiling seemed to absorb extraneous sound, and the lighting created a perfect reading environment. Melissa could imagine coming down here and reading for hours.

Aaron said, "Yes, it is. It's a gift from one of our church families. It's the envy of all the other churches in the district, and it gets a lot of use." He sat down in the chair next to Melissa.

"So, what are you guys reading?" she asked as she pulled some of the books nearer.

"Aaron was just showing me some books that he recommends for new believers. He's going to let me take a couple home."

"You two seem to have hit it off," she said casually as she leafed through the pages of a paperback. "Where did you have breakfast?"

Aaron coughed and then cleared his throat. "At the diner."

Melissa chuckled and then said, "Of course. What did you think of it, Brad?"

"Well, I don't think you could stay a stranger for too long in this town, if Shelia has anything to say about it." Brad chuckled. "She's quite the welcome wagon."

"Yeah, by the time she served us our second cup of coffee, she was telling Brad the history of the town and giving him some leads on jobs and houses for sale. I think she's working on making him a regular at the coffee shop."

Melissa couldn't help but giggle at the picture of Sheila offering to give Brad a tour around the community, pointing out all the important aspects of Sovereign.

"Yeah, and when she realized you and Brad were friends, we three compared notes." Aaron leaned back in his chair, grinning. "It was very interesting."

"That couldn't have taken too long."

"I don't know. Brad filled me in on some very interesting details of your personality, but I doubt I was able to enlighten him like he did for me."

Melissa felt her face growing hot and hoped that her cheeks weren't betraying her feelings of embarrassment. But when she looked into those mischievous brown eyes and saw the sly grin, she was certain that Brad had been spinning tales. She turned to Brad to admonish him for betraying a trust and saw the grinning face of a man who was enjoying her discomfort.

"Brad Webster! What have you been telling Aaron?" Then upon remembering where their conversation took place, she groaned out loud. "Oh, no! In the coffee shop, no less. My name will be lambasted from here to Timbuktu!"

"Now, hold on there," Brad protested, his eyes dancing with laughter. "I didn't tell everything. I didn't mention a word about the time you tossed your keys into the Chicago River, or the time at the company softball game, when you hit a fly ball right into the boss's lemon meringue pie, or—"

"Oh! I'm warning you!" She looked around for something to throw, picked up sheets of paper, wadded them up, and flung them across the table.

Brad feinted left and then right with so much force that he fell out of his chair. "Stop, stop! Please!" He laughed. "I promise I won't say another word." He peeked over the table, still giggling. "I promise I won't tell him about your temper tantrums …"

"What? She has a temper?" Aaron grinned at her. "I never would have guessed it." He walked around to help his comrade off the floor. "It's okay, Melissa. He was very complimentary of you." He picked up one of the paper was and smoothed it out. "But if it's all right with you, could you use something rather than my notes for tonight's social for your ammunition?"

Melissa's eyes widened. "Oh, no!" She looked down at the remaining sheets and saw neatly typed lines, with handwritten notes in the margins—lists of people Aaron wanted to thank and information about missionaries the church was supporting. After covering her face with her hands, she slumped down in the chair. When she dared to lower her hands, and look up, she was met with two sets of grins. "Oh, I am sorry, Aaron. I'll retype those." She shook her head. "I guess I just added proof to those stories about my bad behavior."

"Ah, forget it. No damage done, except to your pride. I'm sorry if we embarrassed you," he said smiling down at her.

"Oh, don't be so apologetic," came Brad's impudent response. "A little harassment's good for her. Keeps her humble." He patted her on the shoulder. "Come on, Melissa. Much as I hate to break up this happy time, we still have to finish up that project." He took her hand and pulled her to a standing position. "Besides, you know I'd never tell the really good stuff."

Melissa rolled her eyes. "That's a good idea, before I really get into trouble."

Brad snorted at that and then said to Aaron, "Thanks for the talk and the books. I'll put them to good use and get them back to you."

"Not to worry, just enjoy them. I'll see you both tonight?"

"I wouldn't miss it for anything. All I want to eat, a chance to crank an ice cream churn, and eat Melissa's pie."

"Oh, my pie. Can I bring it in now?"

"Yeah, just put it in the kitchen, and put your name on it and the kind of pie."

Brad and Melissa worked on their project the rest of the morning and into the afternoon. By 3:30, they felt that they had all the specs and designs in place for the marketing focus, the website, the graphic designs, and the media presentations. All that needed to be finished was presenting it to Mr. Johanssen and Sven for approval. They talked briefly about dates on the calendar that Melissa would travel to Chicago for that presentation if she needed to be there. She felt a little shiver go up her spine at the thought to returning to the city and the office.

As they relaxed after their busy two days of brain draining work, Melissa asked about Bonnie. "Do you two spend a lot of time together?"

"Well, not while we are at work. But as much as we can when we are finished with our jobs. We go to a Bible study that is a couple's group, and sometimes we just hang out—you know, go to a movie or play, and go out to eat. Once a week, we get together and cook a meal. I really enjoy that because Bonnie's a great cook. She's fun to be with."

As he talked, Melissa watched his face change from the focused, on-the-job guy to a man who was obviously talking about the woman he loved. She sighed, and although she was happy for him, she knew that their friendship would probably never be as carefree as it had been before.

"Penny for your thoughts."

"What?"

"You were deep in thought there. Just wondering what you were concentrating on."

"Oh, I was just thinking about how happy you seem, especially when you talk about Bonnie. I guess I'm a little envious of you."

Brad smiled. "No need for envy. It will happen to you too."

Melissa shrugged and started tidying up the kitchen table.

As Brad packed his briefcase and his laptop, he said, "Aaron sure seems like a nice guy, and he's certainly knowledgeable about a lot of different subjects."

"Yes, he is very nice. He seems very interested in all of his parishioners."

Brad nodded. "I can see that. He has a heart for people." He paused. "But I think he's more interested in you as a person than as a parishioner."

Melissa turned to watch Brad's expression. "Really? What makes you think that?"

"Well, he certainly had a lot of questions about our relationship, and he seemed very relieved when I told him I have a steady girlfriend in Chicago."

Melissa nodded. "Well, he's the only single man I've met here, and I have enjoyed the time I've spent with him." She blushed. "And Josie is so cute! I have really taken to her."

"Obviously she is taken with you too. But I think she might be reflecting her dad's interest in you. Kids are very intuitive that way. I wouldn't minimize his interest in you."

Melissa had to admit that the idea of a relationship forming with Aaron seemed wonderful. So far, they had only had pleasant times together. She turned back to Brad and said, "I hope you're right. It would be so nice to have a nice man to spend my life with. It's just so soon, though, to know for sure. I guess I'm just being cautious."

Brad smiled and held out his arms, inviting her for a hug. She hesitated but knew that he was her friend and had her best interests at heart. She moved toward him and let him hug her. *Thank you, Lord, for my friend Brad. Bless him and Bonnie. If Aaron and I are supposed to pursue this relationship, please make it very clear to me.*

When Brad stepped back, allowing her to have more space, he smiled and said, "May God bless you, Melissa. You have been a great friend." He paused as though he had to think before he spoke. "I'm going to pray for you every morning. I'm going to ask God to give you the peace you seek."

She squeezed his hand and smiled. "You know, that is probably the best gift you could give me. Thanks, Brad." She ducked her head, hoping the tears in her eyes weren't obvious. When she looked up, she said, "God blessed me when he put you in my life." Then looking at her watch. "But it's time to go over to church for the social." With a giggle, she added, "I hope you're ready for lots of questions, conversation, and food!"

Chapter 16

They moved way through the crowd to the fellowship hall in the basement. Melissa introduced Brad to Linda and Jim. They stopped a few minutes to visit when Don and Rayleen joined them. Melissa tried to hide her smile at Rayleen's raised eyebrows, and then she quickly said, "Oh, Brad, I want you to meet my good friends Don and Rayleen. They live across the section from me and have been so helpful. Don and Rayleen, this is my good friend and co-worker from Chicago. He's been staying here at the guest cottage while we finished up a project for work."

Brad shook hands with each of them, answering questions and offering his delight with the town and community. "Yes, I am totally amazed by this community and the people here. I can see why Melissa is so happy to be here." Melissa smiled at the way Brad's sincere manners had charmed Don and Rayleen.

Aaron made his way over to the group and greeted each of them before calling for quiet. "The ladies in the kitchen tell me it's time to get started with the meal, so let's have a word of prayer, and then we can all dig in. Please don't crush any of the smaller children in your dash to get to the food." The crowd laughed and then quieted again when he held up his hand. He led them in a prayer of thanks and praise for the bounty the Lord supplied. When the "amen" came, the noise level rose as the youth hurried to fill their plates, and parents got their younger children in line.

She was happy to see Sheila and her husband at the social, as well as their daughter, Nancy. Sheila had nothing but compliments for Brad and reminded him that Sovereign could always use more nice people if he was interested. Brad laughed and said, "Well, I know where to find the best coffee shop in town, and the best waitress."

"Oh, go on!" Sheila protested. "It was a pleasure having you in my shop."

Mr. Miller, Melissa's lawyer, stopped to say hello.

"Oh, Mr. Miller. I want you to meet my business associate, Brad. He's been visiting for a couple days so that we could finish up a presentation we're working on. Brad, this is Mr. Miller, my lawyer."

"Pleased to meet you," Brad said.

Mr. Miller nodded and then introduced him to his wife. "And you remember my secretary, Anna Branson? This is her husband, Carl."

"It's so nice to see you again," Melissa said while looking around the room. "I'm amazed at the number of people here."

"Well, Aaron always invites everyone in the community. And this is such a wonderful event. We all love to come for such a great cause."

Melissa watched as Aaron filled Joseline's plate, following her precise directions of what to put on it and what to leave off. He guided her over to a table Don and Rayleen were sitting at and asked if Joseline could join them. Rayleen smiled and said, "We'd be delighted to have Josie join us," Don leaned over to her and talked with her as she got herself situated next to him.

As Melissa waited in line, other people came along to meet Brad. Melissa laughed and talked with them as she watched Brad chat with them as though he had known them his whole life.

Soon it was their turn to select food from the many salads and entrees on the table. They joined a table that had several empty seats. Brad oohed and awwed his way through macaroni and cheese and the beef and noodles. "This is amazing," he said. "I can't believe how good this is." People chuckled at him as he delighted in the vegetable salads and homemade rolls. "I don't think I've ever had food this delicious."

Aaron was circulating among tables, saying hello to everyone. Then he settled his plate and drink next to Melissa to eat his meal. He agreed with Brad on the tastiness of the food and laughed when

Brad groaned that he would not be able to eat another bite for days. Aaron said, "I bet you'll get your appetite back when dessert is served."

"Dessert?"

Just then, Jim Bodine stood and said, "We need all the able-bodied men we can get outside to crank these ice cream makers. Don't be shy. This is your chance to show off your muscles." Then he looked at Aaron. "Pastor, I believe you've had experience, so I encourage you to bring your city friend out to see if he can cut the mustard."

Brad jumped up, flexed his muscles, slapped Aaron on the back, and said, "Come on, old man. I'll show you country boys how this is done." The crowd erupted in chortles and giggles.

Aaron laughed good-naturedly and said, "You're on—and we'll see who's the old man."

Men and boys of all ages rose to follow them out of the dining area. But before anyone could get too far, Jim added, "One last thing. Remember our annual pie auction starts at seven sharp. I hope you all brought extra cash. I've looked over these pies, and I don't believe I've ever seen a better lot anywhere."

In what seemed like no time at all, the men and children were returning to the fellowship hall, bringing with them five icy buckets of churned ice cream. Each one was packed in ice and covered with a burlap sack. Joseline, with Aaron and Brad, came over and sat with Melissa. Jim Bodine stood in the center of the room and motioned for silence. "I have an important announcement to make. In the competition between our pastor and his city friend, I am proud to announce that Aaron was the obvious winner in the ice cream cranking competition, but that Brad was the overall winner in the excuse-making category."

Laughter filled the room, but when Brad stood up cradling his right bicep with his left hand, the crowd quieted. "Yes, I will concede this loss, but I demand a rematch after I recover."

Jim laughed and promised to provide the opportunity when he visited again. "Now for the next important event of the evening: the pie auction. Ernie Baier has graced us with his superb auctioneering skills since we started this auction. Let's have a round of applause for Ernie and get this sale underway. Remember, folks, the proceeds of this auction go to our missionaries, so dig down deep for that extra dollar. You'll be repaid tenfold."

Ernie took center stage and pointed to a beautiful strawberry cream pie that one of the youth held up. The bidding started at five dollars and quickly went to twenty. As the pie was delivered to the highest bidder, another member of the youth group carefully held up another pie. "Sour cream raisin, made by Joan Mathers."

Applause, cheers, and a whistle or two made Joan blush, and then the bidding began again. One by one, the pies were sold, going for twenty to one hundred dollars each.

Aaron moved around through the room, watching the proceedings, and he finally settled near the back of the hall. He scanned the room and found Melissa's pretty profile nodding in agreement in conversation with Mrs. Mathers. He smiled as he watched how easily she involved others around her in the discussion. He sighed and then yawned, realizing this had been a more tiring day than he had expected. Meeting Brad at the coffee shop had given him a chance to size up Melissa's relationship with the visitor. Brad was a likeable guy and seemed sincerely interested in Melissa as a friend, but he had made it known the love of his life was in Chicago. Aaron smiled at the way they had hit it off, and after only a few minutes, Brad had shared his concern for Melissa. Everything Brad had shared about Melissa had fit in with what Emma had told him, including the information about a rocky romance with which she had been involved. Brad had no problem sharing how glad he was that she had ended the relationship, sparing few words in describing the man who had hurt her feeling. He said that this trip was his chance to see how Melissa was doing after moving here for a healthier new start.

His thoughts were interrupted by the auctioneer announcing that they were nearing the two thousand-dollar goal for the missionary fund, and there was only one pie left. Ernie said, "Come on, folks. We need to boost this so that can keep our promises to support our good people in the field. Let's bid this last pie up."

Melissa looked nervously around the room, realizing that this had to be her pie. *I hope someone bids.* She thought that she had at least twenty dollars in her wallet, and she could write a check for more.

The auctioneer picked up the pie and read the homemade label. "Two crust apple, raisin, and walnut pie, made by Melissa Blakesly. What do I hear for this fine pie?"

Immediately Brad called out, "Ten dollars."

Melissa smiled gratefully at her friend, but the silence was torturous. She was about to bid herself when she saw Aaron approaching from the back of the room. "Twenty!" The crowded reacted with a cheer.

Brad looked at Aaron with a grin and said, "Think you can beat me out of this, do you? I'll bid thirty dollars."

"That a way. Don't let him have it too cheap!" Someone yelled from behind him. Brad grinned, nodded and raised both thumbs up to indicate his agreement.

Aaron moved closer so that the two men were facing one another. "Forty," came his response to the challenge.

People in the room stood and moved closer to witness this contest between their pastor and this outsider.

"Forty dollars," said the auctioneer. "Will anyone bid forty-five?"

Brad smiled at Melissa and said, "Fifty dollars!" The crowd roared their approval, and Brad grinned and raised both his arms, fists clenched as though he'd won a great victory. People chuckled at his grandiose posture.

Aaron laughed at the show-off antics and said, "Fifty-five dollars."

An immediate response of an elongated "Oh!" came from crowd at this high bid.

Melissa was beginning to feel a little uncertain about this jostling, but she didn't know what to do about it. All eyes were fixed on Brad as he contemplated making another bid, and then he finally said, "Sixty dollars, and that's my final bid."

Aaron grinned at his opponent, extended his hand for a congratulatory handshake, and said, "It's yours!" Everyone cheered, and those closest to the two men congratulated them on a good contest. Several people made a point to stop and thank Brad for his generous contribution.

Brad returned Aaron's handshake and accepted the thanks of those around him. He said, "So when do I get to eat my sixty-dollar pie?"

"Right now," answered Jim, and the process of cutting pies and scooping ice cream began.

Just as Melissa was finishing her dessert and Brad his third plate, Aaron joined them at the table again. "I hear the weather forecast for tomorrow isn't good. It's supposed to be foggy all day with poor visibility until noon, and then it'll pour all afternoon. There may be some hail and high winds, with possibility of dangerous lightning."

Brad looked at Melissa. "Yuck! I hate to drive in that kind of weather," she said.

"I don't think you should," replied Aaron.

"I don't either," Brad agreed. "Maybe I could rent a car, or perhaps there's a taxi or shuttle service I could catch to the airport. I really hate the idea of you being alone on the highway if the weather is that bad."

Melissa smiled at her friend. "I'm sure there's not a rental agency or shuttle service you could use in town." She paused and straightened her shoulders, "I'll be okay. I'm a good driver, and ..." She stopped midsentence when she saw Aaron shaking his head. "Really, Aaron. I'll be okay. After all, I used to drive in Chicago traffic. If I can do that, I can handle a little rain."

"No. It's not the same kind of driving. I don't want you going alone. I'll go with you."

Melissa was a little surprised at having this decision made for her. She was about to tell Aaron Chambers that she was quite capable when Brad intervened. "He's right, Melissa. You shouldn't be by yourself in that kind of weather. Why, you could go into a ditch and be there for hours. I think you should let Aaron go with us."

"You guys are being a little dramatic, aren't you?"

They both shook their heads no in unison.

"All right! I guess I know when I'm outnumbered. I'll pick up Brad at the cottage at 11:00, and then we'll come to your house. Okay?"

"Okay!" Aaron nodded with a smile on his face. "I'll see you two at 11:00, then."

Chapter 17

The trip to the airport took twice the usual time. Aaron had offered to take his Jeep, and Melissa accepted the offer, glad that she didn't have to drive in the dense fog. By the time they arrived at the airport, the fog had lifted, but the storm front was threatening from the west, as predicted.

At the terminal, Melissa got out with Brad while Aaron waited in the car at the curb. The agent assured Brad that his flight would be leaving on time. Brad pulled Melissa into a one-armed hug and said, "Thanks for everything. Now, don't worry about the presentation. I've e-mailed all our notes to our accounts. I'll have the technology and any paper copies we need ready when you get there. Now, when do I expect you?" Melissa shared with him her flight number and time. He nodded and said, "You two had better get started for home." He hesitated and then added, "Melissa, give yourself a chance to know Aaron. He seems like a good guy."

She gave him a playful punch on the arm and said, "Thanks, buddy." She quickly headed toward the door, but then she turned back and added, "See you in a few days."

As soon as she shut the car door, they were moving. "This storm looks bad," Aaron said, leaning forward to look up at the sky. Black clouds were somersaulting toward them. Lightning punctuated the horizon on the west and north, and thunder rolled in immediately after the flashes. Rain drops started splattering the windows, and the wipers had a hard time keeping the windshield clear.

Melissa watched the trees blowing and nearly bending over. "Do you think there could be a tornado?"

"I don't know. I can't get anything but static on the radio. I think we will be all right, but pull your seatbelt tight. You don't want to be thrown around if it starts rocking us sideways."

Melissa followed his direction. The sky got darker, and the rain came down with greater force. Sheets of water obscured their view of the road. Aaron slowed down to a crawl. The headlights barely made a dent in the rain and the darkness. White light lit up countryside with each lightning strike, and the thunder seemed to be right on top of them.

"I'd like to pull off the road, but I don't want to risk getting hit by another car. Wait—there's a parking lot we can pull into." He steered the Jeep into an empty spot next to a big truck, which would shield them from the wind.

They sat there in silence for a minute. "I think we should pray for a safe trip home. Grandmother always said God acted when we prayed in time of need."

"You're right." He took her hand in his and said a simple prayer, praising God for his love and protection and asking for guidance through the storm, as well as safety for them and others. "Amen."

Melissa squeezed his hand and repeated the amen.

The wind seemed to be lessening, and the lightning moved off to the east. They were both startled when someone rapped on the driver's window. Aaron rolled down the window a few inches. Immediately raindrops hit his face and shoulders.

"Excuse me." A man in a rain poncho grinned. "Pardon me. I'm sorry about getting you all wet, but I watched you pull in, and it looked like you were heading north on the interstate. They nodded, and he continued. "The radio just said the highway patrol has closed the road at the next exit because of a crash involving several vehicles. It would probably be safe for you to cut over to Center Point Road and try to turn back to the interstate north of the next interchange."

"Thank you so much. We will do that. Is there anything we can do for you?"

The man backed away and smiled. "Just pray for me." With that, he climbed back into his cab and shut the door.

Melissa covered her face with her hands. While thinking about the risk they'd just avoided because a truck driver took time to warn them of possible danger. Finally after a deep breath, she said, "God is just amazing!"

Aaron smiled. "That he is! Our God is an awesome God."

She nodded. "It is incredibly amazing that God took time to listen. Why did he pick us?"

"I think he is eagerly waiting for us to talk to him." He watched her face as she brushed away tears, smiled, and tried to appear brave. "Melissa, you don't doubt that God answers our prayers and puts people in our path, do you?"

She heaved a deep sigh. "Well. Maybe it was just a coincidence. I'd rather believe, but I've heard people talk about things happening just because they happen." She hesitated and watched the rain streaming down the windshield. "It's just so mind-boggling to think that God could do that for you and me here, and for a billion people all over the world, at the same time."

Aaron nodded, "You're right, it is. I guess my answer to that is that God is mind-boggling." He smiled and leaned against the door so that he could face her. "I know that he is able to hear and answer our every prayer."

"But what about all the sick and hungry and injured people? Don't they pray, or doesn't he listen to them?"

He shook his head sadly. "I've questioned his methods at times too. But in Philippians 4:6, Paul tells us, 'In everything by prayer and supplication with thanksgiving let your requests be made known to God.' So it's not a matter of ask and receive, ask and receive. We must be thankful and ask God continually for what we need. It is God's plan to care for us, but he's not a magnified Santa Claus who spoils us. He watches us, waiting for us to acknowledge him so that he can work in our lives for good." He waited for her reaction to his explanation.

Melissa smiled at him and said, "I want to believe as strongly as you do, but I guess I just don't understand."

Aaron thought for a moment. "You're one among many, but you are working hard to listen and understand." He paused and then added, "The church has a Bible study addressing prayer on Wednesday evenings. Maybe that would help to clear up some things."

"Linda mentioned that Bible study to me last Thursday." She looked again at the raindrops streaming down the windshield and then tried to hold back a smile. "Are you two in cahoots? Does she get a commission for each new person she gets to that meeting?"

Aaron looked at her seriously, ready to deny any such plan, when he saw her smile. He realized she was teasing, laughed, and said, "No, we're not, but that might not be a bad idea. Hmm, let me see. A couple of bucks per head, and a dollar for everyone who continues for three months or longer."

They laughed together about the idea, and then Melissa said, "I told Linda I would try to come. I could use a lot more knowledge about how and when to pray. I know that he answers my prayers, I've experienced it a lot recently, and I'm becoming more aware of my need to bring everything to him before I try to handle it myself." After a moment, she asked, "Now tell me, was that a coincidence, or was God working through Linda in my life?"

"I know God puts us with people and allows situations to occur in our lives to help us see his work in us."

"So did Linda tell you that she'd invited me to Bible study?"

Aaron chuckled. "Sovereign is a small town, and Peace has a small congregation. You're going to find that people are interested in what you are doing. Occasionally, some might make suggestions to you. Others may make judgments about you." He stopped and reached over to take her hand. "But that's part of being involved in this type of community. It can be a drawback, but in my opinion, it's a minor one when you consider all the benefits."

Melissa frowned and looked at the glimpses of sunlight streaming down to the ground. The harshest part of the storm was over, but the rain continued in a steady rhythm. She was surprised when Aaron had reached over to hold her hand, but she was pleased at the caring touch and did not pull away.

"There's something else you may need to think about too," Aaron started again. "We have spent some time together, and if we continue—which I hope we do—you are going to be the focus of attention. People will be watching us. That may be something you need to consider as we continue our friendship."

Melissa pursed her lips and then said, "I've thought about that too." She looked up at Aaron and continued in a serious tone. "I'm not sure I could handle that kind of intrusion into my life. I'm a very private person, and I don't want to always be wondering if I'm being good enough." She shrugged her shoulders, looked back at Aaron, smiled, and squeezed his hand. "But maybe I should wait to cross those bridges when I come to them."

"That's a good idea. I've heard that if God leads you to it, then he will lead you through it. And speaking of getting through it, I think we'd better get moving while the storm has lessened."

He started the engine and drove out of the parking lot, heading back to Center Point Road. They drove on in silence, watching the road and the effects of the downpour they had just experienced. The ditches were full of runoff rainwater, but the highway was clear and traffic was moving easily. As they approached the village of Center Point and turned back toward the interstate, Melissa said to Aaron, "I don't want you to get me wrong. I've enjoyed our time together, and I do want to keep on seeing you." Aaron nodded his head. "I guess you'll just have to put up with my ..."

"Temper tantrums," Aaron interrupted, looking at her with a sly grin on his face.

Returning his smile, she said, "That wasn't what I was going to say, but yes, that and other things about me that you don't know."

"So how is that different than anyone else? Do you think my whole life is posted on the bulletin board at church?"

She laughed at the picture his words painted. "I haven't notice it there, but yeah, I guess that is what I kind of thought. I know you sort of belong to your congregation."

"Yeah, some people do believe that, and the main part of my position is to serve my people as a shepherd serves his sheep. But I am allowed to have a personal life too. It may be more highly scrutinized than others, but I still get one."

Melissa nodded and then smiled. "Look, a rainbow! God's promise to us!"

"Yes! I think he's smiling on us or maybe at us."

As they moved north toward Sovereign, Melissa noticed a few limbs down, and petals of flowering trees carpeted the ground underneath. Fortunately, there didn't seem to be much damage anywhere.

Aaron pulled his Jeep into the church parking lot next to Melissa's car. He shut off the engine. "Thanks so much, Aaron, for driving today," Melissa started. She had her hand on the door handle and was about to open it as she talked. "I know you saved me a lot of stress, if not my life!"

I was glad to do it," he returned. "It's always my pleasure to help out a damsel in distress." He had that familiar glint in his eye. "But before you go, when do I see you again?"

She turned back toward him. "Well, I'm going into Chicago the middle of next week, and I'll probably be back on Saturday evening. That gives us the rest of this week and weekend."

Aaron thought for a moment and then suggested, "How about tomorrow night? Friday is Mrs. Mason's day off, and I take it off to spend with Josie. Then in the evening, I grill out. It's our tradition. Why don't you join us for supper?"

"Sounds good, but ..."

"But what? Don't tell me you have another good friend coming into town that I have to contend with."

"Why, Aaron Chambers! I can't believe it. You can't be jealous, are you?"

"Oh, you found me out!" He grinned sheepishly. "I confess, I was concerned about this friend of yours. Here I thought I had met an eligible young lady, and then I find out she's getting ready to entertain a gentleman friend."

Melissa smiled broadly now, enjoying every minute of Aaron's confession.

"You love this, don't you?"

Giggling, Melissa admitted, "Yes, I do! You don't know what this does for my ego!" She spontaneously grabbed his hand and said, "Thanks, Aaron. You made this a fun day."

They laughed together, and then Aaron said, "So are you going to join Josie and me Friday night? We have the best burgers in town, and Josie will be thrilled to have you come. We could eat supper together, and then I could get a sitter. We could go to the park to listen to the community band concert." He sat waiting for her answer, not letting her break eye contact.

She hesitated only a moment before saying, "I'd love to."

Chapter 18

Melissa settled herself into seat 13A for the short flight to Chicago. As she watched other passengers find their seats, she thought about recent events.

The last few weeks had been some of the happiest she had spent in years. The combination of Brad's visit, involving herself again in work, and getting to know Aaron had all worked together to help her find joy again. She smiled as she remembered Josie's sad goodbye, her tears streaming down her face as she clung to Melissa's hand. The Friday night barbecue with Aaron and Josie, treating her like special company, was so sweet. The concert in the park later in the evening had been beautiful. She couldn't remember a time when she had felt more content than sitting on a blanket with Aaron under the clear, starlit skies and listening to the community symphony. Even though she'd only known Aaron for a little over a month, it felt like he'd been part of her life for longer. When he took her home that night, they lingered on her front porch, sharing plans and hopes for the future. He'd made her laugh with his stories of people he'd encountered over the years, and he brought tears to her eyes with the revelations of his sadness over his failed marriage and of having to raise his daughter alone.

He'd listened to her as she talked about spending years in a city and feeling alone and disappointed by relationships that seemed to follow all the wrong paths, leaving her feeling even more alone. He'd nodded at her concerns over whether she had made the right decision to move to a small town where she had no connections. They had sat in comfortable silence, enjoying the sounds of tree frogs and owls.

When he stood to leave, she'd stood to walk him to the steps. He'd lingered, turned to her, and without either of them saying a word given her a tender kiss. When he'd said good night and walked out to his car, she'd known she would miss him while she was in Chicago.

Her thoughts were caught up in that lovely moment when she realized the attendant was explaining about emergency exits and oxygen masks. Back to reality, she reviewed the week and mentally checked off all the things on her list that she had finished in the last four days. She had talked to Don and Rayleen about renting her pasture, talked to the neighbors who were renting her tillable acres about possible expenses and projects that might need some attention, and chatted with Mr. Miller about some legal issues still pending. She'd talked to her parents on the phone and shared with them her plans. Her mom had expressed concern about her returning to the city to work, but she seemed to feel better when Melissa told her she would be working with Brad again. Her dad asked about the preacher who'd broken in her door, and she'd assured him that he was really a gentleman.

Melissa thought about the week ahead. She was looking forward to Thursday's presentation. She'd always enjoyed performing for her clients, presenting her ideas and Brad's plans. She knew that she loved the reward and sense of accomplishment that her work brought her. She had to smile at the long list of activities that Brad had planned for her. She was looking forward to meeting Bonnie and getting to know her better. She realized that she loved her work and the satisfaction it brought her when she was able to contribute to the success of a project. She also realized that she didn't miss the environment of living in a metropolitan area, or the continued feeling of Sven looking for ways to manipulate her. Once they were in the air, she acknowledged the conflicts she would face in the next few days. She questioned the wisdom of working with Sven again, especially after their last unhappy encounter. But she was anxious to see the friends she had left behind. She sighed and said a silent prayer. *God, thank you for all the blessings you have poured out for me. Please help me to enjoy this time and make the* most of this opportunity. Help me say the right things to Sven and everyone else. I know that I am capable, and with your help, I will be able to prove that to myself. Please take care of Aaron and Josie and all my friends in Sovereign. Praise your holy name. Amen.

When she walked through the baggage claim area, Brad was there to meet her. "Hey, Melissa. Right on time!" he said as he pulled her into a one-armed hug and took her bag. "Boy, has this been a busy week. Sven loved the work, and he's really looking forward to the presentation to corporate board tomorrow."

"I am too," Melissa admitted. "In fact, I've been surprised at how much I've been looking forward to it."

Brad smiled. "I thought you might be ready for a bit of a challenge. It seems I remember you love to get up to push your ideas in front of a bunch of bored, expensive suits, blasting them with a lot of pizzazz!"

"Oh, Brad! You are so good for my ego—better than a whole bag of licorice jelly beans!"

Brad laughed at the analogy. "I think Sven will buy you a ton of whatever you want, if you can convince this bunch tomorrow to go with our ideas. I told him not to worry because you'd have them eating out of your hand and begging you for more."

The mention of Sven's name and the realization that she would be in close encounters with him sent a feeling of dread skittering across her mind. "I hope you didn't promise more than we can deliver."

"Not to worry. I have confidence in you."

Melissa smiled. "But what about you? I'm not rowing this boat alone."

"Of course not, but like I said before we got this project rolling, you're the one with the great ideas and words. I simply put it into motion. We have to persuade them before they'll let us convince them, and you, missy, are just the woman for that job." He finished with a big grin and flourish of his hands.

Melissa shook her head at her very confident friend. She followed him out to the curb, where they caught a taxi to her hotel. She rode along, half listening to Brad's chatter. However, she couldn't keep her mind on him because of the traffic. She cringed when a car zoomed past inches from her window, and then she gripped Brad's hand and pressed her body back into the seat when the cab stopped centimeters before crashing into the back of a van.

"Melissa, relax! You're acting like you've never seen this traffic before."

She covered her eyes with her free hand. "I feel like I'm out of my element. I can't believe how fast I've blocked all this out."

"Just lean back and concentrate on me. Let the driver do his job." Melissa turned toward him. "Bonnie is meeting us at your hotel. We'll have dinner together and then let you get some rest. Tomorrow's our big day."

Once the cab pulled up under the canopy of the hotel, Brad gathered her bag, and they entered the lobby. A slender redhead with long, straight hair rose from a couch and approached them. It wasn't until Brad stopped and turned toward her that Melissa recognized her as Bonnie. She accepted the hand extended her hand and said, "Hello, Bonnie. It's so nice to see you."

The two women smiled at each other, talking about the last time they had seen one another. "I wasn't sure you would remember me," Bonnie said.

"Of course, she remembers you!" Brad said, grinning from ear to ear. "You're hard to forget with all that red hair shining like a beacon."

"Oh, stop it. You're embarrassing me." Bonnie giggled and blushed.

"Let's get Melissa checked in to her room, and then we can talk over dinner."

Melissa's room was on the fourteenth floor with a beautiful view of Lake Michigan. The clear air made for a spectacular picture. Melissa stood and watched the boats bobbing up and down on the waves. The room was very nice, but she was surprised at the large bouquet of white roses on the table. Brad whistled and said, "Look at the size of that bunch of flowers! Do you have some secret admirer?"

She pulled the card and was surprised to see the message:

"Welcome back to town. Looking forward to working with you again. I hope we can mend some fences. As ever, Sven."

She stuffed the card back in the envelope and buried it under the vase. "It's from Sven. Just more of his fake pleasantries."

"Hmm. Well, I told you he was impressed with your ideas. I guess this is just his way of trying to smooth the path for both of you."

She frowned but then said, "Let's get on with our evening. I want us to make good memories, and Bonnie and I have lots of things to catch up on."

He smiled. "I agree. I'm a lucky man to get to spend time with my two favorite women. Besides, I'm starving. What do you say we find some place we can eat, and you two can get better acquainted?"

Bonnie spoke first. "He's such a charmer. Aren't we blessed to have such a nice man in common?"

Melissa agreed, "We are very fortunate."

They walked to a nearby restaurant. Melissa was still ill at ease with the noise and amount of traffic in the area. *I don't remember being bothered by this before,* she thought. *It didn't take long to make a country girl out of me.*

During their meal, they talked about Brad's recent trip to Sovereign. Bonnie had lots of questions and commented on her lack of experience with anything outside of the city. Melissa smiled and said, "Brad said you two might come out some weekend. You'd both be welcome anytime."

"I was hoping you would repeat that invitation. I'd love to spend a weekend out of the city. Brad was sure impressed. I don't think I've seen him so excited."

"It's a beautiful area," Brad chimed in. "I only hope we don't have storms next time."

They talked through the meal and afterward. Melissa couldn't help but notice the loving looks the couple gave each other. They both seemed so at ease with the other, so in tune to each other's interests. She found herself thinking about Aaron and the lovely evening she'd just spent with him the night before. *I wonder if he's missing me as much as I miss him?*

"Melissa!"

"Oh, I'm sorry—I was lost in my thoughts. What were you saying?"

"I was just saying that it's getting late, and we have that presentation tomorrow. Do you want to go over it before we present?"

"What time is the meeting?"

The committee meets at 9:00, and we are on the docket at 10:15. We have the rest of the morning, if we want it. Sven expects that it will take at least until noon, and maybe part of the afternoon, to cover everything we are proposing."

"I see. Well, would you mind coming to the hotel at 8:15? We can go through it one last time."

Chapter 19

The next morning, Melissa woke before the desk call. Her shower, hair, and makeup took extra care, and once she was ready for her day, she called down for room service. Even though she wasn't hungry, she knew she needed to eat or she'd be exhausted halfway through the morning. She ordered hummingbird muffins with butter, a fruit cup, and hot lemon tea, hoping that would help to calm her nerves. The thought of seeing Sven increased her anxiety as well. Would he use this opportunity to embarrass her in front of the clients? Would he ply her with charming words and unwanted touches? Their last encounter had been ugly. After several months of dating, she had finally admitted that he wasn't the man for her, and she obviously wasn't meeting his needs. Sven wanted someone who was more sophisticated, less inhibited, and more willing to fit the mold he had designed. Melissa knew he wasn't the companion she had been seeking. When she'd shared with him that she was not going to continue the relationship, their last date had deteriorated, resulting in them both feeling unhappy and disillusioned.

But still, he had sent the flowers, and he had solicited her consulting on this important project. She and Brad had spent weeks researching the field of recreation and personal therapeutic and fitness equipment. They'd used up hours and hours of expensive time going over ways of converting an existing Johanssen-owned defense assembly factory into a more profitable one that would produce middle-priced but effective equipment focused on home use. Much of her last three months with Cohen Marketing Inc had been spent on this project, and she wanted to finish it and see it through. She had to be able to put her personal feelings aside.

When Brad knocked on the door, her jitters had calmed. Brad's handsome good looks matched his exuberance for life. "Wow, you look like you're ready to take on the world," she said.

He grinned and thanked her. "I think we make a pretty good pair for this presentation. You are going to knock their socks off."

"Thanks, Brad. Shall we go over our notes?"

He set up his notebook with the slides he'd made for their presentation. They practiced their facts and figures and synced them with the slides twice until they were satisfied that they were well prepared.

Brad checked his watch. "Not bad. We still have a few minutes before we need to head to the office."

"I will be glad to get there and start the presentation. We have worked hard, and I hope they will be impressed with our ideas." Melissa sat down opposite Brad and then changed the conversation. "Brad, Bonnie is lovely. I really enjoyed last evening."

Brad beamed at the mention of her name. "She really enjoyed you too. When I dropped her off at her apartment, she said she hoped you two would get to spend some time together."

Melissa smiled. "That would be wonderful. I am looking forward to it."

The taxi dropped them off, and they took the elevator to the twenty-first floor and entered the outer office. The receptionist greeted them and said she would let Sven know they were here. Meanwhile, she escorted them to a room larger than Melissa's hotel room. The furnishings were beautiful, soft chairs and sofas upholstered in something that looked like tapestry. The view behind a large mahogany desk was downtown Chicago. One wall was lined with shelves filled with beautiful books and gorgeous glass vases in blues and greens. On the opposite wall, brilliantly colored trophy fish were displayed. She scanned the room with all the examples of Sven's personal favorites and realized how little she had known about him.

Her thoughts were interrupted by Brad saying, "This is just a little fancier than my office."

Melissa laughed. "As I remember, your office was comparable to mine. About one-fourth as big as this room, with worn tan carpeting and a no-view window."

"Well, you're right, but if I squinch my eyes together tight, sometimes I think I can see something other than a brick wall out my window." He reached over and took her hand. "Are you nervous?"

"A little," she admitted. "It's been a while. But we'll be okay."

He nodded and was about to say something else when the door opened, and Sven strode into the room.

Melissa caught her breath and watched Brad rise and extend his hand. "Sven." She watched as the two men shook hands and chatted about the nice weather. Sven, as blond and handsome as ever, turned to Melissa.

She stood, accepted his hand, and looked up into his azure blue eyes. "Nice to see you again. Thank you for the flowers."

He smiled and held her hand in his warm, firm grip for a moment longer than Melissa wanted. "My pleasure. I've missed you."

She smiled and couldn't help but think how much warmer Aaron's brown eyes were than Sven's brilliant blue. She gently pulled her hand away and said, "I'm looking forward to this presentation." She looked down at her clasped hands in her lap. When she looked up at him, she saw that he hadn't taken his eyes off her. Sitting tall, she smiled and said, "So, are you ready for us now?"

Sven smiled again, "Not just yet." Then he turned and placed a hand on Brad's shoulder. "They're still going over the financial report. I must go back in there, but I wanted to greet you. I trust you're ready?"

"Yes," they said in unison.

"Good. I'll hurry this up, and we'll get started in a few minutes. In the meantime, would you like something to drink or eat?" Melissa asked for a glass of water. Sven made her wish known to the receptionist and then said, "I'll see you two in a few minutes. I'm counting on you to convince these guys that this program is a good idea. Good luck!" Then he left.

Melissa sank down in her chair and groaned. "Now I'm starting to get nervous."

The receptionist brought in a tray with a crystal pitcher filled with ice water and two matching glasses. When she left, Brad poured, handed her a glass, lifted his, and toasted. "To us. May the Lord bless our efforts today."

Melissa clinked her glass to his. "Thank you, Brad." Then she added, "Lord, guide my lips. Help me to say the things that are true and pleasing to you. Give me courage, and thank you for Brad, for Sven, and for this opportunity."

"Amen," Brad finished.

Twenty minutes later, Brad and Melissa were summoned into the meeting room. This was a corner room, and two of the walls were glass with a breathtaking view of the city and Lake Michigan. Melissa consciously made herself focus on the people sitting around the long walnut table. She noted that there were three women and seven men, including Sven. They ranged in age from midthirties to midseventies.

Sven ushered them to the end of the table. Before offering them seats, he introduced them to the group. Melissa made mental notes of each name, position, and a visual clue to help her retain their identity. Once the introduction was complete, Sven pulled out her chair for her and indicated the one next to hers for Brad. He sat in the seat next to Melissa and then stated, "Brad and Melissa have worked up a marketing approach for our newest product line. I feel it will take us leaps forward into a successful promotion. Because recreation equipment is a new venture for our corporation, I would like to give their ideas serious consideration." He nodded in their direction and said, "I'll let you take it from here."

Brad stood up and directed them to the website synced on their tablets. He talked them through the main points of the presentation. He then gave an informed overview of their plan and how they could be facilitated within the structure of this corporation, and specifically in the physical plant of the factory. When he had laid the groundwork, Melissa stood and started describing the marketing proposal. One by one, she ticked off their plans to use social media, as well as printed media, television infomercials, shopping network blasts, and personal testimonies. She directed them to look back at their tablets to see slides of mock-ups of equipment and the logo that would identify their equipment and separate it from the competition. She listed specifics of costs, timelines, and a profile of the probable professional and the home purchaser. The more she talked, the more confident she became, and she realized that she was in her element. She talked to each person, hoping to convince him or her that this approach was the one to invest in because it was the one that would sell the most product.

When she finished, she turned to Sven and offered their services for questions and answers. She slipped into the seat between Sven and Brad and waited for the first question. They spent the next hour clarifying and reviewing procedures, outcomes, costs, and predicted profits. At 1:00, a motion was made that they break for lunch and that the committee reassemble to review the materials and make decisions at 2:30.

Sven walked Brad and Melissa out to the area in which they had waited prior to the presentation. Once the doors were closed, he turned to them with a big grin on his face. "Congratulations! I'm sure they were very impressed. Now all we have to wait for is for them to review and make a final decision."

"How long will that take?" Brad asked.

"My bet is they will have made a decision by the end of the day. I've sat in on these presentations before, and I've gotten pretty good at reading their faces and reactions. Believe me, they were impressed with your knowledge and figures. It was obvious that you had done your homework and knew what you were talking about. I don't think any of them had given a thought to half the details you presented today. I'm sure we'll have a favorable decision by the end of the afternoon."

Melissa looked at Brad and met his smile with one of her own. Then to Sven she said, "Thank you for your encouragement."

"You are professionals. I know quality when I see it." He flashed his brilliant smile and added, "You may as well go to lunch and take some time. I'll be in touch with you."

"Won't you join us for lunch?" Melissa asked.

"I'd love to, but I need to talk with my father. I want to get his reaction and let him hear mine. I know he's not too anxious to branch off into a field unknown to us, but he knows we need to diversify. His vote will probably be the hinge point. If he has any concerns, I want to be able to address them."

Melissa and Brad walked to a lunch wagon near a green space and joined the throng of people waiting to order. They ordered and then took it to the only vacant table close by. The chatter of other diners and the traffic noise made it hard to have a conversation. "I've forgotten what lunch hour rush is like," Melissa said as she unwrapped her sandwich. She inspected the contents and took a bite.

"This isn't half bad. If I don't take time to pack a lunch and come here, I usually end up eating while I walk back to work. At least we found a table." Brad tilted his head and looked at her solemnly. "Don't tell me you're missing your countryside retreat already."

She smiled and then took a sip of her drink to help her swallow her bite of sandwich. "I don't like all this commotion." She wrapped the rest of her sandwich up and took another swig of her drink. "I'll be all right. It just takes time to get used to the hubbub again." Smiling, she changed the subject. "Your slides and video presentations were great. You did a fantastic job working all that up. I really liked the way you linked the design and manufacturing process with the financial advantages."

"Thanks." He tipped his drink to her. "But we both worked on the research, and it took both of us to carry that off. We make a good team." He sat back and looked at the cloudless sky. "What do you want to do with the rest of the afternoon? I need to check in at the office. Want to come along and check out your old digs? I know the boss will want to say hello, just to rest his mind that you're really here working and not back home lounging in a hammock."

"Sure. I want to say hi to everyone. And I wouldn't want the boss to worry that I wasn't earning my salary."

Despite the level of business going on at Cohen and Associates, she had a chance to say a few words to many of her co-workers. When they approached the boss's office, the receptionist greeted them with a smile and picked up the phone to let Mr. Cohen know they were waiting to see him. She smiled again and told them to go in. Mr. Cohen greeted them in a very warm manner. They shared a quick summary of their morning's work and Sven's promise to call them as soon as he knew whether their proposal would be accepted.

Mr. Cohen, a middle-aged, balding man, leaned back in his leather chair and studied them for a few minutes. After pushing his glasses up on his forehead, he said, "You know, I really liked the materials you worked up. If your presentation was as good as they were, we should have a winner." He swiveled to look out the window studying the cityscape. Melissa looked at Brad, and he shrugged as if to say he wasn't sure either whether they'd been dismissed or whether they should wait for more information. When Ralph Cohen turned around, he leaned forward on the desk and said, "Melissa, are you sure you don't want to come back full time?"

Melissa's eyes widened, and she said, "Uh, no. I mean yes, I'm sure. At least for the time being. I'm not ready to resume full-time work yet."

Mr. Cohen nodded in seeming agreement and then said, "Well, you and Webster seem to click pretty good together, and we always need good ideas and bright young faces to develop them. You come see me first if you change your mind. I promise I'll make it worth your time." He smiled at her and rapped his knuckles on his desk a couple of times. "Agreed?"

Melissa returned his smile and said, "Agreed!"

Mr. Cohen turned to Brad and said, "I think we need to look at a raise for you. I was really impressed with all your media work, as well as the layouts for the presentation. We'll talk about specifics on, let's see ..." He pushed his glasses back down on his nose and scanned his calendar. "How about 10:30 on Monday?"

"That would work for me. Thank you, sir." Brad turned to Melissa, wiggled his eyebrows, and then grinned like a kid who'd just heard he was getting two birthday parties. She couldn't help but feel elated for her friend's good fortune, but they were called back to task when the phone rang.

"Ralph Cohen here. Yes, Sven. Well, good, good! Yes, they're right here. Sure, I'll tell them. Great! We'll be looking forward to working with you." He turned to them. "Congratulations! They loved it. They want Sven to work out the details with us tomorrow. So, you two take the rest of the day off and be back here tomorrow at 9:00 sharp!" He stood and ushered them out of the office.

Melissa turned to shake his hand and said, "Thank you, Mr. Cohen."

"That's quite all right, Ms. Blakesly. Of course, this means we'll have to extend your contract—at least until this job's done. Then I hope you'll consider other projects."

"Of course." She smiled at him and then turned to watch Brad shake his hand and thank him again.

"Great work." He nodded toward the receptionist. "I'll let Aleeza know that you'll be coming in on Monday at 10:30. Have a good day."

Chapter 20

While sitting in an upholstered chair with her feet propped up on her empty carry-on bag, Melissa thought about all that had happened in the last couple of days. Brad was a joy to work with, and she could see the effect of his relationship with Bonnie and how it affected every part of his life. Sven had been cordial and solicitous of her ideas and her time. Mr. Cohen's complimentary words had encouraged and supported her. And of course, there was Aaron. So sweet and handsome, strong and caring. She smiled and remembered all the pleasant times and conversations they had shared. She was pleased at how their relationship seemed to be evolving, and she admitted that she liked the idea of growing closer to him.

She was jarred out of her daydream by her cell ringing. She glanced at the ID and was pleased to see it was Aaron. "Hi, Aaron!"

"Hello," came his warm and gentle voice. "How are things going?"

The sound of his voice brought a huge smile to her face. "What a nice surprise. Oh, I'm so happy you called. Things are going very well. They accepted our proposal, and we start the revisions and contract assignments tomorrow morning."

"Congratulations! How's Brad doing?"

"Oh, Aaron, you should see how happy he is. He, Bonnie, and I had supper together last evening, and those two are as happy as Josie riding Rusty. He did a great job today too. I'd forgotten how much fun it is to work with him and present in front of group like that." There was a long pause, and so Melissa asked, "Aaron, are you there?"

"Yeah, I'm here. I was just listening to the excitement in your voice. It sounds like you're enjoying being back."

Melissa thought that she detected a note of concern in his voice. "Aaron, are you all right? You sound kind of sad."

"Nothing to worry about. I'm just missing your company and feeling a little envious that you're having such a good time away from me."

"I won't be here for long. I am enjoying myself, but I've already recognized things that I left Chicago to avoid. I'm sure I'll be more than ready to come back to Sovereign in a few more days."

She heard him sigh. "That's a relief. I hated to think of the other possibilities."

She smiled, flattered that he was happy she would be returning soon. "Aaron, I really had a wonderful time Friday evening. Supper with you and Josie, and the concert, was wonderful. It was all so much fun."

"Me too." Melissa thought she could almost hear the smile in his voice. "Joseline misses you already, and you've only been gone two days. Today she asked me when you were coming back and then added that she was sure Granny doll was sad you were away."

"I will call you as soon as I know when I'll be coming home. Tell Josie that I miss her too."

"I will." He paused and then said, "She's not the only one who misses you. Have a good night."

"Good night, Aaron." She looked into the mirror and saw the face of a happy Melissa, one that she hadn't seen for a long time.

Aaron put the phone back in the holster just as Joseline came into the room. "Hey, Josie. What's up?"

"Nothing. Daddy, there's no one to play with. Mrs. Mason is doing dishes, and Paisley is asleep. Will you play with me?" She put a pretty pout on her face designed to melt his heart.

Aaron smiled. "Sure. I've an hour before my next appointment. What do you want to do?"

"Could we go to Don's house? Maybe I could ride on Rusty."

"Nope, Don's a busy man. He's probably worked out in the field all day and wouldn't have time to chase Rusty."

She heaved a huge sigh. "Well, can we go to Missa's house …"

She stopped halfway through her sentence when she saw her dad shaking his head no. "Melissa's gone. Remember when we took her to the airport? I tell you what. Why don't you get one of your books, and I'll read to you?"

"No! I don't want to read a dumb, old book. Daddy, I wish I had a mommy. Then I'd always have someone to play with." She stuck her thumb in her mouth and stared at him with a determined look.

Aaron smiled at his daughter with a mixture of tolerance, sadness, and humor at her drama. "Now, Joseline, we've had this talk before. Your mommy is in heaven."

Sniffing for effect, Joseline tried a more direct approach. "Well, you could get me new mommy." Watching her dad for his reaction, she continued. "Missa would make a good mommy."

Aaron smiled at this pint-sized actress and said, "She might, but we don't know if Melissa wants to be a mommy."

After standing up and leaning on his knee, Joseline looked into her daddy's eyes with the honesty of a four-year-old. "Why don't we ask her?"

Laughing, Aaron picked her up and held her against his shoulder. "It isn't that simple. Ladies like Melissa have lots of things to think about besides being a mommy. Now, why don't we go see what's outside to do?"

Melissa had just finished her hair and makeup and was fastening the black crystal necklace and matching earrings. *That was sure nice of Aaron to call. I never expected him to. I simply thought someone should know how to get in touch with me in case of an emergency or something …*

She looked at her reflection in the mirror, laughed, and said aloud, "Melissa Blakesly, who do you think you're fooling? You know perfectly well you were hoping Aaron would do exactly what he did!" Then she smiled at her reflection. "He misses me!" The thought came to her that she missed him as well. She sat back on the bed, imagining his smiling face and rerunning his words over and over in her mind when her cell rang again.

"Hello?"

"Melissa! I'm glad I caught you. Did Cohen tell you the board accepted your plan?" The sound of Sven's triumphant tone annoyed her.

"Yes, Brad and I are very pleased."

"So am I. It was a unanimous decision, and my dad is very enthusiastic about your information and ideas."

"That's good to hear. I am going to meet Brad and his fiancée for dinner later. He'll be happy to hear that too. Mr. Cohen said that we'll be meeting with you tomorrow morning to go over specifics."

"Yes, it will probably take most of the morning to get things in order. I'm looking forward to working with you more closely again. You make a very favorable impression."

Melissa felt the heat rise on her cheeks, and she was not sure exactly what he meant—and anxious about what it might mean to him. "Thank you."

There was a pause. Melissa was about to make an excuse about needing to go when Sven said, "Melissa, I was hoping to take you out to dinner tonight."

"Uh, well." She gritted her teeth and thought, *This is so awkward.* Then she said, "Would you like to join us?"

"Great! It will be my treat. What time, and where shall I meet you?"

She told him Brad and Bonnie were picking her up at her hotel at 7:00.

"Perfect. I'll meet you there."

She hesitated and then said, "Yes."

"I was really happy to see you today. I'm so sorry we parted with such angry words. I really want to make it up to you."

She closed her eyes, trying to think of an appropriate response. "Sven, you're not the only one who needs to apologize. I said as many of those angry words as you did. I think we both just need to let it go."

"But I don't want to let it go. I really was happy to see you today. There's no one else I care for as I do for you. I'm not kidding. I have really missed you."

"Sven ..."

"Yes?"

Melissa sighed, upset with herself for giving him this opportunity to be a part of their evening. "I'll see you tonight." She clicked off and stood thinking about Sven. *This is not what I came to Chicago for.*

Sven sat at his desk bouncing the phone in his hand. *I don't understand her. She seems so hesitant to accept my wish for restoration of our relationship. Oh, Melissa, such an innocent. She is an interesting little thing and would certainly make a good wife to leave at home to raise my heirs and present a nice family picture for good old Dad and those pompous board members. While she is ensuring my rightful place in Dad's will and as the heir apparent of the head of the corporation, I can pursue his businesses as well as other interests.* He smiled at the thought of the beautiful women he had spent time with in other cities where corporate business took him. They were wonderful diversions, but he needed someone solid and reliable for a wife in Chicago. *Yes, Melissa fits that mold.* He frowned, remembering their last meeting. He certainly hadn't expected her to react so angrily to his overtures. After all, he had been planning to ask her to marry him. It would benefit both of them, but she didn't seem compliant. He realized she'd been upset about her grandmother's death, but to move away? He also realized that she was unhappy with the city hustle and the noise and commotion. But surely being engaged to him should have made up for those small discomforts?

Brad and Bonnie were waiting for her in the lobby. She greeted them both with hugs. Brad seemed to notice that Melissa didn't see her cheerful self and asked her if she felt okay. She shrugged her shoulders and then told him about her reluctant invitation to have Sven join them. Brad asked, "How do you really feel about it?"

Trying to deal with the ill feeling, Melissa said, "Well, he was very civil today, but I don't trust him completely. Yet this is business, and having dinner would be a courteous thing to do. I guess because there will be four of us, it should be okay." She turned to Bonnie. "I'm sorry, I didn't mean to leave you out."

Bonnie smiled. "No problem. I couldn't help but hear some of your conversation. We will be here for you." She looked at Brad and frowned. "Although I promised my sister that we would stop by her place this evening. I don't know how long we can stay with you."

"Don't worry. I'll find some way to excuse myself too. It will be all right."

Just then, as though he was the celebrity of the hour, Sven made his entrance. Because of his height and striking good looks, he seemed to take the attention of everyone in the lobby. He made his way over to Melissa, Brad, and Bonnie and greeted Melissa with a hug that seemed too long. Then shook hands with Brad. When Brad introduced him to Bonnie, he lifted her hand to his lips and whispered, "Enchanted." Bonnie blushed, and Brad cleared his throat and wrapped his arm around her. Sven stepped back and drew Melissa next to him. "Well, where shall we eat? This is a night of celebration."

Brad nodded. "It certainly is. Unfortunately, Bonnie and I have to leave shortly after dinner, so we would prefer somewhere close. We were thinking of something like pizza."

Sven said, "Sounds good to me. Melissa, okay with you?" She

nodded. "My car is parked right outside, but one of my favorite places is very close. Why don't you let me take you there? That way, Brad, you and Bonnie can leave when you need to. We can walk; it's on the next block."

"Sounds good. Melissa? Bonnie?" When neither had an objection, the foursome started down the street in the direction Sven led. As they crossed a busy intersection, Sven reached over and took Melissa's hand. She had an impulse to pull away—not because of his touch, but because it felt like she was a child needing his assistance. Once again, she felt as though she was not being assertive with him and as a result was encouraging these actions she disliked.

Fortunately, it was very close. When they arrived at Giordano's, she was pleased because she knew they would all feel comfortable here. They were seated quickly, which surprised Melissa, but she soon realized that Sven must have arranged this plan and called ahead, probably with the promise of a hefty tip for a quick table. They ordered beverages, looked at the extensive menu, and decided on a large Chicago classic. The hectic part of the day seemed to be behind them, and they relaxed and enjoyed lighthearted conversation. When the pizza came, it was enormous but looked and smelled so good. Sven lifted his glass for a toast. "To the success of this project and our continued friendship."

By 9:00, Brad and Bonnie thanked Sven and excused themselves to go to her sister's home. They said goodbye to Melissa, and Sven assured them he would see her safely back to the hotel.

When Sven and Melissa were left alone at the table, they sat quietly for a few minutes before he broached the subject of their broken relationship. "Melissa, I really meant it when I said I was glad to see you today." Melissa smiled, and he continued. "I'm sorry I wasn't more understanding of your feelings about your grandmother's passing. You were—are—such an important part of my life. I couldn't believe how miserable I'd be without you."

Melissa watched him uneasily. Their last conversation had been one of angry words and accusations. She began softly. "Sven, neither one of us was happy in that relationship. We were both looking for someone to fill a void in our lives."

"That's not true. I was happy, and I want to make you happy again too." Sven covered her hand with his and began stroking her fingers sensually. "I know if we spend more time together, we'll come to an understanding. Oh, Melissa, we just have to work at it harder. I know I can make you happy. I have missed you so much ..."

Melissa jerked her fingers away and realized that the action seemed very abrupt. "Sven, I'm sorry. I don't want to start again. I don't think we ever had an understanding, and I have a new beginning. I'm not interested in going back." The pain in Sven's eyes caused her to pause for a moment. "Please, I think we would be better off if we tried to keep this a business relationship."

Sven stared at her. "That's what you want? A business relationship?" Melissa nodded. Sven seemed at a loss for words. He stared at the remnants of their pizza, shaking his head. Finally he said, "All right, if that's what you want, that's the way it will be. At least until you change your mind."

"Sven ..."

"Hush. Don't worry so much. I'll respect your wishes, but don't be surprised if you find yourself thinking more and more of me." He smiled at her and then summoned the waiter. He laid a couple of large bills in his hand, thanked him for the superb service, and told him to keep the extra. He smiled when the waiter's eyes widened at the generosity of his tip. Sven stood, helped her out of her chair, and then said, "Come. I'll walk you back to the hotel. After all, we have a long day together tomorrow, and who knows how many days it might take to get that proposal up to standards."

Before she slept that night, she pulled out her grandmother's Bible with the scripture verses Aaron had left with her. She crawled into bed and propped herself up against the pillows. Methodically she read through the first two.

> Until now you have not asked for anything in my name. Ask and you will receive and your joy will be complete. (John 16:24)
> Trust in the Lord with all your heart and lean not on your own understanding. In all your ways acknowledge Him and He will make your paths straight. (Proverbs 3:5–6)

After reading the verses, she laid the Bible on her lap and closed her eyes to think about their significance in her own life. *Ask, and your joy will be complete. I will make your paths straight. Oh, Lord, I need your reassurance. Help me to find my way through this project without saying the wrong thing while maintaining my values. I don't want to worry, but I'm nervous about working with Sven.*

She waited for an answer and realized her muscles had started to relax. The comfort of the Lord slowly enshrouded her, and she started to pray. *Lord, I praise you for these opportunities, and I thank you for your answer. I praise you for your all-knowing and caring ways, and for your ever-present protection and love. I ask now that you continue to be with me. Let me be a strong and bright reflection of you. I praise you and thank you. Amen.*

She checked the time on her phone and on impulse dialed Aaron's number. The phone rang once and was picked up before it completed the second ring. "Pastor Chambers. How may I help you?"

Melissa smiled and said, "Aaron …"

"Melissa, are you all right?"

"Yes, I'm fine. I'm sorry to bother you so late. Were you sleeping?"

She heard him yawn and then say, "Just drifted off. Are you sure you're okay?"

"Uh-huh. I just wanted—needed—to talk to you. I was so glad you called this afternoon, and, well, I wanted to hear your voice again and to tell you I miss you too. That's all."

Silence.

"Aaron?"

"I'm here. I was just thinking how nice that sounds. Do you want to tell me again?"

Melissa smiled. "I miss you."

"Me too. So, what's keeping you up so late tonight?"

She took a big breath and then started. "Aaron, I have never told you about Sven Johnson." She told him everything about meeting him at work, how he had pursued her, and the resulting relationship they'd had during the winter and spring. She mentioned the innuendos during the week and their encounter earlier this evening. After describing the silent and uncomfortable walk back to the hotel, she shared with him her devotion and prayer time.

"Aaron, I just had to tell you about how at ease I feel now. Remember when you told me things work out, but prayer makes it work better?"

"Uh-huh."

"Aaron, can't you say anything else?"

"Uh-huh. Yeah, I told you so!"

"You! Just wait till I get back." Melissa laughed, and she could hear him chuckling with her, but his next words were more serious.

"Melissa, I'm glad you prayed, but be very careful. I want you back as healthy and as happy as when you left. This guy doesn't sound too upright."

"I will, I promise. Good night, Aaron. Thanks for listening."

"No problem. I'll be praying for you. Call me anytime you want to tell me important stuff like that. In fact, call me anytime."

Chapter 21

Melissa awoke the next morning from dreams of Aaron smiling in the moonlight, from the pulpit, and from across the table in her kitchen while they shared a cup of coffee. She smiled and felt refreshed, ready for what the day would present and knowing that God was making her path straight.

When she walked into the conference room, Brad, Sven, Mr. Cohen, and several of Sven's associates were already seated. She accepted the coffee she was offered and found a seat near Brad. Throughout the morning, she answered questions and suggested ways to proceed with marketing the products. She quoted her research and assisted with plans to efficiently present this equipment as essential to the fitness of the targeted population. Every time she looked across the table, she met Sven's blue-eyed stare with a businesslike smile and nod. She responded to his questions in a courteous and professional manner. When they took time to break, she made sure she was prepared to greet his attention with pleasant return.

On her way back, she took time to say hello to some workers whom she knew. She glanced at her watch, excused herself, and moved toward the conference room. In the alcove adjacent to the room, where everyone was regrouping, Sven stepped out in front of her. "Melissa. Looking radiant as always."

She smiled and nodded toward the view. "Another beautiful day." He added his silent agreement, and she continued. "Things seem to be progressing well. I hope you are pleased."

He smiled and moved in closer. "Well, it does seem to be moving along quite well, but I'm not sure I am so happy."

"Oh, why? It is falling together nicely. I was thinking that we might be able to wrap it up today."

He placed one finger under her chin and tipped her face so he could look directly into her eyes. "I'm trying to throw some wrenches into the works so that it won't go so well. The longer I can delay, the more time you will have to spend here." He smiled.

Melissa stepped back and broke his contact. "Are your wishes worth foiling all the time and effort everyone is putting into this plan?" She turned toward the conference room, but then she turned back and added, "Sven, we've both apologized for our earlier behavior. Let's just finish this up so that we can all go home."

He shook his head and said, "I wasn't kidding last night, Melissa. I'm going to do everything I can to convince you to give me another chance. If it means messing up the world's schedule, then so be it. But I am going to do my best to keep you from leaving Chicago again so soon. Now, maybe you should think how you could work with me instead of against me."

Melissa was about to reply with an angry response when Brad found them. "Hey, you two. We need you in the conference room. Come on. Some of us want to get home in good time tonight."

"I'll be right there. Sorry for the delay," she said as she turned and followed Brad.

When she returned to her seat next to him, he whispered, "What was going on out there? You looked plenty miffed."

"He told me he's going to try to sabotage our progress so that I will have to stay in Chicago longer. Sven just can't believe I'm not ready to start up with him again." She rubbed the bridge of her nose. "Brad, I'm sorry, but he doesn't want to let things go and he says he's willing to throw a wrench in things to prevent me from leaving. I just don't know what to do!"

They were called back to task by Mr. Cohen. "It seems we've accomplished quite a lot today. Let's try to wrap this up before we go home tonight."

Sven stood up and intervened. "Before we get in a hurry, I think we need to address the fact that my company has to turn one of our existing factories fitted for defense contracts into one that can turn out high-end home fitness equipment." His comment caused a stir around the table.

When the buzzing stopped, Mr. Cohen stared at Sven for a moment and then said, "I don't think overhauling your factory is part of a marketing work-up. You would be better to leave that to your design team and engineers."

"You're right," Sven countered, "but I've got to have more specific figures to take to my engineers and design team to enable them to make the switch." He placed both hands on the table in front of him and seemed to lean halfway across the table to make a point. "Mr. Cohen, I need more precise specifics of the equipment we'll be manufacturing. I can't expect my people to grab this information out of the air."

Melissa watched the encounter, and several times she would have joined the discussion except for Brad's restraining touch to her arm.

"Mr. Johanssen, Sven," Mr. Cohen started again. "I thought we had given you all that information yesterday. At least, you and your board seemed to agree to it all yesterday."

"Indeed, you did give valuable information. But I need more detail and specific numbers. I need more time from your staff." He stared icily across the table as he continued. "Either you supply the information I need, or I'll go elsewhere."

Mr. Cohen wiped his bald head with a handkerchief and stared down at the table. After shaking his head, he glanced over at Brad and Melissa with a grimace. "We've invested too many hours in this already to stop now. All right! I'll discuss this with my staff."

"Good!" Sven stood up to his full height. "Now, I suggest we adjourn for the morning and meet again this afternoon. Two o'clock would be good for me." Sven dropped his papers in his briefcase and snapped it shut. He turned to Melissa. "Ms. Blakesly, I would like to take you to lunch, if you would join me."

Melissa stared at Sven. "I think I might make better use of my time collecting the data you need."

Sven's icy stare cut right through her. She saw the threat in his eyes and thought of the harm he could render the firm by not completing this deal. *Lord, help me. I'm leaning on you.* She finally said, "I'll get my purse." She rose to retrieve her bag, and Brad caught her hand. She squeezed it for reassurance and whispered, "I'll be all right."

Sven silently accompanied her out of the building, and then he pointed to his white Mercedes was parked in the executive lot. Once in the car, he pulled into traffic. Melissa stared straight ahead and kept repeating her Bible verses over in her mind. She was concentrating so hard that she didn't notice they had parked until Sven pulled open her door. After stepping out, she saw they were near the Wrigley Building. He guided her down the inclined walkway to a bench near the river.

"I thought we were going for lunch."

He smiled and beckoned to a young man standing nearby. He brought over a wicker basket full of fruits and cheeses, bottles of flavored seltzers, and sandwiches wrapped in pretty paper napkins. "I wanted you to see that I am not such an ogre. I thought we could avoid the rush of lunch and have some time to talk."

Afraid to encourage him, yet impressed with his thoughtfulness, she said, "This is lovely. Much nicer than a restaurant or food truck." They situated the basket between them and shared its contents. For a few minutes, dining with Sven was as nice as anything she could remember. They talked and enjoyed the parade of people out enjoying the nice spring day.

After closing the basket, Sven set it down beside the bench. He smiled at her and laid his arm along the back of the bench. "Maybe we can talk about us, now that you see I can behave myself."

Melissa sighed and looked down at her hands. She felt his fingers worrying the tiny hairs at the nape of her neck and moved away to break contact. Sensing his impatience, she started. "Sven, there isn't any *us*. I'm happy that I've moved in a different direction and that I'm not involved with you anymore." Feeling the futility of making him understand, she continued to look everywhere but at him. "I love my new home, and I've started a new chapter in my life." Then she finally looked at his face. "I have a good chance at some happiness there. I'm not changing my mind."

Sven quietly studied her. "So what is this new happiness you've found? A new love? What? Surely you couldn't have discovered anything so wonderful in such a short time."

"But I have. There, I have friends who are truly interested in me and have the time to show it. I have a sense of being home and a feeling of peace that I've never experienced before. It's hard to explain."

"So, you've found new friends. Is one of these friends a new man in your life? Is that why you're so willing to give up everything that I could give you?"

"One of them is a nice man, but that's not the only reason I don't want to come back. If you think about it, you'll remember I hadn't been happy here for some time. I don't want to live in Chicago anymore."

"If that's all it is, we can move to the suburbs. I'll buy you a huge house with a big lawn, and …"

Melissa shook her head and agonized over how to make him see. "Sven, you never loved me."

"That's not true. I did love—"

"Yes, it is. Sven, I knew about the other women when you went away on business trips. You couldn't have loved me and spent time with them. But that's not it either. I simply don't want to become involved with you again. At least, not in that way."

Sven looked angrily out over the green Chicago River and then let his shoulders sag as though he has admitted defeat. He heaved a deep sigh and said, "All right. But what about the proposal? I still want the data I need, or do I have to start over with some other firm. I'm not going to give in on my demands."

"You won't have to. I know Brad and I can give you what you need.

It will simply take another week or so." She turned to him and added, "Please don't let our personal feelings interfere with this project. I don't wish any bad for you, but I can't be what you want me to be. I just can't."

He looked down at his feet and shook his head slowly. After forcing the breath out of his lips, he stared at a passing tour boat before he spoke again. "So you'll be spending another week here?"

"No, I'm going home. I have a secure Internet connection and can work on this more efficiently in Sovereign."

Sven rubbed his hand through his neatly coiffed hair. "Well, I guess I may as well give in on this." He raised his head, smiled, and said, "But if I don't like the figures I see, I won't accept them."

Melissa nodded. "I wouldn't expect you to accept anything but our best, and that's exactly what Brad and I will give you."

That evening on the way to drop her off at her hotel, Brad finally asked what happened. "What did you say to him? He was like a different person after lunch."

Melissa shrugged. "I simply told him how I felt and buffered it with a lot of prayer. He eventually accepted it."

"Well, that's good. We got quite a bit more accomplished. I'm glad we don't have to meet again tomorrow."

"Me too. I was happy that Mr. Cohen was all right with my request. I can finish this up next week if we can work together online. I'm ready to go home."

Brad smiled. "Going home?"

"Yeah." She returned his smile. "It really feels like home."

"So, is Aaron picking you up?"

Melissa tried to suppress her smile when answering his mischievous query. "Well, I don't know if he'll have time. Maybe he'll ask Rayleen to come after me."

Brad laughed. "He'll have time."

Melissa smiled at Aaron as she came down the escalator from the gates. *Brad was right: he did have time!* She walked up to him and let him encompass her with a hug.

"Man, I'm glad you're home!" he said.

"I am too. It's been a long week away. I've had enough of Chicago for a while." She looked around. "Where's Joseline? I brought her a little gift."

Aaron grinned. "I guess you're going to have to make do with me. Joseline had a prior engagement with Rusty, and for the night with Don and Rayleen."

"You've got to be kidding. I've been upstaged by an old, shaggy pony?"

"Yep, sorry to say. Rusty is her current best friend. She barely said goodbye to me when I dropped her off on the farm." He shook his head sadly and then broke into a huge smile. "So I get to spend some time with you by myself. I'm going to do my best to make it up to you."

She smiled into his warm brown eyes. "And how are you going to dull my disappointment?"

Aaron laughed and guided her to his Jeep. "Well, I have a nice dinner planned that we are going to pick up on our way out of town. I thought we could take it to your place, if that's okay with you."

"That sounds divine."

"Good. I have a couple of bottles of sparkling grape juice in my cooler in the Jeep. I thought we could sit on your front porch and eat chicken alfredo and salad, and then drink a toast to your return to Sovereign."

Melissa didn't think her smile could be any wider. "I can't tell you how happy I am to be back. I have missed everything and everyone. Thank you for being so thoughtful, Aaron. I'm not sure I could have endured eating out one more time." After wrapping her arms around his waist, she stood up on her tiptoes to give him an impulsive kiss on the cheek.

Chapter 22

The first of the week was filled with necessary phone calls and a call to the Internet provider to increase her Wi-Fi capacity. It was amazing how quickly she had converted her grandmother's country cottage into a home office. She had her laptop and printer set up in the corner secretary, but other than that, everything had remained about the same. She spent most of Monday afternoon working on the specifications Sven had demanded from them. Using her tablet, her phone, and her laptop, she and Brad worked together easily. Their phone calls and Facetime chats made it seem as if they were in the same office. However, as the days continued, the phone calls were less and less optimistic. Finally, on Wednesday afternoon, the dam broke, and Brad shared all his frustrations with Melissa.

"I don't know what to tell you. The man is acting crazy. He has made a complete turn-around and now says that he never agreed to our plan, adding that until he sees what he wants, he's not going to give his approval."

She shifted uneasily in her seat. "I wonder if you are not right about Sven. I don't know if he's never actually been told no, or what. But he seems to be less able to cope with disappointment. Does he give you any ideas what he wants different than what you're already giving him?"

"No. That's the part that doesn't make sense. There's only so many ways we can present these numbers. I think he's playing games."

"What does Mr. Cohen say?"

"He's about ready to call it quits and cut our losses on the deal."

"I hate to see the company lose this job after all this time and work we've put into it."

"Yeah, me too. Mr. Cohen has really bent over backward on this one, and it doesn't seem fair that Sven won't settle. Now to make matters worse, Sven just announced that he will not be available until next week—and that he will be expecting a solution."

Melissa frowned. "Where did he go?"

"I don't know. He didn't share his plans, just that he would return next week."

She shrugged. "Well, I don't know how many ways we can give him the same information, but we can try. I'm going to knock off for today. Maybe I'll talk to you tomorrow, if I have any new ideas."

Melissa closed her laptop, stood, and stuck her phone in her jeans pocket. She strolled around the house, noticing the obvious signs of growth in her flowers and weeds. Her vegetable and herb garden were competing for space with the weeds. She kneeled to clear out some of the unwanted vegetation, systematically pulled weeds, and cleared the little garden so that the tomatoes, peppers, and herbs were more defined. Her spinach was growing, and she quickly pulled out some of the intruders from that row. She could hardly wait for spinach salad with an herb dressing. She was pleased to realize she felt she had accomplished a lot from the simple weeding. It not only cleared the garden of weeds, but it also helped to clear her head of the worries about the project.

Satisfied with the garden, she returned to the porch. While leaning against the rail, she thought about her future. No doubt the projects that Cohen Marketing offered her would keep her busy a few days a week, and maybe that would be enough for now. She sat in the swing, pushed back, and let go so that it swung in a big arc. She thought about the last few days since her return from Chicago. Aaron had brought her home Friday evening and they sat on her front porch sharing the lovely dinner he had planned. They had talked and held hands, chatting and laughing about their evening. On Saturday, Linda called to welcome her home and remind her of the farmer's market in town. They made plans to meet for lunch at the diner. While they were there, several people stopped by to greet them and to welcome Melissa home.

Church the next morning had been like a family homecoming. Don and Rayleen fussed over her and acted like she'd been gone for weeks. Joseline made a beeline for her immediately after Sunday school and let her know that she had missed her. Everyone seemed eager to say hello.

Aaron and Joseline joined Melissa at her house for hamburgers on the grill. Melissa had made a fruit salad, and Aaron brought marshmallows, chocolate bars, and graham crackers for s'mores. They ate their delicious meal and shared all their adventures of the week. After lunch, they wandered through the wooded trail behind the house and ended up at the creek, where Joseline discovered a school of minnows. She nearly fell in while trying to follow their synchronized turns and dashes through the clear water. Aaron coaxed her away with a promise of a piggyback ride to the house. Melissa surprised them with popsicles, and they sat on the porch and listened to Aaron telling silly stories and Josie sharing about Paisley the cat, who seemed to be getting very fat.

Melissa hadn't seen or heard from him since that Sunday afternoon and was beginning to feel an ache for his company. She remembered his sweet greeting of how much he had missed her, and then sharing the delicious alfredo and sparkling wine on her front porch. She found herself wanting more and more of his time and his presence.

Knowing Aaron was planning to attend, she decided to change into slacks for the Wednesday evening Bible study Linda had invited her to that evening.

When Melissa walked into the church, she followed the buzz of conversation to the library, where she discovered a group of people of all ages gathered around the table. In a few minutes, Linda welcomed them and opened with prayer. "Father, we thank you for another blessed day in your love. We praise you for each person here, and we thank you for your word and for the answers you will reveal to us. Amen." Then she started out with a direct question. "Who had an answer to prayer they would like to share this week?"

A teenage girl raised her hand and then giggled when Linda acknowledged her. "I prayed that the dentist would take my braces off earlier than he had planned to in October." She blushed and then said, "Well, look!" With that, she grinned broadly, and the group erupted in jubilant laughter at the two rows of pearly white teeth.

Linda smiled. "Thank you for sharing, Kristen. God is faithful in knowing what we need, isn't he?" Kristen blushed even deeper and nodded. "Anyone else?"

A middle-aged gentleman said, "Yes, I have one. As you remember, I have been praying that my son, John, would have a good report from the doctor. Well, he called today and said that his blood pressure is down. He won't have to take medicine after all." He finished with a big smile and nods of thanks to all around the table who rejoiced with him.

The sharing continued until Linda brought up her daughter Julia's prayers for their family dog. "Julia has been so upset about Poppy. A week ago Monday, we were trying to bring a cow and her calf into the barn. The cow got scared, butted the dog, and broke a couple of her ribs. The vet told us that she had punctured a lung and probably wouldn't last more than a few days. We thought about putting her to sleep, but Julia begged us to take her home and let her care for Poppy. Julia nursed her and prayed for her every day." Linda blushed a little and then continued. "I hate to admit that my faith wasn't nearly as strong as Julia's, because I was sure that Poppy was a goner. But this afternoon, Julia got off the bus and ran right out to the shed to check on Poppy. In a minute, she came tearing in saying that the dog had eaten most of her food and drank some water, it and seemed to want to get outside. Well, I was a little skeptical. I was afraid that Julia was seeing what she hoped to be true and not what was real. The vet was out in the barn, vaccinating the spring calves, so I had him check her. He said he couldn't find any sign of serious injury. He said it must have been a miracle." Linda ducked her head and wiped a tear away with the back of her hand. "Praise God for the faith of little children."

Melissa looked around the circle. Everyone seemed to be genuinely rejoicing over Linda's account. She remembered all the things that had happened in her life that she'd credited to answers to prayers instead of coincidences. She was in deep thought when Linda brought her back to the present. "Melissa, did you have something you wanted to add?"

Melissa took a deep, cleansing breath. "Well, I am just so impressed with all of your experiences. I find myself amazed when I say a quick prayer and then realize I'm right in the middle of the answer. It's hard to understand how often the right solution appears with or without my help." She shook her head. "I guess I still have trouble asking for help, but God has never had a problem helping me out, whether it be through someone stopping to visit or a message on the radio. It all works together to guide me to a solution."

"The Lord knows our needs and meets them," Linda said, and others murmured agreement. "Let's look at a piece of scripture, one that you may be familiar with. Philippians 4:6-7." She waited until they had found the verse in their Bibles. "'Be anxious for nothing, but in everything by prayer and supplication with thanksgiving let your requests be made known to God. And the peace of God, which surpasses all comprehension, shall guard your hearts and minds in Christ Jesus.'" She raised her head and looked around the group. "I'd like us to analyze these verses and see how they apply to our lives. Pastor, can you tell us how we can use these verses in our lives?"

Aaron sat up straighter in his chair and grinned. "She always likes to put me on the spot." The group chuckled, and when they quieted, he continued. "I feel this is saying to me, Don't worry about stuff. Talk to me about your concerns and your happiness. Always be thankful for your circumstances, whether they are good or sad. If we tell him what worries us, what we need, what makes us happy, and what scares us, he will work in extraordinary, if not supernatural, ways to give us what we need. And he'll give it to you and comfort you and reassure you at the same time. He wants us to talk to him about everything, just like a best friend."

"Thank you, Pastor. Does anyone have any questions or comments?

The gentleman who had shared about his son's answer to prayer said, "Good verse to keep close. I'm going to write it down and put it in my wallet so I can memorize it. I waste too much time fussing over things when I simply need to give it to God." Several people made comments in agreement.

"Thank you for sharing. Thank you all for coming, but I see we've used up more than the hour we allotted. I think we should adjourn for this evening and meet again next week. Same time, same place."

As the group dispersed all seeming to go home with a fresh take on how that verse would affect their lives, Melissa stood to leave. Aaron stopped her and said, "Can you wait a minute?"

She agreed and watched as he said goodbye to each participant and then escorted her out of the church. "Joseline is just dying to show you something. She asked me if you could come over after Bible study tonight, and I told her I would ask you."

Melissa grinned. "What now? Don't tell me she has some more pictures for me. My refrigerator is covered now, and I hate to take any of them down."

He took her hand and shook his head. "Nothing like that. This is something much different. Something that even Josie was nearly speechless about." He laughed and then said, "But not for long."

As they walked across the yard to the house, Melissa smiled and thought to herself, *I am so glad I am here and not in Chicago.*

Her thoughts were interrupted by Josie's greetings. "Missa! Missa, come quick!" The little girl raced to the door to meet her and then nearly pulled her through the kitchen into the pantry. "Look!" she said, pointing at a laundry basket lined with a soft blanket. "Paisley had some babies!"

Melissa let out a sound of pure glee when she kneeled to see the little girl's treasure. Lying next to the calico cat were five tiny kittens: one grey and white; one white, one caramel and black; one black with white paws; and one pure black. "Oh, Josie. They're beautiful. When did they come?"

"Yesterday. Daddy and I watched them get borned." She looked up at Melissa with eyes wide with delight. "Poor Paisley was so tired, and these baby kitties just cried and cried and made her stay up all night licking their faces. Daddy says that's how she gives them a bath. I sure am glad ..."

Aaron stood leaning against the door jamb, watching the two of them ooh and ah over the kittens. He smiled at their womanly concerns over the poor mother, and he had to suppress a chuckle when he listened to Joseline explain in a very grown-up voice how the kittens had gotten inside of Paisley in the first place. He watched the gentle way that Melissa handled the babies and assured the mother cat that her kittens were just fine. *Thank you, Lord, for bringing her into my life. She is a prize—one that I'll not let go of easily.*

Chapter 23

Melissa spent Thursday morning trying to find different ways to combine figures and dimensions to fit the schematic drawings that Sven had provided. After gaining no new insight into how to improve the information, she decided to follow her impulse and call Brad. "I've been over these figures a million times, and I can't see any different way to put it together. I feel like I'm at my wits' end. I really don't know where to go from here."

"I know what you mean," agreed Brad glumly. "I hate to admit defeat, but unless there's a miracle, I don't have any new ideas either." After a long pause, Brad offered, "Maybe we're too tired of it. This is all we've talked about all week. I think we need a break."

"Agreed! What's new with you?"

"Oh, not much. Bonnie and I are going shopping Saturday."

"You, shopping? I don't believe it. What are you looking for? Something special?"

"Yeah, kind of."

Melissa sat up straight. She could hear the smile in her friend's voice. "Brad, you can't hide anything from me. What's up? What's so special that Bonnie is getting you into the shopping mode?"

"Well, I don't know if I should tell you," he teased.

"Brad?"

"Okay, okay! I know that tone of voice. We're shopping for a ring."

"A ring? Like a wedding ring?"

"No, silly!"

"Oh," Melissa groaned. "I'm sorry. I shouldn't have jumped to a conclusion."

"That's all right. Don't feel bad. I know you people out on the frontier don't understand the intricacies of civilized life." He paused to add a little drama to his next statement. "Actually, we're going to start with an engagement ring."

Melissa jumped up. "An engagement ring! Oh, Brad, that's wonderful, I'm so happy for you, congratulations. When did you decide? Tell me everything."

"Thanks, Missy. Me too. We've been talking around it for a couple of months, but I decided to ask her last week after you told me I glowed when I talked about her. After we left you on Friday, I took Bonnie for a walk and asked her. She said yes right away."

"Well, of course she did, you goof. Bonnie's not a dumb girl. I am so happy for you. It's the best news!"

"Yeah, it is. Thanks. We're both floating a couple of feet off the ground. We're going to tell our families this weekend, but I'm happy I could tell you first."

She smiled as she listened to his plans for the months ahead.

"I can just imagine winter whites, a sleigh to take you and your bride away." She hugged herself in happy anticipation. "It sounds delightful. I can hardly wait."

"Me neither!" They talked for a few minutes longer before saying goodbye.

Melissa sat for a while, basking in Brad's happiness. She truly was happy for Brad and Bonnie. However, she felt a bit of envy that he had found his special person, and she was still waiting. She knew for sure that Sven was not going to be a part of her future, at least not romantically. As for Aaron, he had so much on his plate. *Oh, well. Be anxious for nothing … But with prayer and supplication with thanksgiving, make your requests known to God.* She sat meditating on that scripture and then said out loud, "And the peace of God will give me comfort." She laughed at herself. "Hmm, talking to myself. No, talking to God." She stood up and headed out to the garden. While walking the perimeter, she marveled at how everything was changing. She stopped to be thankful for the beauty around her and the peace that he showed her. "Dear Lord, I should have come to you before, but I have done all that I can on the Johanssen account. I give this project to you. I will wait on you for ideas and let you guide me in submission. I thank you for the solution you are going to show me. I thank you for the happiness you've brought into Brad and Bonnie's lives. I ask you for that kind of happiness in my life. In Jesus's precious name, amen."

Aaron pulled his Jeep into the church parking lot and sat for a minute under the shade of the oak tree. While laying his head on his arms over the steering wheel, he reviewed the events of the day. Jacob Mettlesmith wasn't doing well, and his dear wife, Anna, wasn't ready to let him go. He sat back in his seat and thought, *What does one spouse do when the other is closing in on the end of his life here after so many years together?* He thought about the prayers he'd said with Anna as they sat with her husband of fifty-two years, who was hooked up to a mass of tubes and machines. The last words Jacob had said to Anna had been of how much he loved her and how he wanted her to continue to live a happy life.

Although Aaron had no qualms about Jacob's preparedness for stepping into the next world, he knew it wasn't going to be easy for Anna to let him go. *What can I say, Lord, to make it easier for her?* Length of marriage didn't make separating from a loved one any less painful. He opened the car door, carried his briefcase in to his office, and checked his answering service for any calls. He smiled at the one from Josie reporting on the progress of the kittens. One was from the church's insurance agent about increasing coverage, one was a hang-up, and one was from Melissa reminding him of dinner at her place Friday evening. He allowed himself a couple of minutes to daydream about his last afternoon with her, and then he immersed himself in the work he had waiting in the office. He picked up the notes he'd compiled that were the beginning of a new sermon series for the next five weeks.

He spent the afternoon with his tablet, laptop, faithful concordances, and versions of the Bible, outlining, listing, and writing. The ideas seemed to generate more, and each enhanced the main topic. He couldn't spend time being amazed at his writing, but he praised God with each new idea that turned into another sentence.

He was so engrossed in the development of the series and the refining of the first of five sermons that he didn't realize the time until Joseline came skipping in. "Daddy, Mrs. Mason says it's time for supper. Come on!"

"Hey, since when do you come in giving me such big orders without a hug first?" Joseline giggled and then crawled up on his lap to give him a hug. "That's better," he said, savoring the comfort of holding his little girl. "Your daddy needed that."

"I love you, Daddy," Joseline whispered with even a bigger hug. "Mrs. Mason says you're the best preacher, but I think you're the best daddy in the world."

"That's good to hear," he said, easing her down off his lap. Joseline clung to him for a minute. Aaron ruffled her hair and said, "Hey, Josie, you okay?" She peered up at him, her thumb firmly in her mouth and her brown eyes large and sad. Aaron frowned a little and said, "Something wrong, sweetie?"

"I missed you today. I wish you didn't have to go away so much."

"Well, I'm here now." He rubbed her shoulders. "And I don't think I'll have to go out again tonight. How about helping me straighten up? Then we'll go eat supper before Mrs. Mason forgets we're coming."

Chapter 24

Early the next morning, Anna Mettlesmith called to say Jacob was gone. Aaron stood barefoot in his bedroom and listened to the woman's grief-filled statement. He said, "I'll be right there."

"No, I'm all right," she assured him. "My daughter is with me, and my Jacob is in heaven with the Lord. I need to rest for a bit, and then I'll start the funeral preparations. If you could come by the funeral home, I'll be meeting with Mr. Stevens at 11:00. Of course, we'd like you to do the service. Jacob liked you so much. He always said you were the best preacher we'd had in years."

Aaron squeezed his eyes shut to push the tears back. "Jacob was a wonderful man and a faithful servant, Anna. I'm sure the Lord is well pleased with him. I'll be honored to do the service, and I'll be at the funeral home at 11:00." He listened for a few minutes and then returned her goodbye. When he put the phone back in his pocket, he noticed a bit of pink lurking just outside his door, and he called to Joseline. "Sweetie, what are you doing up so early?"

"I heard your phone and was 'fraid Paisley would be worried ..."

"Oh, Josie, what would Paisley be worried about?" Aaron said. crouching down to her eye level. H stroked the cat in her arms. "I think she's more worried about her babies. You'd better take her back so she can check on them."

After putting on his socks and shoes, he selected a sweater to go with his brown and tan plaid shirt. He pulled it on and hurried to the kitchen to prepare breakfast for his little worrywart.

Aaron shook cereal into her bowl and scraped peanut butter over her toast. While pouring milk over the cereal, he asked, "Now, why in the world did you think Paisley would be worried about the call?"

"Well, one time you had to leave in a big hurry, and she might have been scared that nobody'd be here to take care of her ..."

Aaron looked into the big, wet, brown eyes and felt his heart crack. *She can't possibly remember being left alone. She was too young when Tanja left. Surely she can't be thinking that I'd ever leave her alone.*

He sat down in the chair next to hers and pulled her close to him. "Josie, sweetie, I'd never leave you alone." After stroking her hair, he heard little sobs start bubble up from deep within her. He leaned back, considered her face, and said, "What is it? Tell me what you are worried about."

"I'm scared that you'll have to go away like my Mommy did, and I won't have anybody to take care of me, except when Mrs. Mason comes to fix my supper after school."

"Joseline. Oh, sweetheart!" Aaron pulled the little girl up on his lap and rocked her. "How long have you been thinking about this?"

"Since Sara Quince told me that because I don't have a mommy, I'd be all alone if you went away too." Her little shoulders shuddered with more sobs.

Aaron swallowed hard and asked God to turn his hard thoughts for Sara into a prayer to bless her with a desire to be more kind to his baby. "Shh," he soothed. "I'll never leave you. I promise. I'll never, never leave you."

They sat like that for several minutes, and when everything seemed better, they turned their attention back to breakfast. The cereal was soggy, and the toast was cold. Aaron started the process of remaking breakfast when there came a knock at the door.

"I'll get it," Joseline said, but Aaron stepped in front of her.

"Oh, no, you don't. Remember, we don't open doors without checking who's there first." He looked out the peephole and then said, "Well, it's someone I think we'd like to see."

When he pulled the door open, Josie squealed in delight.

"Missa! Oh, Missa, we're so glad to see you." She turned to Aaron for confirmation. "Aren't we, Daddy?"

Aaron smiled and said, "Yep, we sure are!"

Laughing, Melissa kneeled and gathered Joseline in her arms for a hug. When she felt the little arms tighten around her, she threw a questioning glance at Aaron. His only response was a sad shake of his head. When Josie released her, Melissa said, "Wow, I see I'm interrupting breakfast. I picked up some muffins at the bakery. I was hoping we could share them."

"Can we, Daddy?" she asked, looking hopefully at her father.

"Of course, we can. Come on, Josie. Help me clear the table, and we'll start again."

When the table was cleared, and there was a fresh glass of milk for Joseline and coffee for Aaron and Melissa, they opened the bag of fragrant delicacies. "Just one, Josie," Aaron reminded.

They sat around the table sharing the yummy treats with lots of conversation. "So why are we so blessed to have you come to our house this morning?"

Melissa sighed. "Well, I tossed and turned all night, thinking about this account I've been working on. I decided I need to take some time away from it, and so I thought I'd stop by and see if I could talk you into taking the day off too."

Aaron smiled at her suggestion, "Sounds great, but I'm tied up." He winked at Melissa and said, "I don't know if Joseline would want to spend time with you."

"I do! Oh, Daddy, I do! Please, can I go?"

"Well, I guess you could. That is, if Melissa thinks she can keep up with you."'

Joseline turned toward Melissa. "Can you?"

"Oh, I think I can," Melissa returned her question with a smile.

"Yippee!" Joseline scampered toward her bedroom.

Aaron laughed and called after her. "You can wear your jeans and the pink T-shirt. And wear your pink socks and your sneakers. Oh, and bring your hoodie and a brush too."

When he was sure Josie was out of earshot, he turned to Melissa and said, "Boy, are you a Godsend!"

Melissa raised her eyebrows. "Really? What makes you say that?"

"A long story. One that can wait a minute until you come over here and give me a hug."

She stood to move around the table. As she approached, he stood and pulled her into an embrace. He held her and didn't seem interested in letting her go. "Aaron?"

"Hmm?"

"Are you okay? First Josie gave me a long hug and now you?"

He released her so she could step back from him, but he held on to her hands. "That was nice. Thank you, Melissa. It's been a rough couple of days, especially this morning."

"Do you want to tell me about it?"

"Sure. Let me get you some more coffee." She sat down in the chair next to his. After he set the cup in front of her, he sat and faced her. "Well, Anna Mettlesmith called around seven this morning to tell me that Jacob has passed away."

"Oh!" Melissa touched her hand to her lips. "I'm sorry to hear that."

"Yeah. It will be hard on her, but he was ready to go, and it's so much easier knowing he was with the Lord and she will see him again in heaven. Anyway, I guess the phone or my voice woke up Josie, and she was standing outside my door listening. When I asked her why she was up, she told me in a roundabout way that she was afraid I was going to leave her alone." Aaron looked down at the floor and cleared his throat. Melissa reached over and took his hand in hers. Finally he continued. "We talked about it, and she seems to be feeling better. I don't know what's going on in her little head. I don't want her feeling afraid every time the phone rings or every time I have to go out."

Melissa looked into his worried face and asked, "What are you going to do?"

"I don't know. Somehow, I've got to convince her that she has nothing to worry about." He squeezed her hand and smiled. "I'm sure glad you are here."

"Do you mind if I talk to her? You know, if the topic comes up?"

"That would be fine. Maybe she'll tell you things she doesn't tell me." He picked up his coffee cup and sipped. "What are you two going to do?"

"I'm not sure. I was hoping the three of us could go or a hike or something, but I know you'll be busy with the Mettlesmith family."

"Yeah. I want to be around most of the day anyway, to help make arrangements and plan for the service. I'm still planning on dinner tonight, though."

Melissa smiled. "Me too. I think we should include Joseline. We don't want her to think you don't have time for her."

He gave her a lopsided grin. "Yeah, you're right. I was looking forward to spending time alone with you, but I can't leave my other best girl out."

Just then, Joseline appeared dressed in blue jeans and a pink T-shirt, carrying a hair brush. "Hey, there she is now," said Aaron. "Come here and let me help you finish." Melissa watched as he tucked in her shirt and brushed her hair back from her face. She was surprised at how easy it was for him to brush her hair to one side and secure it with barrettes. He held her at arm's length to check her appearance. "There's my girl. She's all pretty and ready for the day." Then he pulled her into his arms for a big smacking kiss. He looked at Joseline and then at Melissa. "You girls be careful today. Don't go wandering off. I don't want a bear to eat you!" He pretended to bite Joseline, and she squealed with delight.

Melissa smiled and said, "We will watch out for bears, for sure."

Chapter 25

When Aaron drove up later in the day, the girls were playing shadow tag. He sat in his car undetected for a moment and watched them jump on each other's shadows and giggle as though it was the funniest thing in the world. He opened the car door and, as an afterthought, tooted the horn to draw their attention. Laughing, he gathered Joseline in his arms when she ran to him, and he said, "You two looked like you were having so much fun."

"We are. We've been busy, Daddy." She proceeded to tell him all of the day's events. He told them about how sad Anna Mettlesmith was and how many people came to visit her. He talked about some of the people he hadn't seen for a long time, and how some of them said they were going to start coming to church again. After a few minutes, Joseline grew restless and asked to get down. Aaron watched her skip into the yard to try to make friends with the squirrels and rabbits.

Aaron sat down on the swing, and Melissa joined him. "So how did things go today?" Aaron asked.

Melissa smiled and leaned her head against his shoulder. "We had fun. We went to the Top of the World and the animal display, just like Joseline told you."

"Did she talk to you?"

"Yeah, she thought we should pray, and she asked God not to take you away from her." She turned her face toward him when he sighed. "Then over lunch, I asked her about her prayer, and she said some little girl named Sara had told her that since her mommy left, you were probably going to get tired of her and leave too."

"Ugh!" was all Aaron said, but he stood up and started pacing back and forth on the porch. "I'm sorry." He ran his hand through his hair. "I just can't stand the thought of her having to listen to junk like that." He turned to Melissa with a look of anguish in his eyes. "Surely she knows I love her and would never leave her."

Melissa sat in the swing and let him vent his frustration. Then she said in a quiet voice, "Aaron, she knows you love her. She just can't justify in her mind why she doesn't have a mother like other kids. You'll have to keep reassuring her that you'll always be there for her."

Aaron placed both hands on the porch rail and stared at Josie playing in the yard. "I know that. I've tried to give her a sense of security, but it doesn't seem to be enough." He shook his head. "Maybe I've been so wrapped up in my own grief that I haven't taken time to deal with hers."

"Questioning yourself won't help either of you. Josie knows you love her. I don't think she doubts that. She's looking for reassurance and a way to fit into the mold with her friends. When the differences are obvious, other kids notice it. In her own way, she's putting the pressure on you to help her fit the mold."

"Pressure? You make it sound like she's planning something."

Melissa chuckled and said, "Well, she told me today she thought I'd be a good mommy." She finished her statement and watched Aaron for his reaction.

He remained in the same bent position, staring out at his daughter, but his facial expression changed from one of anguish to one of amusement. "She told you that?"

"Uh-huh."

"And what did you tell her?" He straightened and turned to face her, the amusement still dancing in his eyes.

Melissa, relieved that the signs of anguish had been partially erased from his face, smiled and said, "I told her that was a big decision. One that you and I would have to think about very seriously."

Aaron pressed his lips together and nodded his head silently. He seemed to be in deep thought, and then suddenly he smiled and dropped down next to her. He lazily swung one arm around the back of the bench and let it lie on her shoulder. Then he stretched out his long legs and said, "Have you thought seriously about it?"

Melissa smiled at his direct approach. "Well, not seriously. I guess I felt it was too soon. Have you?"

After grinning, he looked down at the floor and said, "Yeah, I have. I guess I thought about it that day we took Brad back to the airport. I liked the way you wanted to take care of things yourself but were still willing to accept my help. Then later, when we talked about the answers to prayer, you really touched me when you were so open to my ideas but still needed to evaluate them yourself. I don't know what it was. You were like a breath of fresh air to a drowning man, and I kept thinking how nice it would be not to have to take you home." He glanced up at her surprised face and shrugged.

Melissa studied his face for a moment, thoughts whirling around in her head. She smiled at him and then said, "That's what you thought?"

He nodded.

She slumped back in the swing and let out a long breath. "Whew! I guess I need to do some hard thinking here."

Aaron smiled and leaned over and kissed her cheek. "Don't rush it. We have time."

She smiled at him, silently thanking him for not pushing her into a decision. They sat both lost in their own thoughts for a few minutes.

When her thoughts were interrupted by the sound of his quiet chuckling, she turned toward him and asked, "What's so funny?"

"Oh, I was just thinking that maybe I actually fell in love with you the very first time I saw you. After all, who could resist a woman crouching behind a couch, trying to find a fireplace poker in the dark, and ordering me to back off?"

Melissa joined in his laughter and then said, "I'm so glad you enjoyed my predicament. Maybe you'll enjoy this too." She pushed both her hands behind his back and tried her best to push him out of the swing, but he was too agile for her. He turned, still able to maintain his seat by bracing his feet against the floor, and he wrapped his hands around her upper arms. It took only a moment before he'd pulled her close to him, and when he lifted his feet, the swing arced radically. Giggling at his surprise move and the sudden movement of their seat, Melissa realized her error in judgment, and she quit resisting. The chain squeaked loudly, and their laughter helped to relieve the tensions of the day.

While enjoying the moment, Melissa turned her face to meet his lips with hers. She was savoring the pleasure of his closeness when Joseline came bounding up the steps. "What're ya doing?" the girl asked, wedging herself between them.

Aaron laughed, and Melissa covered her smile with her hand. "I was checking to see if Melissa had eaten any chocolate today."

"Daddy, you were not. You were kissing."

Aaron laughed and pulled her up on his lap. "All right, you found me out."

Joseline smiled at one and then the other, and she burst into giggles.

Chapter 26

Melissa concentrated on steadying the brush as she finished going around the bedroom window. She was so pleased with this shade of blue. This paint project helped her think in the moment instead of worrying about the fact that the Johansson account wasn't going well. Each time it came to mind, she turned it to the Lord. In order to keep those thoughts from cropping up, she purposely replaced them with ones of her conversation with Aaron last evening. He had surprised her with talk of love and marriage, but she had to admit it had been pleasant. The memory of the teasing and the kiss they had shared brought a smile to her face. *I know he wants a mother for Joseline, but could he possibly love me in such a short time? And what are my feelings for him? He is such an opposite from Sven. Am I rebounding, or am I simply relieved to spend time with a nice man who is so genuine?* The prospect of marrying and becoming a mother in one step would have been unthinkable a few months ago, but would it work now?

She carried her thoughts with her back to the bedroom and was just getting ready to start work again when Linda popped in. "Hi!" came her cheerful voice. "I just came from Aaron's office. I hear you're hard at work again today."

"Yeah, I am," Melissa said, returning her neighbor's friendly smile. "Come in. I'll fix a cup of coffee." She started for the kitchen.

Linda held up a paint roller and paint pan still in the original packaging, "I'm not here to loaf—I'm here to work. I'll help you finish." Then as though justifying her reason for being there, she said, "You'd be amazed at how much faster things go with two sets of hands."

Realizing her friend was serious about helping, she led the way to the bedroom. While Melissa applied the second coat of white on the ceiling, Linda started painting the wall farthest away from Melissa. "This is a beautiful, cheerful color. I really like it."

By 2:00, the girls had finished the first coat and half the second. Linda stood back to admire their work. "See, I told you we could get this done quickly. Do you know how long this would have taken you alone? I think we can finish this up right now."

"Yeah, I think so too." Melissa stretched her back and neck. "I am so grateful to you. I hope I can repay your kindness sometime."

"Pshaw, don't think a thing about it. I was happy to be able to help. I'm glad I stopped by Aaron's office, or I wouldn't have known. Next time, call me. I love working with you."

By the time the clock struck 2:30, the second coat was on. They scrutinized the ceiling and walls to see if there was a spot they might have missed or needed a little more coverage. Satisfied that they had completed this part of the project, Linda said, "The furniture can wait. It's too heavy for us." She took out her phone. "I'll give Jim a call. He'll help wrestle this stuff back in place." Melissa opened her mouth to protest, but Linda had already hit Jim's number on speed dial. She listened to Linda's side of the conversation. "Hi, honey. Do you think you can spare some time to help Melissa and me put her furniture back in place? Oh, I guess you didn't know. I helped her paint her bedroom. Okay, that will be fine. See you in a bit. Love you!" She put the phone back in her pocket and said, "Now I would like a cup of coffee."

"Me too!" Linda followed her into the kitchen while Melissa made the coffee. Melissa took cups out of and asked, "Do you take sugar or cream?"

"Nope, just plain."

Melissa poured the coffee and sat opposite her friend. "So how did you happen to be at Aaron's office today?"

"Oh, I'm head of the serving committee this month. I needed to know how many to plan on for dinner. We got to talking, and he mentioned that you were painting. I stopped at the hardware store, picked up a roller and pan set, and came out to see if I could help." She smiled at Melissa over her cup and then continued. "Aaron sure has a nice big smile when your name comes up." She raised her eyebrows. "Anything new you want to tell me about?"

Melissa had just taken a sip of coffee and nearly choked. Laughing, she said, "Well, things are going pretty well. Actually, very well since I last talked to you." She smiled and swirled her coffee. After looking up at Linda's expectant face, she continued. "I like him a lot. He is so nice, and we have so much fun together."

Linda nodded approvingly and then said, "Well, Josie sure likes you. She watches for you to come into the sanctuary, so she can come sit with you. She is so cute. I just adore her. My Julia would keep her if Aaron would let her."

Melissa nodded. "I spent most of the day with Josie yesterday. She's a sweet little girl, and we had a lot of fun together."

A pickup rumbled to a stop outside. Linda said, "Sounds like Jim's truck." When no one materialized, they went through the living room to the front door and headed out on to the porch, where they found Jim and Aaron visiting.

Jim smiled at Linda and tipped his cap to Melissa. "Hello, Melissa. The preacher followed me right into your driveway." He winked. "Amazing how he calls on the pretty single lady more than the old married couples like us …" Before he could finish his jibe, Linda sent his hat sailing out into the yard. "Hey! What are you doing?" he said, laughing and pulling Linda close to him.

Aaron smiled at Melissa and nodded. "Just one of the benefits of my profession."

Jim looked at Aaron and then at Melissa. "Can't argue with you there, Reverend."

Melissa blushed and then tried to change the subject. "I'm sorry to have taken you away from your work, Jim. I'm sure you're very busy."

Jim ambled down the steps to retrieve his cap and said, "Ah, don't worry about it." He picked up the cap. "That's one of the benefits of my profession. I have some flexible time, so I can occasionally help out the neighbors."

After the furniture was back in place and the curtains were hung, the four settled around the kitchen table with cups of coffee. Aaron shared his visit with Anna Mettlesmith. "Anna is doing much better today. I think she's relieved that Jacob didn't linger in pain a long time."

Linda nodded in agreement, and Jim smiled and said, "You know, Jacob was one of the smartest men I ever met. He knew more about farming techniques than most of us will ever learn." He paused a moment to sip his coffee. "He could grab and stem of the hay, taste it, and tell me about how much protein was in the hay and whether it would be good feed for the cows. He knew a lot about God too. I remember one time when I was just a kid, he hired me to help put up the hay. We'd go out in that field, pick up endless bales, and carry them into one of the barns. I'd tell him about my big plans to improve farming methods, and he would share his faith with me. I learned more that summer than I did all four years at state."

The group chatted about Jacob and Anna and the weather.

Finally, Jim said to Linda, "Honey, we haven't had a cookout at our house for a while. What do you think about Sunday after church?"

"I think that sounds like a great idea. What do you think, Melissa and Aaron? Can you come out after church? Just informal picnic food, casual dress. It will give the kids some time to play."

"I'd love that. It sounds like a lot of fun. What should I bring?" asked Melissa.

"Just whatever you want. I'm sure there will be plenty. We'll supply the hamburgers, and I have all the condiments we need. I'll pick up the buns, and we'll be in business," Linda offered. "We'll make it up as we go along. Maybe we could get these guys to churn some ice cream for us."

Aaron and Melissa stood on the porch and waved good-bye.

"Wow, it's almost three o'clock," he noted.

"Can you stay for a while?" asked Melissa.

"A little bit. I promised Josie I'd pick her up at preschool at 3:45. They keep the kids until 4:00, but I wanted to have a few moments with her before supper." They walked into the living room, and Aaron put his arm around her as they settled onto the couch. "It seems like years since you and I have been alone for more than a minute or two."

Melissa leaned into his shoulder and said, "Three forty-five will be here before we know it."

He pulled her closer. The love that was fluttering in each of their hearts made them each aware of the quick passage of time. Melissa moved so she could see Aaron's face. At the same time, he looked down at her. He smiled, and their lips met. It was the sweetest kiss, but one that made her think of pleasures and passions that she had long put away. It filled her mind with a desire not only for romantic love, but with the hope of being loved just because she was loveable. Aaron deepened the kiss, and she moved her hand to caress his cheek. Melissa was lost in that lovely feeling until she heard a musical note of her phone and felt it vibrating in her hip pocket.

"Oh," was all she said as she pulled the phone out to look at it. She looked at Aaron, who had let his head fall back against the couch. "It's Rayleen."

He shrugged his shoulders and then smiled at her as she answered. "Hello, Rayleen." She pushed her hair back and continued. "How are you?" she stifled a giggle with her hand to her lips. "Oh, really? That many times? I guess I didn't hear it." She smiled, shaking her head. "Well, yes. I was busy, but it's all right." She smiled and winked at Aaron. "What can I do for you? Aaron? Why, yes, he did stop by. Just a moment—let me see where he is." She pointed at the phone and mouthed the words, *She wants to talk to you.*

He grinned and nodded, holding out his hand.

"Okay, Rayleen here he is. He'd gone to look at my paint job in the next room. Nice talking to you too." She handed Aaron the phone and stood up to go into the kitchen to give him some privacy.

She gathered up the coffee cups and wiped off the table. She stood at the sink, swished out the cups, and thought. *What a kiss? Maybe he's not just looking for a mommy for Josie.* She stared out the window as she rinsed the cups and spoon. *Kisses like that could be addictive.* Unaware that Aaron had finished his conversation, she was still gazing out the window when he came in, rested his hand on his waist, and leaned down to steal a kiss.

"I've got to go." He looked a little disappointed.

"But it's not even 3:30."

"I know, but if I stay, I might want to continue where we left off." He looked at her pleadingly. "Please understand."

She laughed. "I do. Boy, do I ever. But just another minute. I have something I need to ask you. Please."

Noting the solemn tone of her voice, he said, "Okay. It sounds serious."

"Well, yes, to me it is very serious. Let's sit down for a minute." He complied, and she continued. "You know I've been working on this account. Remember how I told you that Brad and I were going to submit some new figures?"

Aaron nodded.

"Well, we've proposed two ways to doing it, and Sven won't accept either one. Brad is really frustrated, and Mr. Cohen is ready to throw in the towel."

"And you're ..."

She rubbed her forehead. "I want to try again, but ..."

"But what?"

"Well, I decided to apply that verse from Philippians that we talked about the other night. You know—trust in the Lord."

"Uh-huh."

"So I prayed, and I told the Lord that I was going to turn it all over to Him. I did pretty good on Thursday and okay on Friday, but today ..."

Aaron smiled and nodded, "Today was harder?"

"Boy, was it! I kept thinking that I should be calling Sven or sitting in front of the computer, trying new combinations. Then I'd remember that I'd given it up, and so I handed it back to Jesus. But before long, I'd find myself thinking about it again."

"What did you do?"

"I kept giving it back."

"Good!" Aaron gave her thumbs-up.

"Do you think I'm doing the right thing?"

Aaron wrinkled his brow and paused as if collecting his thoughts. "It's really hard to give up control." He smiled at her. "But that's what the Lord wants us to do. He wants us to depend upon Him for guidance." He sat up a little straighter. "You're doing the right thing. When the answer is clear, you'll know it. Either he'll give you an inspiration, or he'll close the door. But if it's the Lord's will, you'll have peace about it."

"Okay, that's what I needed to hear. Thanks, Aaron."

"I've got to run. See you tomorrow?"

"Of course." She walked with him to the edge of the porch. He gave her a quick kiss and then was in his car and was gone.

After church on Sunday, they joined Jim, Linda, Julia, and Robert at the farm. The children played in the sunshine, the guys grilled the hamburgers, and Melissa and Linda set the picnic table for lunch. Linda was right: there was more than enough food for lunch, plus the promise of ice cream for dessert.

Josie made a point of sitting between Melissa and Aaron. After lunch, when the food was put away in containers, the grown-ups sat on the patio and watched the children play. At one time, Josie wandered up to check on her daddy and found Aaron and Melissa sitting together on a wicker couch. She wriggled herself up between them and bestowed equal numbers of hugs and kisses on them both. They presented as a happy family threesome.

It wasn't long before Jim, Robert, and Aaron went to the back porch to start churning the ice cream mixture Linda had cooling in the frig. Melissa and Linda went in the house to put out the fruit and chocolate and caramel toppings. They chatted while they worked, and Linda shared her observation. "You have brought so much joy into their lives. You may not see it, but Aaron and Josie are much happier now that you are here."

Melissa smiled. "They've brought me a lot of happiness too. In fact, I can't remember a time when I've looked forward to simple things so much." She smiled as she scraped the last of the chocolate sauce into a bowl. "I've really felt fortunate in the last couple of months. I've learned so much about myself and people, and how important the Lord is in my life." She looked up to see Linda's grin and laughed. "What's so funny?"

"Not a thing. I'm just so delighted for you—all three of you." Melissa smiled and embraced her friend. It seemed like everything was going so right. After a moment, Linda said, "Well, we'd better see if those guys finished up the ice cream."

They found Jim and Aaron on the front porch, standing next to a churn of ice cream staying frozen in a galvanized tub of ice.

Linda crept up behind Jim and tickled him in the ribs. He laughed and caught her up in an embrace. "What do you mean, picking on a guy like that?" She soothed his feelings with a peck on the cheek and a pat on the fanny.

"Just trying to keep you on your toes."

Aaron snuggled Melissa against him, and they watched the girls joyfully chasing Robert around the yard.

The cold, creamy ice cream and toppings were delicious. By the time they all had time to finish, the afternoon naps were beckoning to everyone. Josie was drifting off on her dad's lap, and Melissa was gathering her dishes and the leftover food. Robert said, "But we didn't get to make s'mores."

Everyone laughed, and Aaron said, "Robert, you take care of the crackers, chocolate bars, and marshmallow, and we'll be back sometime to make them. Okay?"

"Okay, but don't wait too long!"

Chapter 27

Melissa got up early Monday morning so that she would have time to bake a cake for the funeral dinner. After coffee and cereal, she decided she needed to check in with Brad. She dialed his number and smiled when she heard his cheerful hello.

"Hi, Brad. How are you doing?"

"Blissfully happy to be engaged to the love of my life."

Melissa chuckled and congratulated him once again. "I'm so happy for you two."

"And how are things in Cowtown?"

"Things seem to be very happy here too."

"Oh? Well, tell me more."

Melissa chuckled. "There's not a lot to tell. I am just so happy right now. I love my home. I'm so happy that I've let go of so much, so that God could take over. It feels so good."

"I'm glad to hear that." Brad sighed. "But the realities of work have set in. I haven't come up with any ideas different than the ones we've already reworked over and over."

"I haven't either. In fact, I put it out of my mind the end of last week. Well, it wasn't that simple, but I did give it over to Jesus. I had to work very hard not to take it back. I asked him to give me ideas, so I had to depend upon him. So far, he hasn't revealed anything to me, so I'm just waiting."

"Hmm," was all Brad said. She knew he was thinking and probably rubbing his chin. "Well, I don't see that there is anything else we can do. I'm not sure Mr. Cohen will like it. He may not understand our philosophy."

"That's true." Melissa shrugged. "Aaron says the Lord will either give us an inspiration or close the door."

"I agree." He heaved a deep sigh. "I'm going to meet with Cohen today and ask for his ideas. We may have to just let it happen as it will." There was a long pause. Melissa waited for Brad to end the call, but he didn't. "I had another reason for calling. Actually, two."

"I'm listening." Melissa twisted a curl of hair around her finger.

"Well, work first. Cohen has another account he wants us to work up together. This one should be easier. The client has an established product that he's adding new lines to, and he wants a strong program to revitalize the old one while promoting the new one." They talked on about the possible marketing ploys they might use.

Melissa wrapped up by saying, "I think that sounds feasible. I'm sure we can design a marketing plan that will enhance both the old and the new. It sounds good to me."

"Okay." Brad's tone lightened. "This next one is a personal one."

"I'm listening."

"Does the invitation for a visit still stand? For Bonnie and me, I mean."

"Of course it does." Melissa sat up straighter. "When would you like to come?"

"We were thinking of driving out for the Fourth of July weekend, if you're going to be around."

"That sounds like fun!. I guess they have an old-fashioned celebration here. You know, parades, carnival, fireworks."

"And homemade ice cream?" Brad asked hopefully.

Melissa laughed. "I'm sure there will be some, especially if you're willing to crank it. I can hardly wait."

Melissa drove into town and delivered her cake to the church. She offered to help Linda and the kitchen committee. By the time the dinner was finished, and all the guests had lingered and left, and the kitchen and fellowship hall were cleaned up, it was nearly 2:00. Aaron stopped in and visited with the ladies, thanking them for their hard work. He escorted Melissa out to her car and then hopped into the passenger seat.

Melissa couldn't help but laugh. "What are you doing?"

He turned to her with a big grin. "I'm all yours."

"What?"

"I have exactly ..." He checked the time on his phone. "Two hours and four—no, five minutes until Joseline comes home from preschool. Let's spend it together. All by ourselves. Alone." He finished with a raised eyebrow.

"Sounds good to me." She paused for a minute, curious about this suggestion. "Where would you like to go?"

"The park. The phone reception is not good there. It should be pretty deserted right now, so we can have uninterrupted time."

"Sounds wonderful."

They chatted about Brad's request for the Independence Day weekend, their work projects, and the funeral. They arrived at the yellow gate at the foot of the path to the Top of the World in about fifteen minutes. They joined hands as they walked the path. Aaron was right: it was deserted, at least at that moment. When the path veered off to the Top of the World, Aaron guided her on the lesser traveled path that led down to the stream at the foot of the outcropping.

"It's nice down here, and fewer people come here."

"What's all this need for solitude suddenly?"

Aaron smiled and lifted her hand to kiss the back of it. "It just seems we get too little time to spend together without someone interrupting. I'm carving out a moment for us."

They followed the path until they came to the grassy bank of the where the brook babbled between a group of large and small boulders.

"Here we are." Aaron swept his arm toward the rocks and the stream.

"It is beautiful. Idyllic, really." She breathed in the fresh air and the peaceful sounds of nature.

Aaron took her hand and guided her across some of the rocks to a large picnic table–sized boulder. He held her hand as she plunked herself down on the rock. Then he eased himself down next to her and pointed out trout swimming in and out of the shelter of the rocks. Melissa pointed out a heron standing in the shallow water on one leg next to the other bank. The peace of their surroundings ministered to them as though God had designed it specifically for them. They sat in silence, drinking it in and savoring this divine therapy. Minutes passed, worries faded, and tensions soothed.

Aaron quietly broke the silence. "Thank you for coming here with me."

She smiled. "This is so soothing. I'd like to bottle it up and sell it."

He nodded, paused, and then said, "Melissa, have you thought any more about marrying me?" He picked up a pebble and threw it into the stream.

Melissa stared at him blankly. This wasn't how she'd expected him to lead out the conversation. She waited, trying to think how to respond. "Of course, I've thought about it. Have you?"

He leaned back on his elbows. "Constantly." Then he gauged her reaction continued. "I have trouble thinking of anything, without it reminding me of you."

Melissa felt little prickles of excitement start at the nape of her neck and travel up her scalp and then down her spine. She turned to face him with a look of joyful amazement on her face. "You do?"

Aaron's face split into a grin, and he sat up so that they were facing one another. After touching his index finger to the middle of her forehead, he let it trail down her nose and, over her lips. Then tipped her chin up slightly with one finger. While looking directly into her green eyes, he said, "Why does that surprise you? Haven't I made my feelings clear?" She sat entranced. He said softly, "Melissa, don't you know what I feel for you?"

She dropped her gaze and turned to break the contact. "I know that you like me. And the other afternoon at my house, I knew that you were attracted to me. I know that you want Josie to feel secure, and ..."

"Melissa! We are not talking about what I want for Joseline now." Aaron leaned toward her. "Melissa, look at me."

When she raised her eyes to meet his, she saw the caring expression she had come to expect from Aaron. "Melissa, I love Josie. She is the joy of my life. Of course I want her to feel secure and loved and happy. All the things that you can offer her. But I would not ask you to marry me if I hadn't fallen in love with you first."

He let the soothing sounds of nature surround them and then continued. "I wasn't kidding the other day when I told you I loved you the first time I met you screaming your head off, telling me to back off or you would do whatever you had to. Then the time you were determined to drive Brad to the airport in the middle of a rainstorm, but you relented and let me help you. Or any of the other times we've been together. That week you were in Chicago, I felt like a lost puppy. I missed you so much. But I think I realized how much I loved you the afternoon you and Josie were playing shadow tag, finding joy in a simple game. At that moment, I knew that I loved you for everything you are—not just a potential mother for Josie or a wife, but a good friend, an amazing companion, and a capable businesswoman. Everything you are or ever will be." He picked up a pebble and studied it carefully. "Just like this rock is a complex combination of different elements, God made you a complex combination of wonderful qualities." He looked directly into her eyes. "You are important to me. I want you to be part of my life. You are the woman I love. The woman I want to be married to." He tossed the pebble into the stream, and the leaned forward so his face was inches from her. He spoke slowly, drawing out each word. "Will you be my wife?"

As Aaron pleaded his case, Melissa's thoughts raced from this moment in the sunshine to that first stormy night when she'd met this man, to when she'd realized he was a pastor, to their first kiss, to when she'd first realized she had fallen in love with him. She felt her lips curve into a smile that grew wider with every word he spoke. Finally, as his speech came to an end and he phrased his proposal, she placed her hands on each side of his face. "Pastor Chambers, has anyone ever told you that you talk too much?"

Aaron gave her a startled look and then grinned as she pulled his face down to hers for a long, slow kiss. When she finally released him, he let out a long breath and said, "You know, I don't recall anyone ever saying anything like that to me." Then he gave a mischievous glint. "But if you'd like to repeat it, I'd be glad to listen."

She placed a kiss on his chin and said, "Yes."

Aaron stared at her as tough he had no idea what she was saying. "Yes?" He frowned and then smiled, "Yes! You said yes?" He pulled her into an embrace. "You have made me so happy."

She felt tears of joy trickle down her cheeks. "I love you, Aaron." The best part of all, she knew that it was true.

They stayed at the park until it was time to pick up Joseline. On the way, they made tentative plans, changed them, and made them again. By the time they reached the edge of town, they had decided when to call her parents and his parents to share the news. But for certain, they knew they would tell Josie before anyone else.

When they stopped at the preschool, Miss Granger was standing in the doorway and talking to Joseline. Melissa honked the horn as Aaron stepped out of the car and waved at the teacher as he greeted his daughter. Joseline crawled into the front seat and gave Melissa a wet kiss on the cheek. "Hi, Missa."

"Hello, Josie. Did you have a good day at school?"

As she settled onto her daddy's lap, she replied, "Uh-huh. I drew a picture. See?"

Melissa glanced at the drawing and smiled. There, in her best art, were a man with dark hair, a little dark-haired girl, and a woman with blonde curls, all holding hands and with huge smiles on their faces.

"That's very nice. Who are those people?"

"Daddy, and me, and you." She pointed to smaller figures in the corner. "And there's Paisley and her babies."

Aaron smiled at Melissa over Josie's head and said, "That looks like a nice family."

Melissa returned his smile as she listened to Joseline say, "It is, Daddy. It's ours." She smiled at her dad and then at Melissa.

After wiping another batch of tears from her face, Melissa leaned over to hug Joseline. "Thank you, sweetie."

Aaron cleared his throat and then said, "Josie, that is a very special picture, especially for today, because Melissa and I have decided we are getting married. We really will be a family."

He waited for Joseline's reaction. She looked from one to the other and said, "I know. That's what I asked God for every night before I went to sleep."

Chapter 28

They were reveling in God's abundant blessings, but just as he promises mountain top experiences, he also allows crevasses. On Thursday, Melissa arrived home after spending the afternoon with Linda and Rayleen discussing plans for showers and wedding options. As she let herself in the house and collapsed on the couch, she remembered she had turned off her phone so they wouldn't be disturbed.

She noted she had two voice messages waiting for her. "Melissa, this is Brad. Call me when you get this. It's important."

The next was from Sven. "Melissa. I'm back in Chicago and need to see you. I want you to call as soon as you can."

She called Brad, and he answered on the first ring. "Melissa! I'm glad you called. Have you talked to Sven?"

"No. I have a message from him telling me he needs to see me, and he wants me to call him. Brad, what's going on?"

"I'm not sure. Sven came into the firm madder than a hornet yesterday. He told Cohen that since he didn't find a better proposal on his desk, he was going to sue the firm, smear me, and expose you as a cheat and a liar."

Melissa leaned back into the overstuffed couch and squeezed the bridge of her nose between her index finger and thumb. "What does he want that's different than what we've already offered?"

"I don't know. He must have brooded about this all the time he was gone." He forcibly exhaled. "Cohen doesn't seem too worried about a lawsuit. He says we have fulfilled our part of the contract, and that we've proven ourselves and should have no problem maintaining our reputations. You know, Ralph is a pretty good guy. He really stood up for us to Sven, and he said he'd do everything he could to help us avoid Sven's slurs." He paused. "Melissa, forgive me for asking this, but did you do something to draw Sven's anger?"

"Brad, I've told you about our relationship. For some reason, he has built it into more than I ever thought it could be. I guess if he wants to say horrible things about me, he can. That last night we were together, he made a comment about how I would find myself thinking more and more about him. Maybe he thinks he can force me to comply with his demands by acting bullish. I guess he can say whatever he wants about me, I hope Mr. Cohen can control the stuff he says about our work." She felt angry and hurt, and tears threatened to spill out. "I don't think I am going to return Sven's call."

"I wouldn't call him, if I were you. I think you should let corporate handle him. And if he's that irrational about you not wanting to continue a relationship with him, you'd be setting yourself up for more harm."

Melissa agreed. She was about to end the call when she remembered why she'd wanted to talk to Brad. "I have some happy news to share with you."

"Good, I could use some of that. Tell me."

Melissa smiled as she related the events of the last few days.

"That is wonderful! I couldn't be happier for you. Congratulations! When's the wedding?"

They chatted for a few more minutes and were saying goodbye when Aaron tapped on the door and came in. She stood and walked into his arms. "I'm so happy to see you."

He grinned and then sensed her unhappiness. "What's wrong?"

She quickly related the messages and phone call of the last hour. She was explaining Sven's threats of lawsuits and professional and personal slurs when her phone buzzed.

She groaned. "It's Sven. I should probably take it."

He nodded and said, "I'll give you some space."

"No, stay. I need your support. I'm going to put it on speaker. It's not confidential, and I would like you to be a witness. Please stay."

He agreed and settled down on the couch with her.

"Hello, Sven."

"Well hello, Melissa."

"How may I help you?"

"Oh, I can think of many ways you could help me. In fact, why don't you come on into Chicago, and I will show you?"

She closed her eyes as if she could shut out the picture he was trying to create. "I'm not coming to Chicago anytime soon. I'm not meeting with you when I do. I thought I made my feelings clear the last time I was there."

"Well, aren't you Miss Independent? If that's the way you want it, then you'll have to take the consequences of your bad behavior."

Melissa rolled her eyes and said, "What bad behavior? What are you talking about?"

"Why, Melissa, you have broken my heart and left me in the lurch, and I don't like it! Now you're trying to pass off this shoddy work on my company. What are people going to think when they find out you do such poor work and then try to exploit my feelings for you?"

"You're not making any sense. I haven't broken any promises to you, and we presented you with two very good proposals for your diversification."

The anger in Sven's voice peaked. "You were supposed to marry me! I wanted you to marry me, but you walked away from me. No one does that to me. I had a plan, and you ruined it."

Melissa asked God for the right words. "Sven, I'm sorry things didn't work out the way you wanted. But I never made a commitment to you. I would never have been the person you wanted me to be." There was no response. "Sven, I pray that you find happiness and peace in your heart."

Silence.

"Sven …"

"I don't have anything more to say to you. You're such a disappointment." He clicked off.

She sat in silence, not sure of how to feel. In one way, she was relieved, but she still felt uneasy with Sven's accusations and angry words. Aaron moved closer and took her hand, but he let her process her feelings on her own.

Finally she said, "I don't know what he was talking about. I'm not sure where he thought our relationship was going. She turned to face him. "Thanks for being here with me."

He pulled her into an embrace. "Is he dangerous?"

"No, I don't think so. I hope not. He simply never accepted that I didn't have the same intent as he did. He always wanted more than I did." She snuggled closer to Aaron. "I am so thankful I have you." She leaned into him, feeling so safe and so happy. "I had shared with Mom and Grandmother my situation with Sven. They both encouraged me to be very careful in making decisions that would affect me the rest of my life. I guess they could tell that I wasn't happy. Granny was such a great support to me. I was so sad that I had to leave her, but I felt like I had to return to Chicago."

"What happened when you went back to work?" Aaron asked.

"When I got back to my apartment, I realized that I had shut off my phone while I was I in Iowa. When I turned it back on, I had several messages from Sven—some angry, some demanding, some pleading. It was overwhelming. I never expected him to want to talk to me that much. Anyway, I didn't call him because I didn't want to deal with his manipulation. I turned off the phone again. When I went into work the next morning, I had several job assignments and was happy to be busy. During lunch, Sven found me and asked to join me. He was nice, more pleasant than he had been. He asked me to go to dinner with him that evening. I didn't relish the idea of being alone with him too much, so I suggested that I meet him at a place near my apartment building. He agreed. That evening was a disaster. He simply wouldn't listen to my feelings and kept insinuating that I should be grateful to him for allowing me to do the projects I had completed. He could not separate my success from what he saw as his influence. I felt so unhappy and frustrated. We finally ended the evening early, but he kept insisting that I would feel differently about him in the morning.

"I decided to focus on my work and have as little to do with Sven as possible. That's what I did. It wasn't easy, but he did stop bothering me at work, and I refused to take any of his calls. Then Mom called the second week in December to tell me Grandmother was in the hospital. I talked to my team and Mr. Cohen. They all encouraged me to go be with her, and so I finished up my current project and flew back to Iowa.

"She was so ill. She knew I was there because she smiled at me and called me by name. She said to me, 'Remember, Jesus wants you to have peace.' I wanted to ask her what she meant, but she didn't recover. Those were the worst days of my life." She cradled her face in her hands and wept. Aaron pulled her close, comforting her.

"You know, it's strange. I don't remember much about her funeral. There were lots of people. Were you there?"

Aaron smiled. "Yes, I was there. I did the service for my friend."

Melissa sat up and looked at him. "Oh, Aaron, I'm sorry. I was just so focused on my own sadness that I didn't realize."

"Nothing to be sorry about," Aaron soothed. "I was hurting too. Many of us shared your sorrow."

"I know that now. But when I got back to Chicago, I decided the only way to handle it was to work and avoid everyone except to deal with work. I must have gone on like that for three or four weeks. Finally, I knew I couldn't handle it on my own any longer. I remembered Granny telling me to take my cares to Jesus, and so I started praying. I didn't even know how to pray; I just started talking to God. I searched my mind for my conversations with Granny about prayer, and I made it up as I went along. He must have thought I was really ignorant, but thankfully he was willing to listen to my imperfect words."

Aaron rubbed her shoulder, pulling her closer to him. "I imagine he loved it. He welcomes anyone who comes to him in need."

Melissa laid her head against his chest. "It must have worked, because my phone rang. It was Brad telling me he was bringing chili over, and he wouldn't take no for an answer." She put her head back.

"He brought homemade chili and butter pecan ice cream. We had a wonderful visit. I remember asking him if he ever prayed, and he assured me that he did and that it was the best thing to do." She smiled at Aaron. "God has been so good to me.

He pulled her closer and leaned in to kiss her when her phone rang. "Bad timing," Aaron said. "You'd better check to see if you need to answer it."

Melissa sighed and checked it. "Oh, it's Mr. Cohen." She gave him a quick kiss on the lips and said, "I'll make it up to you."

Aaron leaned back and said, "I'll hold you to that promise."

Melissa smiled and said, "Hello?"

"Miss Blakesly. Uh, Melissa, this is Ralph Cohen."

"Mr. Cohen. How are you?"

"The question is, how are you? Brad Webster called me and said you were going to call Sven Johanssen. I hope he didn't cause you any, uh, discomfort."

"No, I decided not to call him. I wasn't up to talking to him, and I don't intend to talk to him about anything other than business ever again. But I understand that he's threatened to slander me. I know that I've always worked hard and been professional. If he wants to be unpleasant, then he will."

"Well, if I have anything to say about it, you'll have no problems. You've always done outstanding work and have been an excellent employee. Don't worry about what he says. Cohen Marketing will stand behind you."

"Thank you, Mr. Cohen. You don't know what that means to me. I have liked working for you, and I don't want to cause you any harm, even inadvertently."

"Well, there are many other accounts, but I can't afford to lose good people like you and Webster. I'm looking forward to a long affiliation with you both."

"So has NorAm cancelled with us?"

"Maybe, maybe not. I talked to Old Man Johanssen, Nᵣˊ afternoon. He and I go way back. He didn't know abou' threats the kid has been throwing around. I have a feeling that Sven may be working out of the Oslo office exclusively for a while."

Melissa's eyes misted, and she smiled at Aaron. Then she raised her free hand toward the ceiling and said a silent, *Thank you!* To Mr. Cohen she said, "That would be just fine with me Thank you so much for calling. You have made my day a whole lot better."

"Goodbye, Ms. Blakesly. I hope to see you again soon."

"Goodbye. I'm sure you will."

She turned to Aaron. The smile was back on her face, and the gleam had returned to her eyes. "God is good. I just got the answer to my prayer and the peace that passes all understanding." Aaron opened his arms, and she moved over to sit on his lap. She hugged him tightly and then finished the kiss they'd started earlier.

Epilogue

The Independence Day celebration in Sovereign promised to be everything Melissa had imagined. She had heard the high school band practicing patriotic songs all week, and the carnival and food venders were ready to do a great business. The community band was set to play in the bandstand by the river starting at 7:00, followed by the fireworks show at 9:00. Flags were flying all over town. But, by far the most important event for their family was the parade. The preschoolers were riding on a hay wagon decorated with red, white, and blue crepe paper and balloons. All the children had been assigned a special patriotic character costume. Joseline had been given the honor of posing as Miss Liberty. Her green gown fit nicely over her T-shirt and shorts, but her book and torch seemed to frequently change hands. Melissa worked to secure the foam crown to her braids with hairpins for the third time. Joseline simply couldn't stand still, and Brad's teasing didn't help matters at all.

Finally, Bonnie came to the rescue with her idea. "I have a couple of safety pins. Let's try fastening them to the crown and then through the barrette. I think that might hold it more securely." Thankful for the suggestion, Melissa was able to step back and enjoy the sight of twenty pint-sized patriots. Brad was circulating around the wagon, taking pictures of the little hams and charming all the parents at the same time. Bonnie and Melissa turned to smile at each other and then burst into laughter at his enthusiasm.

Bonnie and Brad had arrived the night before, and after a late supper at Aaron's house, the group had split up. Bonnie and Melissa sat up and compared wedding plans for nearly an hour before they both gave in to their exhaustion. The next morning, they met the guys and Joseline at the coffee shop.

Shelia was in her favorite element. There were more visitors and new faces around the breakfast bar and the tables than she could talk to in one morning. By the time she'd served everyone and found out something about each new person, it was time to close the shop and prepare for the parade.

As Nancy Granger calmed the children and gave instructions to the children, Aaron rushed up. "I'm glad I got here before they took off. The youth group's float is looking great, especially with Rayleen's help and Don driving the truck." He turned to Brad. "Thanks for taking pictures."

Brad grinned. "I loved it. It is pure Americana."

The band tuned up, the majorette sounded her whistle, and the parade participants moved into position. Aaron reached up and kissed Joseline. "We'll be watching for you, sweetie. Remember to hold your torch up high."

The four adults hurried down the street so that they could jockey for a good position to watch the parade. The sun was warm, the sky was a cloudless blue, and Melissa felt complete happiness wash over her. Friends and acquaintances stopped for a word or waved or nodded as they searched for a good vantage point. The anticipation of the crowd increased when the cadence of the first marching group approached. Everyone craned their necks to catch a glimpse of the color guard coming into view and carrying the flag, followed by the high school band playing the national anthem. She felt goose bumps form on her arms and the hairs stand up on the back of her neck. She glanced around and saw everyone standing and smiling with right hands over their hearts as Old Glory was carried by the American Legion color guard. *This is home,* she thought. *This is where I want to be.* She reached over and linked arms with Aaron. He smiled down at her, and she once again counted her blessings. She turned Granny's diamond engagement ring on her finger and smiled, remembering the persuasion it had taken to convince Aaron that this was the only symbol she wanted of their love. After all, hadn't he said that very first night that maybe Granny had hoped they would meet? He'd finally agreed but insisted that they have a diamond band made to made to match the antique ring.

She was lost in her thoughts when the crowd around them tittered and then erupted into laughter. She turned her attention to the parade and she saw the preschool float. There on that converted wagon were miniature George Washington, Paul Revere, Betsy Ross, Abraham Lincoln, George Bush, Barrack Obama, Donald Trump, Uncle Sam, soldiers, and sailors. In the middle and near the front was Miss Liberty waving her torch and shouting, "Happy Independence Day, everybody!"

Melissa, Aaron, Brad, and Bonnie laughed, waved, and shouted to catch Joseline's attention. Josie smiled proudly and shouted, "Hi, Missa. Hi, Daddy! See, Sara? There's my family." The moment was too precious, and Melissa couldn't stop a tear or two from rolling down her cheek. She turned to smile at Aaron, the man she loved, and thanked God for his Sovereign peace.